THE KILLING SHIP

THE KILLING SHIP

Simon Beaufort

Severn House Large Print
London & New York

This first large print edition published 2017
in Great Britain and the USA by
SEVERN HOUSE PUBLISHERS LTD of
19 Cedar Road, Sutton, Surrey, England, SM2 5DA.
First world regular print edition published 2016 by
Severn House Publishers Ltd.

British Library Cataloguing in Publication Data
A CIP catalogue record for this title is available from the British Library.

ISBN-13: 9780727895509

Severn House Publishers support the Forest Stewardship Council™
[FSC™], the leading international forest certification organisation. All
our titles that are printed on FSC certified paper carry the FSC logo.

MIX
Paper from
responsible sources
FSC® C013056

Typeset by Palimpsest Book Production Ltd.,
Falkirk, Stirlingshire, Scotland.
Printed and bound in Great Britain by
T J International, Padstow, Cornwall.

In fond memory of Kenneth Owler Smith –
mentor and dear friend

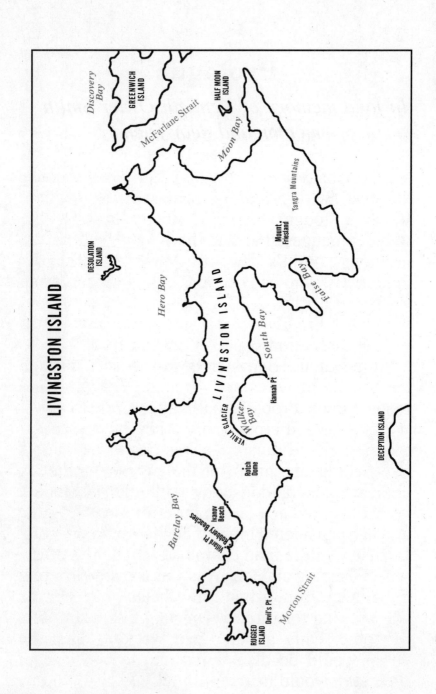

LIVINGSTON ISLAND

GREENWICH ISLAND

Discovery Bay

HALF MOON ISLAND

McFarlane Strait

Moon Bay

Tangra Mountains

DESOLATION ISLAND

Mount Friesland

Hero Bay

False Bay

LIVINGSTON ISLAND

South Bay

Hannah Pt

VERILA GLACIER

Walker Bay

Rotch Dome

Barclay Bay

Ivanov Beach

Villard Pt

Robbery Beaches

DECEPTION ISLAND

Devil's Pt

Morton Strait

RUGGED ISLAND

Prologue

28 February, Livingston Island,
South Shetland Islands, Antarctica

An icy wind gusted across the escarpment, making the dust swirl. Squinting against it, Dr Andrew Berrister fought his way slowly towards the weather gauges that had been damaged in the previous night's storm. Malcolm 'Freddy' Fredericks, who had offered to go with him, tried to stay in his lee.

'Well?' Freddy asked, watching him prise off the inspection panel. 'Can you fix it?'

'Some of it.' Berrister began to sort through the jumble of wires and circuits. 'But the wind meter's gone. Probably halfway to Chile by now.'

Freddy gazed around idly while he waited for the biologist to finish. He was one of the team's two field hands, hired for the austral summer as cook and general dogsbody. Although Australian, he had worked at a Polish base for three seasons, and had considered himself an old Antarctic hand. Berrister's little field camp had taught him otherwise. Sleeping under canvas was a vastly different experience from a bunk in a heated hut, and he was looking forward to returning to the comforts of home. Only another two weeks – then the camp would be dismantled and every trace of their stay would be carefully eliminated. No one

1

coming the day after would ever know they had been there. It felt a bit excessive to Freddy, but the Antarctic was protected by some serious laws and international agreements, and Berrister clearly had every intention of following them to the letter – as he had done each summer for the last fifteen years.

In the aftermath of the storm, the sun shone brightly enough to warrant wearing sunglasses, although the temperature was still well below zero. Far below, their camp was a collection of tiny green and yellow tents huddled behind an outcrop of rocks. Around it, the rest of the team were collecting the supplies that had been scattered by the winds, which had gusted up to 150 kilometres an hour. Beyond the camp, the sea was a vivid royal blue, and the snow-dusted mountains and the smooth dome of the glacier so brilliantly white that they hurt the eyes.

'What's that?' Freddy asked suddenly.

Berrister glanced where he was pointing, then leapt to his feet in excitement. It was a whale – and not just any whale, but the most rare and vulnerable of them all: a blue. As he watched, spellbound, another surfaced. Then another – six in all.

'A pod!' he exclaimed. 'I've never seen so many together before – they're almost extinct. My God! This is incredible!'

'Will they stay around here for long?' asked Freddy, watching them through his binoculars.

'They might, if there's enough food.'

The biggest whale blew, spouting a geyser of mist that hung across the shifting sea for several seconds before slowly fading away. Then the pod began to move off. The two men watched until they were out of sight, then Berrister turned his attention back to the instruments. He finished eventually, and packed away the tools.

'I think I'll wait here a while, to see if they come back,' he said. 'Do you want to stay or go back to camp?'

'I'll have to stay if you are,' said Freddy, a little resentfully. He was cold, and had been looking forward to huddling over the stove for a bit, preparing dinner. 'It's against the rules – *your* rules – for anyone to be up here alone.'

Berrister hesitated. He did insist that the team always worked in pairs when they were away from the camp, lest there was an accident, and in a place where the nearest help was a hundred kilometres away – and depended on the vagaries of the weather – such precautions might mean the difference between life and death. But blue whales . . . it was just too rare an opportunity to miss.

'Just this once,' he said. 'Be careful.'

Relieved, the Australian began to scramble down the long, steep slope. Berrister watched him go, then turned to scan the horizon for tell-tale spouts.

Three hundred kilometres north-east, a rust-coloured ship was doing battle with mountainous waves, tossed about like a cork in a bath. First mate Evgeny Yablokov was worried – *Lena* was old and in poor repair, and he was not sure she could take such a battering. One of her holds was flooded, and warning lights on the bridge showed that her engines were labouring dangerously. More alarming yet was the state of her cargo: the barrels strained at their holding chains and a couple had torn loose. He did not like to think about what might happen if more broke free and started to roll around.

Captain Garik slouched in his chair, his oilskins still wet from his last foray onto the spray-drenched bridge-wing. His 'adviser', Imad Hasim, stood nearby, clearly seasick and clinging to a door to prevent himself from being hurled off his feet. Yablokov did not like the smooth-talking Hasim, and was uncharitably grateful to see him so miserable. Garik barked an order to the helmsman, and the ship veered away from a mat of ice that glowed green on the radar.

Yablokov joined several other officers who were scanning the sea for chunks of ice that might be dashed against the ship. When an especially large wave lifted *Lena*, he could see the craggy peaks of Elephant Island, a desolate scrap of rock where nothing lived but birds and seals. He shuddered. Its jagged skyline looked menacing, and it was surrounded by frothing water that could kill in minutes with its searing coldness.

He glanced around as the communications officer came to hand Garik a message. The man was grinning, cap pushed back at a jaunty angle. When Garik read the note, he smiled, too, and handed the paper to Hasim.

Hasim was too seasick to look at it for long. 'We'd better go, then,' was all he said.

'Set a course for Livingston Island,' Garik told

4

the helmsman. He rubbed his hands together gleefully. 'At last! I was beginning to think we'd wasted our time.'

'How long will it take to get there?' asked Hasim weakly.

Garik shrugged. 'Depends on the weather. A couple of days, maybe.'

'No,' snapped Hasim. 'It needs to be sooner, or we'll be too late.'

'It'll take as long as it takes,' retorted Garik. He had been drinking again, and Yablokov could smell the vodka on his breath. 'We'll do our best, but in these seas . . . well, you can see for yourself that they'll slow us down.'

Wordlessly, Hasim left the bridge. The door slammed behind him as the ship pitched violently, sending coffee cups and charts flying.

'What did the message say?' asked Yablokov curiously.

'Whales,' replied Garik. He grinned, baring teeth that were a combination of metal crowns and nicotine-stained originals. 'All feeding happily off Livingston Island.'

One

Freddy stood at the top of the scarp and looked around him. The sea was a dull, milky silver, the sky was grey, the glacier was white and the mountains were dusted with snow. If it were not for his yellow jacket and the flapping ends of his red bandanna, he might have thought he had lost all sense of colour.

Although a natural outdoorsman, the Australian had not enjoyed camping out in temperatures that regularly dropped below freezing, and thought the Hannah Point camp was a grim place to be. He had been so cold that day that, when he had finished his duties around the camp, he had hiked up the scarp, hoping to see the blue whales again. Making what was a strenuous climb alone – and without a radio – was against regulations, but everyone else was out working, so who would know? Breathing hard from his exertions, he walked along the crest, scanning the horizon for the flash of white that would tell him the whales were about.

Not far offshore, a white plume shot upwards, and he glimpsed a smooth blue-grey back. He nodded in satisfaction. They were still there, feasting on krill – Antarctic shrimp. They had been feeding in South Bay – the inlet east of

7

Hannah Point – for three days now, moving among the grounded icebergs.

He was beginning to think of them as his personal property. Berrister had talked with passion about them – their biology, feeding habits and the fact that they teetered on the edge of extinction – but Freddy felt he knew them better. Berrister had lent him a book on them, too, a dull affair with too many words and graphs, and too few pictures, but reading about them wasn't nearly as interesting as watching.

One whale sounded so close to shore that he fancied he could hear it breathe. It lay on the surface for a few moments before slipping out of sight again. He wondered how long they would stay. Of course, that question would have been irrelevant if Berrister hadn't vetoed his request for a trek west to the Byers Peninsula. Everyone else had wanted to go, but Berrister was officially camp leader, and his 'no' carried more weight than seven 'yeses'. Freddy scowled. Why couldn't one of the other scientists have been in charge? They would have gone in an instant. Freddy had been angry about it ever since, which was why he had stuck two fingers up at Berrister that day by climbing the scarp on his own. He half wished the camp leader would find out – a row would give him another chance to explain how much he wanted the trek, and give the others a chance to say that they did, too.

Pushing his irritation aside, he turned his attention back to the whales. As he watched, he glimpsed something else move out of the corner of his eye. At first, he thought he was mistaken, but seconds later he saw it again.

He reached for his binoculars, and saw someone walking along the South Bay beach far below. The man was at a point where the ice cap ended in a tumbling cliff – waves lapped at its foot when the tide was in, but it was out now, so there was a wide, sandy beach. However, the cliff was very unstable – Freddy would not have walked there. Indigo-blue gashes were scored into its face, marking weak points that would soon collapse, and anyone caught beneath when they fell would be killed.

Freddy frowned. No one from camp should have been down there. Or had another team arrived during the night? But that was unlikely. First, they would have radioed. And second, people did not appear out of the blue in the Antarctic, especially this late in the season.

Puzzled to begin with, then with a growing sense of unease, he watched the man pick his way along the beach. Cursing himself for an idiot, he ducked behind a rock, out of sight. Who was the man, and what did he think he was doing?

When the second report cracked out, sending sharp echoes across the bay, the little huddle of penguins fell eerily silent, then brayed with even greater vigour. Nearby, an elephant seal snapped awake and sniffed the air. He shuffled forward, waking the moulting bull next to him, so that irritable roars soon drowned out the noise of the birds.

Andrew Berrister glanced up to see John

9

Graham watching him meaningfully, eyes narrowed to slits against the wind and the flurries of snow it carried. Graham was slightly built, with pale blue eyes and auburn hair, which had grown wild and shaggy during the three months that they had been at Hannah Point. He was the second of the team's two field hands, hired to help whichever of the four scientists happened to need him. It was usually Berrister, as his work with seals tended to require an extra pair of hands. Berrister was tall and looked bulky in his cold-weather clothing. Despite the inconvenience, he still shaved every day and kept his light brown hair neatly trimmed.

'It *wasn't* gunfire,' he said firmly. 'It was cracking ice.'

The anaesthetised seal in front of him gave a sudden jerk, knocking the syringe from his hand. He swore under his breath as he fumbled to retrieve it with cold-numbed fingers, while Graham pulled out binoculars and trained them on the glacier, trying to see which part might be about to calve. It was a bitter day, with a spiteful wind carrying flurries of snow. Summer was over and winter was on its way, as attested by the fact that most of the birds and seals had already gone. Only a few breeding bulls, always the last to moult and return to sea, and a handful of late-fledging penguin chicks remained. Berrister and his colleagues were fast reaching the point where there would be nothing left for them to study. He was glad the season was almost over, and was counting the days – only ten now – until the RRS *Frank Worsley* came to take them home.

That year, Berrister had chosen to work at Hannah Point, a finger of land that curved into the sea like a hook. It was a stunning place to be, not only because it boasted several large penguin and seabird colonies and was a popular haul-out site for seals, but because of its beauty. It had two long, sandy beaches, one to the west and one to the east, separated by a towering ridge they called 'the scarp'. To the north was the ice cap that covered most of the island, a towering dome reaching 1,700 metres at Mount Friesland.

Graham put his field glasses away and watched Berrister draw a blood sample from the seal. Its eyes snapped open when there was a third report. It shook itself, trying to eliminate the lingering effects of the sedative, then aimed unsteadily for the sea.

'Ice,' said Berrister, before Graham could claim it was gunfire again.

Graham was about to argue when the radio crackled. It was one of the two students, Lisa White.

'She says she just heard a boat,' reported Graham.

'Unlikely,' said Berrister, aware that theirs was the only camp on Livingston still working, and that the nearest base was a hundred kilometres away. 'She probably heard a seal.'

Graham relayed his opinion to Lisa. An aggrieved barking issued from the handset, and Graham laughed.

'She says she and Sarah will be back at camp early today – probably by three o'clock,' he said

11

tactfully, when Berrister raised questioning eyebrows.

Berrister nodded approvingly. 'Good. It's important to keep each other informed of changes in plans.'

Personally, Graham thought Berrister's obsession with safety was a royal pain in the arse, and knew the others did as well. According to Lisa, he had been a lot more relaxed about it before he had had an accident on the ice three years earlier. No one knew what had happened, and he stubbornly refused to discuss it, but it had changed him for good – and as he was in charge of the camp, the others had no choice but to follow the rules he set. Graham was all for caution – he had been hired for his experience in mountain rescue, and no one knew better than him the danger of complacency – but Berrister took it too far.

Graham pondered the situation as he continued to scan the ice. It was common practice, at the end of the season, for people to do something fun for a few days – a hike to a new area, or a visit to another base. Three days ago, Freddy had suggested a trek to the Byers Peninsula, an area of outstanding natural beauty about thirty-five kilometres to the west. Everyone had been excited by the prospect, but Berrister had refused. His excuse had been that there was still work to do, even though they had already exceeded expectations.

It was especially galling as the Byers Peninsula was so magnificent that it was designated a Specially Protected Area, which meant that only those with permits were allowed to

12

visit – and Berrister had one. As far as Graham was concerned, there was no reason whatsoever why they shouldn't go, and if Berrister was too wimpy to cross the ice, then he could stay back at the camp while everyone else went.

But dwelling on Berrister's annoying decision was making him angry, so Graham pushed it from his mind and attempted to smile.

'Lunch?' he asked, producing a bag of water biscuits sandwiched together with peanut butter.

Berrister regarded it unenthusiastically. 'Is there anything else?'

'Yes – this.' Graham poured some brownish-green lumps into a cup from a battered metal flask. 'Sarah's homemade soup, comprising mushy peas, spaghetti hoops, and three sachets of muesli.'

'My God!' breathed Berrister, repelled. 'I knew supplies are running low, but I didn't think we were that desperate.'

'Supplies aren't low, but all the good stuff's gone, so we're left with what no one wanted to eat earlier. At least that's what Freddy says. Personally, I think he should have managed them better. I would've done.'

Berrister ignored the Scot's sour humour. It was always this way at the end of the season, when people were tired and ready to go home. Once away from the camp, they would all be best friends again, the niggles forgotten. He took a water biscuit, as the lesser of the two evils on offer. They ate in silence for a while.

'Will you come back here next year?' asked Graham eventually. 'Or go somewhere else?'

'Neither,' replied Berrister. 'I've decided to

13

make this my last season. It's time to move to lab-based research.'

Graham raised his eyebrows. 'I've heard that people lose their nerve down here after a while. They realise how hostile it is, and it scares them.'

'I'm not "scared",' said Berrister, irked by the transparent attempt to shame him into agreeing to the trek to Byers. 'This *is* a hostile environment, and anyone who thinks otherwise is a fool who has no business being here.'

'Is that why you won't let us go?' pressed Graham. 'Because you think it's an unnecessary risk? Freddy says he's been over there before, and it's brilliant. We'd all love to go—'

'Well, we can't,' said Berrister shortly. 'Not while there's still work to be done.'

Graham shot him a sullen look, but could see that arguing would be futile. 'This stew isn't bad,' he lied. 'Try it.'

Berrister took a tentative sip. It tasted exactly as he imagined it would, although there was a curious sweetness that suggested Sarah Henshaw had added some other ingredient that Graham hadn't listed.

'Now, about that gunfire,' said Graham, packing away the flask. 'Maybe another expedition has landed and is trying to attract our attention.'

Berrister sighed. It was not yet noon, but lunch had been revolting, he was freezing cold, and Graham was being more annoying than usual. Again, he thought how glad he was that the season was almost over.

* * *

14

Three kilometres away, Sarah Henshaw and her graduate student Lisa White were deep in conversation. They were an ill-matched pair. Sarah was tall, athletic and honey blond, while Lisa was a short, plump, African-American. The differences went beyond their physical dissimilarities, though – Sarah was caustic, single-minded and impatient, while Lisa was timid, diffident and shy.

'The only boat within a hundred kilometres is our Zodiac,' Sarah was insisting. 'And Freddy wrecked that when he tried to drive it over some rocks. Are you *sure* you heard an engine?'

Lisa nodded. She scrubbed at her cheek with a thickly gloved hand before grabbing an unsuspecting penguin chick. Sarah knelt next to her, and began to tag the struggling bird.

'Another research team must've arrived,' Lisa said.

'They'd have radioed us,' argued Sarah, fixing a plastic clip onto the bird's flipper. 'And the season is almost over – researchers are leaving, not coming. You must be going stir-crazy.'

Lisa saw she would not convince the older woman. 'I wonder what Freddy will have cooked us for dinner,' she mused, her mind wandering to food, as it always did when she was cold.

Sarah's eyes – virtually all that was visible of her beneath her hood – gleamed with amusement. 'I suspect he'll have just warmed up the remains of my soup – to avenge himself on Andrew for saying no to the Byers jaunt.'

Lisa released the bird, which waddled away to preen ruffled feathers. 'I hope not – it's not *our*

15

fault that Andrew's being such a wet blanket. Personally, I'd love to go on a hike for a few days.'

Sarah sat back on her heels to watch the bird go. Her attitude to Freddy's proposal was mixed. On one hand, she longed to see more of the island, but on the other, she was loath to squander precious time when she could be working. The season had gone very well for her – better than she had hoped – and she was anticipating some very interesting results.

All her previous research had been on captive birds, and this was her first attempt at studying them in the wild. She had been apprehensive, although she had taken pains to conceal it – it would not do to appear nervous in front of her colleagues. For a start, one of them would be awarded a professorship later that year, and she intended to make sure it was her. Thus it was imperative that she had some decent results to publish.

But Lisa's attention was on the bay, eyes narrowed against the wind. Frowning, Sarah followed the direction of her gaze.

'There!' Lisa jumped to her feet and stabbed suddenly with her finger. 'D'you see? A boat!'

'There's nothing there,' said Sarah, after several minutes of seeing nothing but grey water. 'It's too rough for a boat, anyway.'

'But I saw it!'

Sarah shrugged. 'Maybe it was a fishing buoy. But we don't have all day – we can't have Andrew promoted over me because you think some scrap of flotsam is a boat.'

16

Reluctantly, Lisa tore her eyes away from the sea and returned to the business of catching penguins.

Ajay Joshi took a deep breath of cold, clean air, relishing the sharp scent of old ice. He should have been collecting data for his doctorate in botany, but it had not taken him many days in the Antarctic to learn that life as a scientist was not for him, and he had made the decision to abandon his studies and follow his brother into computers instead. Unwilling to be a freeloader for the remainder of the season, he spent his time helping the others, especially the portly glaciologist Geoff Mortimer, who was amusing and easy company.

That morning, he and Mortimer were taking samples of the sediments that were trapped in the glacier in long, dirty streaks. Or rather, *he* was: the laconic Yorkshireman was lounging against a rock, smoking. Mortimer deplored physical activity, and was only too happy to pass the privilege to someone else. Joshi's project might be dead, but Mortimer's was improving in leaps and bounds, and he had samples he would never have dreamed of taking had he been forced to dig them himself.

Mortimer, like the other three scientists – Berrister, Sarah, and the elderly botanist Dan Wells – held a university post. Unlike them, he had little passion for his subject. He did as much as was necessary to keep his job, but no more, and he failed to understand why anyone would want a professorship – a position that would entail a lot more work.

The radio crackled, and he pressed it to his ear.

'Graham heard a gun, and Lisa heard a boat,' he reported, putting it down again.

'Maybe *Worsley*'s come early,' suggested Joshi hopefully.

'Now that *would* be nice, but in my experience they tend to be late.'

'What was that?' demanded Joshi, standing abruptly. 'An engine?'

Mortimer had heard nothing but the wind buffeting his hood.

'Probably my stomach.' He flipped open the lunch bag. 'Watching all this hard work has given me an appetite. You can have that muck Sarah "cooked" this morning. She called it stew, but I saw her adding a bar of stale chocolate. Or you can share my ginger nuts, a tin of peaches, and a hermetically sealed pizza base.'

Joshi gaped at him. 'Where did you get those?'

'I took the precaution of stashing one or two morsels in my tent when the quality of the fare started to go downhill. Soft crackers and peanut butter are no use to a man of my princely girth. Keep your mouth shut, and I'll give you some.'

Joshi grinned conspiratorially, but they had barely begun to eat when a thin, strangled cry came distantly on the wind. It sounded so human that he felt a shiver run down his spine.

'Skua?' he asked uneasily.

'Tern, maybe,' said Mortimer. 'Although it was odd – like one of those cartoons, when someone falls over a cliff-edge, and they scream all the way to the bottom.'

'Or down a crevasse,' added Joshi. He glanced at Mortimer, then both looked away, unsettled.

The storm had abated, although there was still sufficient swell to make *Lena* ride uncomfortably. Hasim had spent the last three days in his cabin, too seasick to speak to anyone. Yablokov did not mind: it was more pleasant without his disapproving presence. He took a gulp of vodka from a battered flask, and offered Zurin the helmsman a swig. The heating was not working again, so it was cold on the bridge, and the vodka took the edge off the chill.

'How much further?' Yablokov asked.

Zurin shrugged and took another sip from the flask. Yablokov knew it was the only answer he would get from the taciturn sailor. Zurin never spoke unless absolutely necessary, but he was a good seaman, and Yablokov was glad he was aboard – not only because he was a fellow Russian, but because he did not have to be supervised constantly, to ensure orders were carried out. Captain Garik was lucky to have Zurin, just as he was lucky to have Yablokov – a drunken captain needed a reliable first officer.

Yablokov walked to the chart table and checked their position. Through the window, he could see the smooth white dome of Livingston's ice cap. It was not beautiful, he thought – it was too stark and formidable. A fat seal slipped silently from an ice floe into the sea, its ease in the frigid wilderness making Yablokov feel more alien than ever. Even though he was familiar with ice and snow, he had been fighting the increasing

19

conviction that he should never have accepted the commission to sail south.

Lena was one of the Barents Sea cod fleet, but overfishing meant it was difficult to make a living from cod any more, so Yablokov and half of *Lena*'s crew had agreed to sign on for a journey south. The other half had declined, so the shortfall had been made up from sailors recruited by the company that chartered the ship. They included French, Nigerians, Filipinos, Norwegians and Egyptians, to name but a few of the nationalities aboard.

At that moment, the door opened and Hasim entered. He looked around critically, and the relaxed atmosphere immediately turned formal. The two Norwegians stopped chatting and turned to their computers; the communications officer slipped his paperback into his pocket and put on his headphones; and the captain sat straighter in his chair. Only the implacable Zurin did not react. Yablokov lit a cigarette, hoping the smoke would disguise the vodka on his breath.

'Why are we still moving?' demanded Hasim in impeccable Russian. He spoke multiple languages with what Yablokov thought might be a French accent, although he would not have put money on it. That, together with his looks and the occasional remark about some past experience or other, suggested that perhaps he was Algerian, but no one was sure.

'Because the swell slowed us down,' explained Yablokov. 'Then we lost an hour by launching the Zodiac.'

He gave Hasim a pointed glance. He was not

20

a pernickety man, always braying about Health and Safety regulations, but to launch an inflatable so far out to sea was madness. He was just glad that the men detailed to go in it were Hasim's people – the ones Hasim referred to ambiguously as his 'team'. Yablokov would not have wanted his crew to embark on such a risky venture.

'Any news from them?' Hasim asked.

'Not yet. They're still out of radio range.'

'Still?' Hasim scowled, as if he considered it Yablokov's fault that they might have come to grief. 'Then get the gear ready – we may have to act fast.'

'Which gear?' asked Yablokov slyly, knowing that Hasim would not have the faintest idea what was required.

'The gear you anticipate we will require,' retorted Hasim coolly. 'And hurry up about it. Time is of the essence.'

'You heard him,' said Garik. He had hairy fingers, dirty nails and callused skin. His eyes were red-rimmed, but he did not appear to be drunk as he gave one of his wolfish grins. 'Let's make this a trip to remember.'

Yablokov doubted he would forget it.

Berrister and Graham crept to where four elephant seals lounged contentedly in the icy wind. Their target was the largest animal, and Berrister held a dose of ketamine calculated from its estimated body weight. Sedating seals was not easy: too much made them go into 'dive mode', after which it was difficult to start them breathing again. Too little meant they might wake up unexpectedly.

21

Approaching from behind, Berrister injected the sedative. The seal reared with a furious roar, but then lay back down again. When he was sure the anaesthetic was working, he began to take his samples. Unfortunately, he had misjudged the dose, and the animal started to come round too soon. It rolled suddenly, and splintering glass told them that the remaining ampoules of anaesthetic had been crushed, effectively ending the day's work.

'Well, I'd had enough for today anyway,' he sighed. 'Let's finish early.'

'Can we climb the scarp first?' asked Graham, once he had finished packing away their equipment.

Berrister regarded him askance. It was a long way up there. 'Why?'

'To have a look around.' Graham's jaw was set, and Berrister saw a determined glint in the pale blue eyes. 'You said the sounds were ice, but I'm not so sure.'

Graham interpreted Berrister's moment of hesitation as concession, and set off towards the foot of the rocky escarpment without further ado.

'Wait!' shouted Berrister irritably. 'The wind's picking up, and the barometer suggests we're in for another storm. It's not a good time to—'

'It won't take long,' said Graham, glancing around but not stopping. 'Are you coming?'

Berrister had no choice. It was against his own rules to let someone make the climb alone, and he could see that Graham had made up his mind. Rolling his eyes, he began to follow, cursing the soft sand that made climbing such hard work.

The incline grew steeper as they neared the top, and they were forced to use their hands to keep from falling. Berrister glanced down, and saw the four seals lying far below, like brown slugs.

Eventually, they reached the top, where they could look down on their camp and Walker Bay to the west and the huge expanse of South Bay to the east. The day was cloudy, but the view was still spectacular. While he waited for his breathing to slow, Berrister sat on a rock and gazed across an uneasy sea, looking for the blue whales. He soon felt himself growing chilled, the warmth generated by the climb quickly wicked away by the wind.

'Look,' said Graham, pointing down to the beach on the far side – the one opposite to where they had been working. 'There are lines in the sand near the edge of the glacier.'

'Seal tracks,' replied Berrister automatically, but then frowned. They were too straight to have been made by seals. Graham evidently thought so, too, because he shot Berrister a haughty glance and began to bound down the scarp towards them at a pace Berrister felt was far from safe. Alarmed, he shouted for the field hand to stop, but the wind tore his words away. Irked, he saw there was nothing for it but to follow him down.

'Andrew!' shouted Graham, gesturing frantically for him to hurry. As Berrister jogged towards him, Graham waved something in the air. 'It's a dog-end.'

Berrister took it from him. It was indeed a cigarette filter, but it might have been there for months or even years. Rubbish decayed slowly in the Antarctic and, despite the universally held belief that its beaches were pristine, human flotsam was washed up on them every day.

'And look there.' Graham pointed again. 'Blood!'

Berrister crouched down to inspect a red patch in the sand. 'But—'

'Gunfire, a boat, a cigarette end and a pool of blood,' interrupted Graham. 'Someone else is here – someone dangerous.'

'There *might* be another scientific team, I suppose,' acknowledged Berrister, 'although I would have expected them to contact us first. But they won't be carrying guns – it would contravene the Antarctic Treaty.'

The Antarctic Treaty was an agreement signed by all the countries operating in the region. It regulated international relations, established measures to protect wildlife and the environment, and set up guidelines for behaviour. One of its rules forbade weapons of any description, and another banned hunting.

'What if they're criminals?' persisted Graham.

'And why would criminals be here?' asked Berrister, exasperated. 'There'll be a rational and innocent explanation for all these things, you'll see.'

Unconvinced, Graham prowled the beach, looking for the evidence that would prove his theory. Berrister shook his head, and headed back towards the scarp, thinking that if another team had arrived, he and Graham should be at the camp to greet them, not messing about elsewhere.

* * *

24

Dan Wells loved the Antarctic, and had done ever since he had first visited it as a young man in the 1960s. Research had changed since then, and tape measures and the 'eye of faith' had given way to the kind of elaborate instruments that Berrister attached to his seals, which even now were tracking their every move and relaying them to a computer at home.

But Wells preferred to work with a field microscope and a pair of callipers. He knew his colleagues regarded him as a dinosaur, but he did not care. He hated relying on technology over which he had no control, and always gloated when the others' equipment broke or misbehaved.

That day, he had decided to examine a colony of lichens on the South Bay beach, although he had told the others he planned to stay near camp. He knew Berrister would disapprove of him crossing the scarp alone, but he did not care. Berrister's accident had made him overcautious, which was just as bad as being careless in Wells' opinion. Only two people knew the details of Berrister's mishap three years before: Berrister himself and Wells, but neither talked about it. Wells liked Berrister, and appreciated being included in his programme when other colleagues overlooked him for younger, more dynamic researchers. If Berrister wanted the matter to remain between them, then that was how it would be.

He had scrambled over the scarp at a pace that was impressive for a man of sixty-two, and then spent a perfect day on a rocky outcrop that was only accessible at low tide. He stood periodically to stretch his back, looking out across South Bay and the glorious mountains that glittered white in the distance.

Veterans like Wells were usually aware of the incoming tide, but he was in a sheltered spot and failed to notice that an increasing wind had driven the sea in faster than he had anticipated. When he looked up the next time, he was startled to see waves licking at the foot of the ice cliffs he would have to pass on his way back.

He stuffed his samples in his pockets and turned for home. He was not unduly concerned about the water: he would have wet feet, but nothing worse. His biggest worry was how to keep it from the others. He did not want them to foist an assistant on him for the last ten precious days, 'for his own safety'.

Water tugged at his ankles as he waded through the surf, one hand against the cliff for balance. Suddenly, there was a tremendous crack and he froze in horror, sure he was about to be crushed by falling ice. But nothing happened. He began to breathe again, smiling at his own lurid imagination.

Yet even as he grinned, a massive section of the cliff broke away in front of him and dropped into the sea with awesome grace. It created a wave that washed along the foot of the cliff towards him. There was nowhere to run – and nothing to do but brace himself for the impact.

The wave punched into him, sweeping him off his feet, and dragging him back the way he had come. A distant part of his mind told him that perhaps Berrister had been right after all, and it was a sensible precaution to work in pairs and keep in touch by radio. Then the wave relinquished its hold on him, and he found himself lying face down on an ice-littered beach.

Gasping for breath, he pulled himself upright, blinking salt from his eyes and trying to ignore the agonising ache of cold in his body. He squinted along the beach. A massive pile of ice now blocked his way. It was too high to climb over and jutted too far into the sea to skirt around – at least, until the tide went out again. But luck was with him: he had fetched up near where he knew there was a path up to the glacier – he would go over it, and get back to the camp that way. It was not an easy climb, but he had done it before, and the exertion would serve to warm him up.

Painfully, he began to ascend, forcing all thoughts from his mind except inching upwards. Unfortunately, he was wrong to think the effort would restore the heat to his body: he could not move fast enough, and the combination of wind, wet clothes, and the chill of the ice was draining him of life. His arm hurt, too – perhaps he had broken it when he had been swept along the beach.

Doggedly, he staggered on, determined to make it back, because he was *not* going to be remembered as the doddering old fool who had made a fatal error of judgement. Then the path levelled out, and he realised that he had reached the top.

He blinked in disbelief. He had done it! Now all he needed to do was to walk across the top of the glacier and down the other side, where the slope was much shallower. He staggered forward on numb legs. He smiled to himself, sure none of the others could have managed what he had done – they would have lain down and given up. Once again, he had shown that there was no substitute for experience and grit. And what's more, he wouldn't allow what had just happened to change his view of the Antarctic, like Berrister had. *He* would simply add it to his enormous store of anecdotes.

He fell forward on all fours when his foot caught on a ridge, aware that ice crystals were forming on his coat – his clothes were freezing, even as he moved. He started to struggle upright again, but then blinked to clear his vision. Was that someone coming towards him?

Two

As Berrister and Graham hiked along the beach towards the camp – four yellow tents for sleeping, and three green ones for storage, cooking and lab work – the wind picked up, sending sand flying into their eyes. Just ten more days, thought Berrister, gritting his teeth, then the camp would be dismantled, and *Worsley* would take them home. He would sleep in a bed, eat fresh food and scour away three months of grime under a scalding hot shower.

When they arrived, he logged and stored his samples, then headed for the biggest tent, which

28

served as kitchen and common room. It was five o'clock, but, unusually, there was no smell of simmering food and no steamy warmth to greet him – the tent was cold and unwelcoming. Lisa and Graham sat at the empty table, while Sarah fiddled with the cooker.

'Where's Freddy?' Berrister asked, surprised. The Australian had never neglected to prepare their supper before.

'We can't find him,' replied Sarah, her attention on the stove. 'He must've gone exploring.'

'Alone?' asked Berrister, frowning.

Sarah shrugged. 'He's still sulking over Byers. Oh, damn this bloody thing!'

Like them all, she wore multiple layers of clothing and a jacket that had suffered from close contact with the Antarctic's wildlife. It was a mystery to Berrister how she still managed to look elegant. He went to the fuel canister, where a shake suggested it was all but empty.

'But I only changed it yesterday,' objected Graham. 'It must be faulty. Bugger! We've only got one more left. We'll have to be careful if we want it to last.'

'I don't believe Freddy wandered off alone,' said Lisa worriedly. 'And even if he did, he would've made sure he was back in time to make dinner.'

'Dan, Geoff and Joshi are still out, too,' said Graham. 'Perhaps they went somewhere together.'

'Unlikely,' said Sarah, abandoning the cooker to Berrister and going to sit at the table, where she nibbled unenthusiastically at a water biscuit. 'Dan finds Joshi too irritating.'

'Have you tried them on the radio?' asked Berrister.

Sarah nodded. 'Several times – no reply.'

'Maybe they're with our visitors,' said Graham. 'I heard them firing guns to attract our attention, and someone landed a boat over in South Bay.'

'I heard the boat,' said Lisa.

'We saw signs that a boat had been there,' Berrister corrected. 'However, the others wouldn't just go off with them – not without leaving us a message.'

The others stared at him. 'So what are you suggesting?' asked Sarah eventually. 'Because you're scaring me.'

'I don't mean to. However, if they're not back in an hour, we'll go and look for them. OK?'

They nodded, so he primed the stove while Graham fetched water. As they waited for it to boil, they prepared a hasty meal – hot tea, water biscuits smeared with strawberry jam and the remains of the soup, eaten cold. No one spoke, all pondering the sudden, curious changes in a routine that had been unbroken for weeks. Berrister swung between annoyance that Freddy had neglected to leave a message, and worry that all was not well. He did not believe that Graham had heard a gun, but he did know someone had visited South Bay recently, and it was peculiar that no contact had been made. The Antarctic was a close-knit community, despite the vastness of the place, and everyone tended to know what other groups were doing. It was against protocol and good manners to land without making yourself known to the current residents.

30

He thought about his decision to abandon polar research, and was more convinced than ever that it was the right one. He would turn forty in a couple of years, which was too old for the rigours of such an environment. He loved the Antarctic, but he was no Wells, who embraced the discomforts of polar living with happy enthusiasm. He was no Sarah either, determinedly ambitious and still needing to prove herself. No, he thought, as he ate his fifth biscuit, it was time to leave the cold for others to endure.

They all looked up in relief as footsteps crunched in the gravel outside. The door flap was pulled aside and Mortimer stepped in, followed by Joshi.

'Where's dinner?' demanded the fat glaciologist, eyeing the meagre meal in dismay.

'Have you seen Freddy or Dan?' asked Berrister. 'Were either working near you today?'

Mortimer shook his head. 'No, and I tried to contact Dan at about two o'clock, but I couldn't raise him.'

'Why did you want him?'

'No reason,' replied Mortimer blandly. 'Just being friendly.'

Berrister looked hard at him. Everyone knew that Wells would not appreciate being disturbed, and, despite his insouciance, Mortimer was no fool: he never blocked the radio with idle chatter.

'Actually, we thought we heard something,' said Joshi. 'A cry.'

'Nonsense,' countered Mortimer, setting his backpack on the table. 'It was a bird.'

'What sort of cry?' demanded Sarah worriedly.

'The kind that means someone had an accident?'

'No, of course not,' replied Mortimer, frowning at Joshi. 'Or we would have gone to investigate. But you know how it is late in the season, when we're all ready to go home. The imagination always gets a bit wild at this stage.'

He smiled, but Berrister was not deceived. He had known Mortimer for years and it was clear that whatever the glaciologist heard had unsettled him. He stood abruptly.

'We'd better go and look for them now. I wish you'd radioed this in sooner.'

'Radioed what in?' asked Mortimer. 'That we heard a gull? Besides, we all know that Dan isn't looking forward to going home this time. It'll probably be his last season down here, given that you're the only one willing to offer him a place at a field camp these days, and he's made it clear that he intends to savour every last minute. He'll be sitting on a rock somewhere, enjoying himself.'

'Yes, but Freddy can't wait to get out of here,' Berrister pointed out. 'So let's get going. Lisa, pack up some food; Joshi, check the radios are working; Graham, change the gas canister so we'll have some heat when we get back.'

Relieved to be doing something, the two students and the field hand hurried out, leaving Berrister, Sarah and Mortimer to talk more openly.

'God!' said Sarah, her face pale. 'What's going on? I didn't hear a boat, but Lisa swears she did.'

'I'm more concerned about the cracks,' said Berrister worriedly. 'Not that they were gunshots, but that the glacier calved. We didn't hear it fall,

32

but the wind's blowing in the wrong direction, so we wouldn't have done.'

Mortimer nodded soberly. 'Last night's storm might have made it unstable, and if Freddy and Wells took someone up there to show off . . .'

Before either could reply, the flap was ripped open to admit Joshi and Lisa.

'Everything's gone,' gulped Lisa, her eyes wide with fear. 'The supplies – there's nothing left. *Nothing.*'

'There are plenty of boxes,' added Joshi. 'But they're all empty.'

The tent opened again, and this time it was Graham standing there, white and shaking.

'The last gas canister,' he blurted. 'It's punctured or something, and there's nothing in it. The dribble of fuel in here is all we've got left.'

Yablokov stood on deck, watching the crew raise the equipment from the hold. The conditions were not ideal for such an operation – there was a heavy swell and the planking was slippery with spray. One of the Turks stumbled and would have fallen had Yablokov not caught him. The first mate glanced up to the bridge. Hasim was there, as always, watching with critical eyes.

When they had finished, Yablokov ordered them to the mess for a hot meal. He saw the last hatch secured, and hurried back to the bridge. The chief engineer had mended the heating, but the thermostat was broken, so hot air now blasted unchecked from the ancient heaters. One extreme to the other, he thought sourly, unfastening his jacket.

Garik was sprawled in his chair, cap over his eyes, and made no response when Yablokov started to make his report. Yablokov glanced at Zurin. A slight pursing of the lips said it all: the captain was drunk again. Yablokov didn't understand it: Garik had always liked a nip, but he had never been insensible on duty in the Arctic. Did he think they were on holiday here in the south, where his behaviour didn't matter? Yablokov sincerely hoped he had more sense.

He coughed loudly, and watched the big man come to his senses, the sweet scent of old alcohol on his breath.

'The equipment is unloaded,' Yablokov reported. 'I've lashed it down because the glass is dropping – we're in for another storm.'

The captain acknowledged him with a nod. 'Anything on radar?'

'Not yet,' replied Yablokov. 'Have you heard from the Zodiac?'

The captain shrugged, and it was Zurin who answered, by pursing his lips again.

'It's been too long.' Yablokov was concerned. 'We should never have let them go. I said it was too rough.'

'And I said it was not.'

Yablokov jumped. Hasim had a nasty habit of gliding about soundlessly and taking everyone unawares. It made Yablokov acutely uneasy.

Hasim whispered something in the captain's ear, which was another annoying habit. Why not speak aloud, so everyone could hear? When Hasim had finished, Garik heaved himself upright and went to inspect the radar. Yablokov was irked

34

– the implication was that Hasim had not trusted his report. He fought down his irritation. Confronting the man would get him nowhere. Worse, it would likely exclude him from future work with the company, and the pay was too good to lose.

He went to the bridge-wing with a pair of binoculars, and scanned the shifting grey waves anxiously, searching for the splash of colour that would herald the Zodiac's safe return.

Everyone was silent after Graham, Lisa and Joshi had made their announcements. Lisa was openly frightened, while the others looked at Berrister for reassurance. Unable to give it, he headed for the store tent, with its neat stacks of boxes. He began opening them one by one. The others watched for a moment, then began to help. They worked in taut silence, acutely aware that they could not go to help their friends without the necessary provisions, so the sooner they found what they needed, the sooner they could mount a rescue.

The first few cartons were empty, but Mortimer grunted in satisfaction when he unearthed three cans of carrots. Unfortunately, other finds were few and far between, and certainly not enough to last eight people ten days.

'Perhaps Freddy cached them somewhere,' suggested Sarah, her voice strained. 'Because I definitely saw three cases of tuna on Sunday – which was only three days ago.'

'But why?' asked Graham. '*Why* hide the food?'

'And what about the fuel?' asked Mortimer. 'Why is there none left?'

It did not take Berrister long to discover the answer to that: the valves at the top of the cylinder were open, allowing its contents to seep out. He could only assume that Freddy had done it by accident, when he had been performing a routine check.

'I don't understand,' said Lisa in a small voice. 'Why didn't he tell us that we were running low on food? It's his job to make sure this didn't happen.'

'It's not a problem,' said Berrister briskly. 'Help is only a hundred kilometres away, and the Chileans will send a boat – or even a helicopter – when we tell them what's happened. But first, we need to find Freddy and Dan. There'll be an explanation, I'm sure.'

'*If* we find them,' said Lisa fearfully. 'Perhaps someone shot them, then drove off in the boat I heard, taking all our supplies with them.'

'Well, I did see a pool of blood,' began Graham. 'Perhaps it was—'

Berrister cut the discussion off abruptly. 'Stop! Why would anyone steal our food? Let's not jump to conclusions until we have all the evidence. Now, who knows where Dan went?' He gestured to the itinerary sheets that he insisted were completed each day before work began. 'These say he was working down on the point, but I saw him heading in the opposite direction.'

'I think he might have gone over the scarp,' said Joshi unhappily. 'He told me last week that there was some outcrop he wanted to survey.'

'And he wouldn't have put *that* on the sheets, because you'd have insisted he take someone

36

with him,' surmised Mortimer. 'Stupid bugger! Still, if he has gone over there, it explains why he's late back – it's a long way.'

'Freddy's taken to going up the scarp recently,' said Graham. 'Maybe he spotted Dan from the top and went to join him on the beach.'

Berrister didn't want to waste time speculating. 'Geoff can stay here in case they come back. The rest of you – you know the drill. Warm clothes, water bottles, the first aid box. Did you get the radios, Joshi?'

He took one and tested it. The one Sarah held crackled faintly, but there was no sound from any of the others.

'The generator was off,' explained Joshi. 'I left the batteries for Freddy to charge last night, but he must've forgotten. Or he did switch it on, but someone else turned it off.'

Now even Berrister was beginning to be alarmed, although he struggled to hide it. 'Get the generator going, Geoff, and charge up the batteries – we may need them tomorrow if we haven't found Dan and Freddy by then. Then contact the Chileans.'

Sarah regarded him uncertainly. 'So are we still going out now – without food and radios, and with the temperature falling and a storm blowing in?'

'We have to – we can't leave them out all night. Lisa can stay here with Geoff, so if they do come back, she can run up the scarp and signal to us. I suggest the rest of us go over the ridge, then Joshi and I will head north, while you and Graham go south. OK?'

'Me?' asked Joshi uneasily. 'With you? Have you done this before? I know Graham has.'

Berrister could only suppose that his obsession with safety had given Joshi the impression that he didn't know what he was doing. Mortimer hastened to reassure him.

'You'll be fine with him, Joshi – just do what he tells you. Now, it's six-thirty. Everyone should look up at the scarp on the hour, every hour. If Lisa has her arms at her sides, it means the others have come home. If she holds them over her head, it means keep looking. Any questions?'

There were none, so they took their leave of the camp. Graham shot up the steep slope like a gazelle, Joshi hot on his heels with Sarah, while Berrister brought up the rear. It was markedly colder than it had been earlier, and the sky was a dull, leaden grey. The wind had picked up, too, and seemed to blow straight into their faces. It slowed Berrister down, especially when combined with the heavy pack he was carrying.

By the time they reached the top, his legs were shaking from fatigue. Graham barely gave him time to catch his breath before beginning the descent. Joshi shot past them, trying to be first, and Berrister yelled at him to slow down. Joshi ignored him, then caught his foot on a rock and took a long tumble.

'For God's sake!' snapped Berrister, hauling the student to his feet. 'We can't be ferrying you back to the camp with a broken leg – not when Dan and Freddy might need us.'

But Joshi barely heard him. He was gazing at something in his hand – a dirty brown hat that might have gone unnoticed if he had not been face down on the ground.

'This is Freddy's,' he said in a cracked voice.

Berrister and Sarah exchanged a glance: the hat was Freddy's good luck charm, and the fact that he was parted from it did not bode well. Berrister shoved it in his pocket without a word.

'Which rock did Dan say he wanted to examine?' he asked Joshi. 'Not the one by that fresh ice fall – the one surrounded by water?'

Swallowing hard, Joshi nodded. 'It isn't surrounded when the tide's out.'

'That ice wasn't there earlier,' said Graham unnecessarily. 'Maybe you were right, Andrew – maybe those snaps *were* the sounds of it shearing off.'

They struggled along the shore, keeping as far away from the towering cliffs as possible, all acutely aware of the danger of another fall. They reached the rock, where Berrister removed his boots and tugged on a pair of waders instead.

'Tie this around you,' said Graham, pulling a rope from the rucksack. 'Then if you fall, we can pull you back.'

Berrister waded into the surf. The cold penetrated the thin boots immediately, and a sudden, agonising ache told him they leaked. The water soon reached his waist. The rock, when he reached it, was wet and slippery, making it difficult to get a good grip. Eventually, he managed, and had almost reached the top, when part of it came away in his hand. He began to slide back down into the icy water.

*   *   *

39

Garik snored softly on the bridge. Had Hasim not been there, hovering possessively, Yablokov would have woken him and suggested he nap in his cabin, as it was hardly edifying for the captain to sleep on duty. Garik grunted and settled himself more comfortably. The two Norwegian officers exchanged a smirk, but stopped when Yablokov glared at them.

Yablokov smothered a sigh. He appreciated that *Lena* was not all she had once been, but he took pride in her nevertheless, and liked to see her well run. But how was he supposed to maintain discipline when the captain set that sort of example?

The wind was rising and there were whitecaps on the waves. Scattered across the surface were chunks of ice, some the size of cars, and every so often there was a thud as one hit the ship. As the barometric pressure continued to drop, Yablokov recommended finding a safe anchorage until the storm blew itself out. Hasim disagreed: they were on a tight schedule, and had no time to wait for squalls. Yablokov scowled: he *knew* they were running late. However, their success depended on good seamanship as well as keeping to a timetable, and they would be no use to their employers if they sank.

Hasim opened his mouth to argue further, but at that moment, a wave tossed a huge lump of ice on the foredeck, where it smashed a hatch. Seething with impotent anger, Hasim woke Garik and told him to look for a place where they could wait out the storm. Yablokov studied the charts and recommended one himself, not trusting

Garik to make a sensible decision. Of course, the men on the Zodiac were unlikely to guess where they'd gone, but the inflatable was now hours overdue, and looking at the monstrous grey waves, Yablokov doubted they would see it again. He said as much to Garik, but the captain only turned to ask Hasim what they should do about it. Disgusted, Yablokov went to the mess for some sensible company.

He found it in Nikos, the chief engineer, a small, bald man with wall eyes, who spoke Russian with an almost incomprehensible Greek accent.

'How long since it left?' asked Nikos, rolling a vile-smelling cigarette. 'Five hours?'

'Eight,' replied Yablokov tightly.

'Well, at least they're Hasim's team, not the crew,' said Nikos, blowing pungent smoke through his nostrils. 'His loss, not ours. I'm worried about the cargo, though.'

'You are?' asked Yablokov, surprised. 'You told Garik earlier that it was fine.'

'It is – for now. But it was loaded with far too much haste. I told them to slow down, to do it properly, but they said they had no time. No one around here has time.'

'Garik doesn't – he needs to get *Lena* to Murmansk for the start of the cod season, or the rest of the fleet will steal the march on us. And Hasim told me that he's got to be home soon, too.'

'Something terribly important, no doubt,' sniffed Nikos.

Yablokov nodded. 'He wants to get his hair cut.'

41

Nikos laughed, then became serious. 'But the cargo bothers me. A few more hours would have seen it much better stowed, then we could have weathered all the storms you like.'

'Is that why you told Hasim that our bows are weak – that *Lena* can't take ploughing through so much ice? It was the first I'd heard about it.'

Nikos waved a dismissive hand. 'You're right – this old bucket has a few years in her yet. And yes, I lied because we can't have the cargo breaking loose and rolling around.'

'Then why not tell Hasim so?'

'I did. He came for a quick look, pronounced all was well and told me not to mention it again.'

Yablokov was about to suggest that they went to the holds themselves when a crewman came to report that the Zodiac had been spotted. Astonished, Yablokov ran to the foredeck, mustering hands as he went. He yelled for the crane to be readied, and told Zurin to arrange for blankets and hot food to be ready, too, knowing that Hasim's people would need them.

The little craft bobbed closer, labouring up the sides of the great waves and racing down into the troughs. Yablokov squinted into the wind, eyes streaming. Something was wrong! Zurin thought so too, and handed him his binoculars.

Berrister did not fall far, and soon regained his footing. He climbed quickly to the top of Wells' outcrop, but it was all for nothing: a quick search revealed that neither Wells nor Freddy was there. Several tiny scratches showed that Wells had recently taken some samples, but that was all.

He checked once more, then waded back to the shore, gritting his teeth against the cold. Shivering, he kicked off the waders and dragged on dry clothes, telling the others what he had found as he did so.

'Then it's obvious what happened,' said Graham. He glanced over his shoulder at the ice fall. 'Dan's under that. Freddy saw it drop on him from the scarp and came to help, but then he was crushed, too. We did hear three separate cracks – which means three different falls.'

'Not necessarily,' argued Berrister, although he was inclined to think the Scot was right. He sensed Joshi was close to tears. 'So you two walk to the end of the beach – maybe Dan found some new species there, and Freddy can't tear him away. Go on – hurry.'

'What will you be doing?' asked Graham, not moving.

Berrister indicated the tumbled ice. 'Investigating that.'

'You can't possibly excavate it all,' said Graham, looking at it in dismay.

He was right, but Berrister did not want to admit it in front of Joshi. 'Be as quick as you can, then come back and help us,' was all he said. 'And don't forget to look up at the ridge in five minutes for Lisa's signal.'

Graham nodded once, then began walking rapidly along the beach. Joshi glanced miserably at Berrister before following, staggering as the wind bore him forward. Berrister and Sarah turned into it, and began slogging back towards the ice fall.

43

It was not a large one, but still comprised blocks three times as high as they were tall, all covered in white, powdery snow. Waves lapped around its edges, making greedy sucking sounds. While Sarah watched for Lisa's signal, Berrister climbed across it, looking for signs that someone was underneath. Sarah joined him after she had watched the lone figure stand with arms raised, struggling to stay upright in the wind.

'We're definitely in for another storm,' remarked Berrister. 'So when Joshi and Graham return, I want you to take them back to camp, while I continue to dig here. Hopefully, Geoff will have contacted the Chileans by then, and they'll help.'

'Yes, but not until the storm dies out,' said Sarah.

'No,' agreed Berrister sombrely. 'Not until then.'

For an hour, they scratched and scraped, constantly glancing upward in fear of another collapse. They levered away some chunks with driftwood, but most were too big and the wood too soft. At nine o'clock, Sarah went to watch Lisa's next signal, then returned to report that Wells and Freddy were still missing. By now, the sun had set and the light was fading fast.

'This is worse than useless!' she snapped, kicking one slab in an agony of frustration. 'We need a mechanical digger to excavate this, not bare hands.'

She was right, but there was nothing they could do except keep trying. Berrister's gloves were soaking, and he could barely feel his fingers. He began to dig again, concentrating on a point where the ice was looser.

44

Eventually, Graham and Joshi arrived, exhausted from their battle against the wind. Their grey, tired faces and a rip in Joshi's waterproof trousers suggested that they had done their best, although to no avail.

'We need to stop now,' said Graham in a low voice, looking at no one in particular. 'We're too tired and cold to be effective, and it's getting too dark to see. If we stay out much longer, we'll end up in trouble, too.'

'He's right,' said Sarah wretchedly. 'We've done all we can.'

By giving up, they were effectively acknowledging that Wells and Freddy were dead, something Berrister was unwilling to do. He started to shake his head, but then his eye was caught by something he had just uncovered. He bent to pick it up. It was a plastic specimen bag with a red resealable top.

'One of Dan's,' said Sarah softly. 'With today's date on it, and a time of eleven-thirty.'

'That's just before I heard . . .' Graham faltered, wiping his nose on his hand.

'When you heard what you thought was gunfire, but was probably the ice calving,' Sarah finished. Her expression was bleak. 'I'm sorry, Andrew, but there are only two places Dan and Freddy can be: under this or washed out to sea. Either way, they're beyond our help, and we need to go back before we get into trouble, too. Look at Joshi – he's all in.'

'You take them,' said Berrister. 'I'll keep looking for a bit longer. Besides, while the bag might mean that Dan *is* under here, there's nothing to say that Freddy is with him.'

'No,' acknowledged Sarah. 'But we did find his hat – his *lucky* hat, which he'd never have abandoned without good reason.'

'That's a good point,' said Graham, a little too eagerly for Berrister's liking – the Scot was clearly more concerned with his own welfare than his missing friends. 'Staying here any longer is pointless. We *have* to go. Now.'

Leaving was one of the most difficult things Berrister had ever done, and he could not rid himself of the conviction that a few more moments might save a life. But Joshi's nose had the dull, whitish look of frost-nip and the daylight had almost gone. Without waiting for permission, Graham began to lead the way home. Berrister stared at the ice for some time before following.

That night, a short but fierce storm swept across the island. The wind screamed down the glacier, ripped across the beach and tore out into the bay. Pieces of rock and ice buffeted the tents so violently that the poles groaned under the pressure. It was not the first gale the scientists had experienced at Hannah Point, nor the wildest, but with two of their friends missing, it felt like the worst.

But by five o'clock the following morning, it had abated somewhat. Berrister emerged from his tent, and when he went to check the temperature, he found the thermometer had blown away. So had the store-tent, because the empty boxes had been insufficient to anchor it down. It lay in a soggy heap several hundred metres away. He went to the cook tent, and found Mortimer already there. The fat glaciologist gave him a haunted look.

'We're in a fix here, Andrew.'

Berrister nodded. 'We'll ask the Chileans to evacuate us today. But we'll search for Dan and Freddy until they arrive.'

Mortimer narrowed his eyes. 'Didn't you hear what I told you last night? We *can't* call the Chileans – neither long-range radio works and the generators are down, so we can't power them up. We can't call anyone.'

Berrister recalled very little about the return journey and their arrival back at the camp, assailed as he was with the sense of having condemned two friends to death. He scrubbed at his face with his hands. 'What about Joshi's Iridium phone? I saw him talking to his brother on it a few days ago.'

'Quite – he ran down the battery and forgot to recharge it. The bloody thing's useless. The phone, I mean, not Joshi.'

'Then we'll repair the generators.'

Mortimer's expression was grim. 'I've been trying – all night, as it happens. But they'll never work again. Never.'

Berrister frowned. 'They were working OK yesterday. What's the problem?'

'Sabotage,' replied Mortimer. Berrister gaped at him. 'I'm serious, Andrew – someone mixed sugar with the fuel. To put it in layman's terms, the inside of each motor is full of sticky gunk.'

Berrister felt his stomach churn. 'Are you sure the cold hasn't affected the consistency of the fuel? Perhaps if we warmed it . . .'

'It's sugar,' said Mortimer firmly. 'And whoever put it there knew what he was doing, because neither will ever work again.'

But Berrister shook his head, unwilling to believe it. 'You must be mistaken. You're upset over Dan and Freddy—'

'I *am* upset, but I'm not mistaken: someone deliberately destroyed our only means of communication. And obviously, whoever it was also stole our food. You clearly think I'm mad, but the facts are that we're marooned here with no supplies and no way of calling for help. Go and look at the generators yourself if you don't believe me.'

Berrister went, but it did not take many minutes for him to see that the glaciologist was right. He returned to Mortimer, his stomach churning.

'Do you think Freddy did it?' asked Mortimer. 'Or Dan?'

'Of course not! Lisa heard a boat, Graham and I found tracks and a cigarette end . . . but who would want to do this to us? We're scientists, for God's sake.'

'Good question,' said Mortimer. 'But two of us are missing, and Graham says he found blood on the beach. Perhaps Dan and Freddy aren't so much missing as . . . dispatched.'

'Dispatched?' cried Berrister, shocked. 'But that's insane!'

'Yes,' acknowledged Mortimer. 'But so are two sabotaged radios, no food and a pair of vanished friends.'

'No,' said Berrister, stubbornly refusing to believe it. 'There must be a rational explanation – an innocent one.'

48

'Such as what?'

'I don't know,' Berrister admitted. 'But help will come soon. When we fail to contact Rothera, they'll ask the Chileans to send a plane to check on us.'

Rothera was a British research station on Adelaide Island, off the Antarctic Peninsula, some 550 kilometres south. Several of their colleagues were working there, and the arrangement was to check in with them by radio every night. Three missed calls would result in rescue protocols being initiated – a reconnaissance plane from Chile's Eduardo Frei base on nearby King George Island in the first instance, followed by a message to all ships in the area if necessary.

'They won't do anything until the day after tomorrow at the earliest – and then only if the weather is clear enough for a flight,' Mortimer insisted. 'It might be days before anything happens.'

Berrister gave a wan smile. 'Fortunately, I've been collecting krill for Noddy Taylor. He's an absolute fanatic, and when he doesn't get last night's data he'll want to know why. He'll be all over Vince until he has an answer.'

Vince was Rothera's communications officer, a quiet, businesslike man, known for the brevity of his messages. No one dared clutter the airwaves with inconsequential chatter when he was at the console.

'Yes,' acknowledged Mortimer. 'There's not much Noddy lets between him and his krill. He—'

He faltered as the tent flap was wrenched open. It was Joshi, eyes alight with excitement.

49

'There's a ship on the other side of the scarp – a little rust-coloured thing, anchored about a kilometre out. It must've come in during the night. We're saved! Now we need to work out how to contact it.'

'Let's look at it first,' cautioned Mortimer. 'And if it seems friendly, we'll let off a flare. I'll fetch some while you wake the others.'

'Is it true?' asked Sarah, as she emerged from her tent. Her eyes were red; she had been crying. 'Rescue is at hand?'

'Maybe,' hedged Berrister. 'We're going to look. Coming?'

Graham emerged fully clothed. His hair was matted and his ginger beard was more straggly than usual. There were dark rings under his eyes, and he looked pale and unhealthy. He also smelled of whisky, and Berrister was not entirely sure that he was sober.

It did not take them long to don warm clothes and begin their ascent, although Berrister, ever safety conscious, was the only one who thought to grab a knapsack containing their emergency supplies. It was a dishevelled, gasping group that reached the top of the escarpment to gaze down at the ship.

She was a curious vessel, red with rust, and with an odd collection of winches and hauling tackle on the afterdeck. Berrister had never seen anything quite like it. He was about to suggest that she was a fishing trawler, when he happened to glance behind him, back down at the camp. Two figures were moving about in it, setting it on fire.

Three

For a minute, all Berrister could do was gape at the blazing tents so far below. There was a Zodiac on the beach nearby – he could only surmise that it had arrived while they were climbing the ridge. Then came a distant crack. One of the men was pointing at Sarah's tent. A split second later, there was another bang as the second man did the same to his own.

'They're *shooting*,' breathed Joshi in horror. 'They think we're inside, still asleep, because it's only six in the morning. They want to kill us!'

'Oh, God!' gulped Graham, gazing accusingly at Berrister. 'You should have listened yesterday. I *told* you I heard gunfire. Those men killed Dan and Freddy, and now they're coming for us.'

'Down! Get down!' Berrister hissed. 'Behind the rocks. Quick!'

Once out of sight, Sarah wriggled forward on her stomach to look down and see what was happening. She gave a stifled cry.

'What is it?' asked Lisa fearfully.

'They're burning the cook tent now. No! This can't be happening!'

Lisa clutched Joshi's hand and turned a terrified gaze on Berrister. 'What's going on? I don't understand.'

Berrister was looking in the other direction, at the ship, which had swung around on its anchor

51

to display the side that had been hitherto invisible.

'Christ!' he breathed, appalled. 'Look what's tied to its side.'

The others peered over the edge. The vessel was listing slightly, pulled over by the ropes and chains that stretched from it to the whale that was tethered there. The water around it was stained red with blood.

'But that's illegal,' blurted Joshi, shocked.

'Not necessarily,' countered Lisa. 'The Japanese have permits to catch whales down here. It must be one of theirs.'

'They do – to kill minke whales,' said Berrister. 'But that's not a minke. It's a blue – one of the pod I saw with Freddy the other day.'

'It can't be,' argued Mortimer. 'Blues are seriously protected beasties. No Japanese whaler is going to take one of those.'

'Who says it's Japanese?' asked Berrister. 'It's got no identifying flags that I can see. And that most definitely *is* a blue whale.'

Graham, who had not taken his eyes off the camp, gave a yelp of alarm. 'They're coming! They're climbing up the scarp.'

He was right. Finding the camp abandoned, the two men were beginning to walk towards them. Even from a distance, they could see the pair of them carried guns.

'Obviously, they don't want witnesses to their illegal whaling,' whispered Joshi. 'Oh, God!'

'We're trapped,' gulped Lisa. 'Men with guns on one side, and their ship on the other. What're we going to do?'

52

'Roll rocks at them,' determined Berrister. 'Or start a sand-slide.'

'Why bother?' asked Graham wretchedly. 'These guys mean business – even if we beat these two, others will come. Then what?'

'We'll face that when – *if* – it happens,' said Berrister firmly. 'Come on. And keep your heads down.'

He crawled to the edge of the scarp. The two men were already halfway up it, and he could see their weapons quite clearly – ugly things, larger than revolvers but smaller than rifles. He supposed they were semi-automatics. He began to push the soft sand in front of him, easing it down the slope. His first attempt caused quite a slide, taking small stones with it, but it veered off to one side. The others joined him, heaving and shoving for all they were worth.

It was not as easy as he had hoped. Their avalanches followed the tracks of the gullies that had been carved by rain, which allowed the gunmen to stay out of their way with ease. They were now three-quarters of the way up, and he could see their faces – dark featured, perhaps Mediterranean, although it was difficult to tell.

In desperation, Joshi clambered to his feet and threw stones at them. It was a mistake. One man pointed his gun at him and sent off a rapid spray of bullets. Joshi toppled forward, and began sliding down the slope.

Sarah screamed, and started to dive after him, but Mortimer hauled her back. The gunmen scrambled towards the slithering student, while

53

Graham began frantically heaving a barrage of stones over the edge.

'Stop!' Berrister yelled in alarm. 'You'll hit Joshi.'

'It's too late for him,' Graham shouted back. 'Now help me!'

At that point, Joshi managed to arrest his wild tumble, and Berrister saw the student's terrified face looking up at him in mute appeal. The man in the lead had reached him, and was preparing to shoot him in the head. Then Berrister saw the flare they had brought with them. He snatched it up, took aim and fired.

Early morning was Yablokov's favourite time of day. He had expected twenty-four-hour daylight so far south, but autumn had arrived. It was quite dark between ten and four, after which came dawn. The light had a beautiful silvery-gold quality that he had never seen before. He stood on the bridge-wing and savoured it.

The storm had not been as severe as he had anticipated, and by five o'clock the wind had dropped sufficiently to let them be about their work. Nikos, the chief engineer, came to stand next to him.

'This is a bad business,' he said, trying to light one of his foul cigarettes.

'The whale?' asked Yablokov, looking to where the huge carcass bobbed as the crew struggled to tether it more closely to the ship. Garik, who had boasted of his experience with the Arctic whaling fleet, was directing the operation from the deck, Hasim at his side. The whole business was a shambles, and Yablokov was sure it had been luck, rather than skill, that had given Garik a successful hit on his first attempt with the harpoon.

'No, not the whale,' said Nikos shortly. 'The scientists.'

Yablokov nodded agreement. 'Hasim told me that Livingston Island is uninhabited – that the bases here would be closed by now.'

'They are, but he forgot to mention that some of the field camps might still be running. We can't let them see us, Evgeny – illegal whaling carries a prison sentence.'

Yablokov knew it. When he had been invited to sail south, and heavily veiled hints suggested that *Lena* wouldn't be fishing for shrimp, he had looked up Southern Ocean whales on Wikipedia. The whole region was an official whale sanctuary, and the penalties for hunting were severe. But *Lena* would only take a couple, and he could not see it would do any harm. And he had a family to think of – cod in the Arctic was so badly overfished that it was only a matter of time before the industry went under. He had to take precautions, and if killing whales meant food on the table, then so be it.

Of course, his kids would starve for sure if *Lena* were caught and he was arrested, especially given that the animal they had caught was a blue whale. He was angry as well as worried. Hasim's men had taken the Zodiac specifically to make sure the area was deserted, so *Lena* could work unseen, yet he had known something was wrong as soon as he had seen the inflatable lumbering back to the ship. He had demanded an explanation from Hasim, who had denied anything was amiss. Yablokov knew he was lying, so he had asked the captain, but Garik had simply raised his glass in a sloppy salute and drank a toast to the riches he said would soon be theirs.

The door opened and Hasim stepped outside to join them. Nikos tucked his unsmoked cigarette behind his ear and left without a word.

'You told us there'd be no one here,' Yablokov said accusingly, watching Hasim don a woollen cap. 'Now what? They're bound to see us.'

'You worry too much,' said Hasim. 'Just trust me.'

Yablokov almost laughed. Trust him? Yeah, right! 'We'll spend the next ten years in prison if—'

'It doesn't matter if they see us or not,' interrupted Hasim. 'Because I have a plan.'

'What plan?' demanded Yablokov.

There was a slight pause before Hasim answered.

The flare shot from Berrister's hand and by some miracle caught the gunman square in the chest. Surprise, rather than force, made the man lose his balance. He tumbled backward, and he and flare intertwined as they bounced down the slope together. His scream continued for a long time after he was lost from sight.

Berrister's hands shook. Until that moment, the deaths of Wells and Freddy had seemed remote, and he had not given up hope that they would appear, alive and well. Seeing men shooting into their tents and setting the camp alight brought

56

home the fact that their colleagues were dead, and that they themselves might soon follow.

'Andrew!' hissed Sarah. The urgency in her voice pulled him from his shocked immobility. 'Get the other one.'

The second man had almost reached Joshi. Berrister fumbled the spare cartridge into the flare and took aim, but the success of the first shot had been a fluke. The next went so wide that his target did not so much as flinch. And that was it: they had only brought two flares, and the rest were in a box at the camp. Lisa's wail of dismay told the gunman that his quarry were now out of ammunition, so he began to climb again, ignoring Joshi to deal with the bigger threat first.

Berrister hurled a rock at him, then ducked as a frenzy of bullets clattered so close that he fancied he felt the wind of them passing above his head. The man continued his relentless advance, while Berrister tried frantically to think of something else to do, but his mind was numb with shock and fear. All he could do was watch the man climb ever closer.

But the would-be killer had reckoned without Joshi. The student began pelting him with stones from behind, his terrified sobs audible from the crest. When the man spun around to shoot him, Mortimer shoved a large slab of basalt down the slope. It bounced once, and then caught the man on the back of his legs – they went from underneath him and gravity did the rest. With a yell of shock, he went the way of his accomplice, clawing and grabbing at the slope in a desperate attempt to slow his descent.

Berrister scrambled towards Joshi. 'Are you hit?'

He pulled the student this way and that, looking for blood.

'I just slipped,' replied Joshi sheepishly. 'I'm not hit.'

The second man had dropped his gun before he had fallen, so Berrister snatched it up. It felt cold, unfamiliar and heavy in his hands.

'Andrew!' yelled Sarah. 'Look!'

Berrister whipped round and saw a second boat landing on the beach, bringing another four armed men. He slung the weapon over his shoulder by its strap, and clambered back up the slope to the others, Joshi at his heels. The newcomers were already running across the beach, heading for the ridge.

'We need to move,' said Sarah shakily. 'Farther along the crest – towards the glacier.'

'Why?' asked Lisa in a small voice. 'It's only delaying the inevitable, and we can't run forever.'

'Nonsense!' snapped Sarah. 'We're *not* sitting here, waiting for them to kill us. We're going to outwit them. We've got a gun and we know this place – they don't. Now pull yourself together.'

'I know what we can do,' said Graham suddenly. 'Follow me.'

Without waiting to explain, he turned and began to jog along the crest, impressively sure-footed on the uneven terrain. Joshi and Sarah followed, so Berrister hauled Lisa to her feet and pulled her after him. Behind them, Mortimer brought up the rear, huffing and blowing like a steam engine.

58

The scarp ran north for several hundred metres before it met the glacier. It changed as it snaked towards the ice, from a scree slope to a rocky ledge, with almost sheer drops on either side. One false step, and there would be no need to worry about being shot. As if to prove it, Lisa lost her footing, saving herself only by grabbing Berrister's leg. For one agonising moment, he thought they were both doomed, but Mortimer dragged her up before she could pitch down, taking Berrister with her. Gasping and shaking in terror, she straddled the ledge on all fours.

'They're gaining on us,' yelled Mortimer, urgently. 'Come on!'

'I can't—' she began.

She was interrupted by three sharp snaps, and a puff of dust rose close to her foot. It galvanised her into motion, and she set off at a speed that left the other two standing.

By the time they reached the glacier, Graham had kicked footholds in it and the others had followed him up a short cliff to the smooth white dome beyond. Berrister wondered what the Scot was thinking, because they would be even more exposed there than on the scarp. He gave Lisa a shove to urge her upwards, and waited for Mortimer, who was trailing behind. The glaciologist's face was red from effort, strands of lank brown hair poking wetly from under his hat. He glanced behind him. The men had reached the crest, and were making better time along it than their quarry had done.

'Go on without me,' gasped Mortimer, swiping

59

sweat from his eyes. 'Maybe I can hold them off for a while – give you a bit longer to escape.'

'Don't talk, just move!' Berrister suddenly remembered the gun. If he and Mortimer were sitting ducks, then so were their attackers. He pointed the weapon and pulled the trigger. Nothing happened.

'The safety catch,' rasped Mortimer. 'You've got to take off the safety catch.'

Berrister looked helplessly at the weapon and its unfamiliar components, so Mortimer snatched it from him, and let off a burst that forced their pursuers to throw themselves flat on the ground.

'That should slow them down,' he muttered.

Berrister began to climb the ice, aware of Mortimer wheezing behind him. It was not far up the little cliff to where the glacier flattened into a much gentler slope, and Graham and the others had already travelled some distance across it. Berrister ran to catch up with them, hoping Mortimer was following. Two sharp shots rang out, and he whipped around in alarm. There was no sign of Mortimer. He was about to go back when the glaciologist appeared on the dome and began to trot towards him, white-faced.

'And then there were three,' he muttered.

Berrister pulled him along, acutely aware of the crevasses that would be hidden beneath the snow – great cracks in the ice created when it moved over the rocks below. At the edge, most were shallow, but further in, they were very deep – some too deep to measure. He and the others had no choice but to chance it, but their pursuers did. Maybe they'd decide it wasn't worth the risk, and would give up. A glance behind him killed any such hope.

'Can you shoot them, too?' he asked Mortimer.

The glaciologist shook his head. 'Too far for me. Waste of ammo.'

In the distance, he heard Graham shout a warning – Joshi was forging recklessly ahead. The student had only gone a few metres when he gave a scream of terror and disappeared from sight.

Berrister felt his heart thud painfully, and cursed himself for agreeing to venture onto the glacier in the first place – if there was a way to die that terrified him above all others, it was by falling down a crevasse. He stumbled to where Graham was kneeling next to a dark hole, the others standing indecisively around him.

'Keep moving,' he ordered. 'Or they'll pick us off.'

'We can't,' said Graham tersely. 'This part of the glacier's riddled with fissures – but that's why I brought us here. It's how we'll escape.'

'You mean we go down there?' whispered Berrister, appalled. 'But it might be hundreds of metres deep.'

'It's not,' said Graham. 'Not on this bit of the ice.'

'He's right,' said Mortimer, suddenly hopeful. 'It's fairly thin here. We *might* be able to hide down there – but only as long as those bastards don't see where we're going.'

Graham nodded quickly, before snatching the gun from him and taking careful aim. There was

61

a sharp snap, and one man jumped convulsively before crumpling. The other two hurled themselves flat. They stayed down: clearly their enthusiasm for the chase had waned once their prey had acquired the wherewithal to fight back.

Graham slung the weapon over his shoulder. 'Now follow me. Hurry!'

Berrister faltered when he saw where the Scot intended to take them. Joshi's crevasse was a jagged, turquoise-blue gash in the snow, deadly and uninviting. Sarah needed no more urging, though: she dropped to her knees, skittered over the edge and was gone. Lisa was quick to follow and then only Berrister and Mortimer were left. Berrister knelt and peered downwards. Joshi stood at the bottom with Graham and Sarah, while Lisa slid towards them. It was not deep – perhaps four metres – and a ceiling of snow made it more tunnel than crevasse. The bottom looked solid, but appearances could be deceptive – it might be a wafer-thin crust that would disintegrate when he stood on it, sending him crashing to his death.

'They'll see us,' he objected. 'Then we really will be sitting ducks.'

'Not if we ease further along it,' argued Mortimer. 'Now, hurry up, for God's sake, or they'll guess what we're about.'

'I'm not doing it,' said Berrister, standing abruptly. 'I'll run on ahead, lead them away from you.'

'But that's suicide.'

'So is this. I'd rather take my chances up here.'

Mortimer moved fast. Berrister felt a sharp

shove, and then was tumbling downwards. The light turned from white to violet and he landed with a jolt that drove the breath from his body.

'I won't be party to this,' snarled Yablokov, drawing the curious attention of the other officers on the bridge. He lowered his voice. 'And neither will my crew.'

'*Your* crew?' asked Hasim. 'I always understood it was the captain's. Am I mistaken?'

Yablokov glanced out of the window to the foredeck, where Garik was trying to supervise the flensing. The barrage of contradictory orders stopped while he fortified himself with a nip from his flask. Then the hollering began afresh.

'No,' replied Yablokov stiffly, although he itched to remind Hasim of who was actually running the ship at the moment. He did not know whether it was Garik's constant drunkenness or his unhealthy association with Hasim that had alienated the captain from his crew. Regardless, the last few hours dealing with the whale had lost him the final vestiges of any respect he might still have held.

'Well then,' smiled Hasim. 'We'll do what he says, shall we?'

'But murder!' Yablokov was still shocked. 'That's something else.'

'*Your* pretty white hands will remain unsullied,' said Hasim, disdain in every word. 'So just sail the boat. Leave the rest to me and Garik.'

'You expect me to look the other way while you kill scientists?' Yablokov was outraged. 'What do you take me for?'

'A man who wants to see his family again,' replied Hasim coldly. 'And who *doesn't* want to spend the next ten years in prison – because that's where you'll end up if these scientists blab.'

'It shouldn't have happened,' snapped Yablokov. 'Your men said the island was empty.'

'They were mistaken.'

They were lying, thought Yablokov sullenly. It had been obvious from the way they had delivered their report that they knew the island was occupied, but had been under pressure from Hasim to declare otherwise. Like Hasim, all they wanted was to catch a whale before it was time to sail north again. And all of them would rather murder witnesses than look for different whales to kill.

'Why can't we just head north right now?' Yablokov asked desperately. 'We'll make a clean escape, and that'll be that.'

'And our cargo? Do you want to take that home again?'

'We'll leave it somewhere else,' argued Yablokov. 'No one will know.'

'*I* would know,' said Hasim coldly. 'Ergo, so would our employers. You've been paid handsomely to do a job, and I'm here to see you do it properly. It's too late to "escape" anyway – if we let these people go, we might as well surrender right now. Is that what you want?'

He turned abruptly as one of his team hurried towards him.

'The scientists have disappeared,' he reported tersely. 'We can't find them.'

'Disappeared?' echoed Hasim incredulously. 'From six men with guns?'

'They got one off us and fired back. Two are dead, and Ibram is hurt bad.'

Yablokov closed his eyes. It was getting worse by the minute – a nightmare! When he opened them again, Hasim had gone and Nikos was there instead. The engineer was smoking, his movements jerky and agitated.

'A dead whale's one thing,' he muttered. 'But dead people is something else. I don't like it at all.'

Yablokov nodded. 'We should forget the whole thing and go home while we can. I don't want blood on my hands, and none of the scientists have died yet. It's not too late to throw in the towel.'

'Who told you none of the scientists have died?' asked Nikos bitterly. 'Because they have, and it *is* too late, Evgeny. We can either kill the rest of them or go to prison. Those are our only two choices.'

Yablokov gazed at him in despair, cursing the day Garik had come to him with the 'offer of a lifetime'. He should have known it was too good to be true, especially given that he had distrusted Hasim on sight. He should have disembarked the moment the man had come aboard.

'The cargo's ready,' said Nikos, when the Russian made no reply. 'Do you want to see to it, or shall I speak to Garik instead?'

'God, no!' muttered Yablokov. 'I'm coming.'

When he stopped falling, Berrister opened his eyes, then closed them again quickly. He was lying on his back at the bottom of the crevasse, its narrow walls rising to the slit of grey sky above.

'Andrew! Hurry!'

He felt his shoulder shaken hard. Reluctantly, he forced his eyes open a second time and saw Graham's anxious face looming over him.

'Come *on*,' the Scot hissed urgently, and was gone.

Berrister sat up slowly. The base of the crevasse was just wide enough for a man to lie down, and was lit dimly by the light that filtered through the thin ceiling of snow above. He stood unsteadily. The crevasse disappeared into gloom in both directions, and the others had chosen to take the wider route to the left. Graham turned and made an urgent sound, begging him to follow. Despite the chill, Berrister felt himself break into a cold sweat, and it was not easy to make himself venture deeper into the ice, as memories of his accident assailed him.

The crevasse bottom soon narrowed to a sharp v that caught his boots and made them difficult to extricate. It was slippery, too, and with every step he was sure that either he would be crushed by ice falling from above, or the 'floor' would collapse under his weight and send him plummeting to his death. Then, Graham stopped so abruptly that Berrister collided with him. The Scot raised a finger to his lips.

There were angry voices just above their heads – their pursuers were arguing, although not in a language Berrister recognised. He held his breath, sure they would be able to hear his heart pounding in his chest. He gazed upwards in an agony of tension, expecting one to crash through the fragile ceiling at any moment.

But the voices moved away after a while. Wordlessly, he and Graham caught up with the others, where Mortimer took the lead. It grew colder and darker as they ventured deeper inside the glacier, and their fissure intersected with others. For Berrister, every step was a massive effort of will – Mortimer had never been a very good glaciologist, so why was everyone trusting *him* to go first?

Eventually, Mortimer determined that they had gone far enough, and motioned for them to stop. They were in a wider fissure now, which was big enough for them to hunker down and talk in low voices, although Berrister could do no more than sink wearily to his knees. He felt numb, not just from the horror of the last few hours, but because of where he was. He felt the walls pressing in around him, and was acutely aware of the danger from above and below.

'Now what?' asked Joshi, and Berrister realised that everyone was looking at him. He supposed he should not be surprised. He was camp leader, and had established the rules by which they had lived for the past three months, as well as making most of the decisions. Now they expected him to step up and take command again. He looked at them one by one.

Sarah leaned against one wall, exhausted but quietly determined; Berrister envied her cool courage. Lisa and Graham were openly terrified but trying to hide it. Joshi was jittery and pacing restlessly, while Mortimer was still catching his breath.

'Now what?' Joshi repeated, as if he imagined that Berrister had not heard the first time.

It was on the tip of Berrister's tongue to point out that it had not been *his* idea to hide in the glacier, so someone else could decide how to proceed, because he would just as soon take his chances on the surface. Instead, he took a deep, unsteady breath, and pulled himself together.

'One of us needs to climb that,' he said, pointing at a part of the crevasse that should be easy to ascend, with plenty of hand- and footholds. The snow ceiling – roughly ten metres above – was so thin that it was almost transparent, and therefore perfect for scraping out a hole big enough for a head to fit through. 'To see what's happening above. The others should eat something and try to rest.'

'Rest?' echoed Lisa incredulously. 'Here? With *them* prowling about above us?'

'He's right,' said Mortimer firmly. 'It's as safe a place as any, and we're all warmly dressed. We'll be fine for a while.'

'Let me go,' begged Joshi, as Berrister prepared to climb. 'I don't think I can stay down here any longer. Not yet, anyway.'

Berrister did not want to stay in the crevasse either, but sensed that Joshi was near the end of his tether. He nodded acquiescence and stepped aside, albeit reluctantly.

'We'll take it in turns,' he said. 'Half-hour shifts until it's safe to leave.'

Joshi had gone before he had finished speaking,

clambering up the wall like a monkey. The others watched him poke his head cautiously through the snow at the top, then relaxed when he signalled that no one was there.

'How long do you think they'll stay?' asked Lisa eventually. Her voice was unsteady.

'Several days,' replied Berrister. 'Flensing a whale that size will take a while – especially as their ship isn't properly equipped for it. It's just a fishing vessel.'

'A fishing vessel with a private army,' remarked Sarah.

'And a harpoon on the front,' said Berrister. 'Which I suppose will be dismantled and stowed away when they leave.'

'Is it worth it?' asked Sarah. 'The risk of being caught . . . they must be mad!'

Berrister did some quick calculations. 'At the current rate, the meat alone is worth roughly four and a half million pounds on the black market. Not to mention the oil and—'

'They killed Freddy and Dan, didn't they?' said Lisa in a small voice, not much caring about whale economics. 'It wasn't the ice fall.'

The others' silence was all the confirmation she needed.

'You heard a boat,' said Sarah. 'I can only surmise that they landed in South Bay, where they killed Dan and Freddy. Then, while we six were still out working, they came to our camp, where they destroyed our communications and stole our supplies.'

'They're thorough,' said Graham gloomily. 'We're likely to die anyway, with no food and no shelter, but they still made sure we couldn't summon help. They thought of everything.'

'I don't want to die,' whispered Lisa softly. 'Not here.'

Mortimer reached out to pat her knee, a gesture of kindness that brought tears. No one said any more. Half an hour later, Joshi ducked down from his vigil, and Berrister took his place. The student went to Lisa, and held her while she cried herself to sleep.

Four

'We've eluded them so far,' Mortimer said three hours later. 'It's like a maze down here, so why shouldn't we continue to do it until they leave? And when they do, we can return to camp and see what can be salvaged.'

'You mean hide down here indefinitely?' Berrister was unable to keep the horror from his voice. 'But a glacier is a dynamic force – it moves. New fissures are opening and closing all the time, and we've pushed our luck by staying here this long.'

'This part is relatively stable,' said Mortimer. 'We'll be alright.'

He met Berrister's eyes, daring him to contradict. Both knew that the glacier edge was exactly where most movement occurred, so Berrister was right to be concerned. But Lisa did not, so why tell her? To avoid further discussion, Berrister went to relieve Graham again.

70

The wind blew steadily and sharply on the surface, making his eyes water and the tears freeze on his cheeks. By mid-afternoon, there had been no further sightings of men with guns, so they decided that someone should venture out to see if they were still at large. Berrister offered to go, and picked Graham to accompany him. Joshi regarded Berrister doubtfully.

'Are you sure you're up to it?' he asked baldly. 'You never like hikes normally – you prefer to stay in camp.'

'He knows more than you do,' said Mortimer, before Berrister could defend himself. 'And more than me.' He turned to Berrister. 'If you do manage to reach the camp, look in my tent first. I've got some food stashed there – in the box at the far end. Bring that and any clothes you can carry.'

Berrister and Graham began to prepare themselves. Graham swapped his bright red parka for Joshi's whitish one, while Berrister turned his yellow coat inside out, so that the pale brown lining was on the outside. In that way, they would be less easy to spot from a distance. They considered taking the gun, but decided against it when Mortimer discovered there was no more ammunition.

Berrister climbed out of the crevasse with relief, and stood slowly. The ice was smooth and white, with no dark-clad killers to mar its bright surface. Acutely aware of the maze of fissures below his feet, he made his way gingerly towards the escarpment, Graham at his heels. When they reached it, he lay on his stomach and wriggled forward until he could see South Bay.

71

The ship was still there. So was the whale, with long, reddish-purple slits along its side, where the flensing process had been started. The killers had made scant headway, though, suggesting that they were either incompetent or inexperienced. Or both.

'I knew something was wrong when I heard those gunshots,' whispered Graham for at least the tenth time since the nightmare had started. His voice held a strong note of censure. 'You should've listened.'

'Yes,' acknowledged Berrister shortly, tired of hearing it. 'I've said I'm sorry.'

'We shouldn't even have been here,' the Scot went on bitterly. 'We should've been off on a nice jaunt to celebrate the end of the season. But oh, no! *You* had to work to the bitter end.'

Berrister rubbed his head. 'I suppose.'

'Freddy was desperate to go. If only we'd done what he suggested. Then we'd all be over enjoying the Byers Peninsula, and he'd still be alive.'

Berrister regarded him covertly. Could he smell whisky on Graham's breath again or was it his imagination? He hoped he was wrong – he did not want a drunk with him while he played hide-and-seek with armed men. Yet he was sure Graham would not be saying such things if he were sober.

He made no reply, and Graham eventually fell silent. They took it in turns to watch the ship through the binoculars. People moved about on it, but what caught Berrister's attention were the two Zodiacs that bobbed near the stern. Did that mean that the men had given up their search and were back on their ship?

They remained where they were for an hour, trying to count the number of crew. All they learned was that there were a lot of them. At the stern, a hatch was open, and drums were being rolled into the sea. It was against international maritime law to dump rubbish in the Antarctic, and Berrister despised them all the more for what they were doing.

He was about to suggest that they cross the scarp to look down at the camp on the other side, when he heard a sound. Graham heard it, too, and gazed at him in horror. It was laughter. Berrister glanced behind him and saw two men coming their way. Now what? He and Graham could not hide in another crevasse, because they would be spotted long before they could reach one; and they could not go forward, because that would mean crossing the exposed crest of the scarp. They were trapped.

But Graham had a plan. He inserted himself in the gap between ice and rock at the glacier's edge – where the ice had melted away, leaving a hollow underneath.

For the first time since they had left the camp, Berrister regretted wearing so many clothes. The ice broke as he tried to squeeze beneath it, sending shards skittering down the rock face. He winced, wondering if the men could hear them. Then his coat snagged, leaving him halfway in and halfway out. The voices came closer. With a strength born of panic, he squirmed sideways, tearing his sleeve. Then he was free. He wriggled further in, squeezing under the ice until he was jammed tight between it and the rock beneath him.

The voices were very clear, and he thought they were speaking either Arabic or Turkish. Then there was a soft creak, and the ice pressed down on his chest. The men were directly above him! If the ice snapped . . .

One of the men laughed again, and boots crunched down to his left – two pairs of them, side by side. There was more laughter, and someone spat. Then Berrister smelled smoke. They were sitting on the ice above him, enjoying a cigarette. Berrister tried to ignore the sense of being crushed beneath their weight, wondering when the nightmare would end.

Back in the crevasse, Joshi was on watch again, and Sarah was growing restless. Lisa and Mortimer had managed to fall asleep, but she was too agitated. She hated waiting, doing nothing. She thought about Berrister's accident three years before – something that had been the subject of much gossip at the university, mostly because he had steadfastly refused to tell anyone what had happened. Had it left him incapable of moving about the glacier safely with armed men on his heels?

He made no secret of the fact that he considered the Antarctic dangerous and unpredictable, and was also probably the least physically fit of them, with the obvious exception of Mortimer. She wished *she* had insisted on going with Graham instead. Of course, the Scot had hardly risen to the challenge. He had been hired for his mountain rescue experience, but he had proved himself to be morose and defeatist. He had been right – the sounds he had heard had *not* been cracking ice – but his 'I told you so' attitude was unhelpful, and Sarah had expected him to be above such pettiness.

She glanced at her watch. It was almost six o'clock, which meant they had been gone three hours. She sat on a lump of ice, then stood again, thinking about all the work she had done that season. Had it all been for nothing? Would Berrister get the professorship, just because the micro-transmitters on his seals were already amassing data at home, whereas all hers had been burned by criminals? Or would it not matter, because neither would see home again? They could not survive for nine days inside the glacier without supplies – and that was assuming *Worsley* came on time – the thing might be late. She grimaced. Worse, the whalers might still be there, and a research vessel was unlikely to win a confrontation with armed men.

She sighed. It was shockingly cold, and her empty stomach was not making things any easier. She looked at her watch again: six-ten. Maybe, Berrister and Graham had been caught and were never coming back, so how long should she wait? Until nightfall? The morning? A week?

Although still an Antarctic novice in many ways, she was fit, cool-headed and resourceful. She decided that the chances of everyone's survival would be greatly improved if two attempts were made to reach the camp, not just one. She woke Mortimer.

75

'Please wait,' he begged. 'Two forays might result in all of you being caught, and then where would I be? Stuck here with a couple of frightened kids.'

'We need supplies, Geoff. I'll take Joshi – you stay here with Lisa.'

'The fact that Andrew and Graham haven't come back suggests that the gunmen are still at large. Taking Joshi out there isn't clever.'

'I *have* to. The temperature's dropping, and we need to do something now – before it's too late to do anything at all.'

'I'm not happy about this,' grumbled Mortimer, although he suspected that his happiness, or lack of it, would not induce her to change her mind. He scowled. 'Go on, then. I assume I don't have to tell you to be careful.'

'No, you don't.'

If the situation had not been so terrible, Yablokov would have laughed. The crew were wholly unequal to the task of butchering the whale, and Garik was a useless supervisor, despite his claims to have done it before. Chaos ruled. Several men had fallen in the blood-stained water, and were lucky to have been fished out alive. The rest skidded around on the whale's slippery back, chopping ineffectually with unsuitable knives. The lumps they hacked were irregularly sized and impossible to stack neatly.

Hasim watched in growing dismay, their inefficiency obvious even to him, and turned accusingly to the captain. 'I thought you said they could do this.'

76

'They can,' replied Garik airily. 'Just give them time.'

'We don't *have* time,' snapped Hasim. 'We're on a schedule, remember? If they don't get their act together, we'll have to go home empty-handed.'

'It's because we don't have the right equipment,' grumbled Garik defensively. 'You wouldn't let us bring it.'

'And I told you why,' retorted Hasim. 'How would we explain having whale-flensing gear if we were boarded by a patrol ship? It *is* illegal down here, you know.'

He made an exasperated sound when one of the crew lost his grip on a slippery cube of flesh. It splashed into the sea and sank.

Yablokov also watched, thinking Hasim was a fool to believe that a bunch of cod fishermen and hired hands could butcher a whale, no matter what Garik had claimed on their behalf. They might have managed a smaller one – they could have winched it aboard to deal with. But Garik and Hasim had been greedy, and had harpooned the biggest blue without thinking about how they would handle such an enormous carcass.

'Any news of the scientists?' asked Garik, lighting a cigarette. The whites of his eyes were yellow, and he had a sallow, unhealthy mien. Yablokov had overheard the cabin steward say that Garik was now getting through two bottles of vodka a day.

'Only that they're still at large,' replied Hasim. Pointedly, he flapped away the smoke that wafted towards him. 'But they won't get far – there's nowhere for them to go.'

'They don't need to go anywhere,' said Yablokov, lighting a cigarette of his own, with the sole intention of making Hasim uncomfortable. 'They just have to wait for their supply ship to appear. It'll be here in nine days – I looked it up online. All they have to do is wait us out.'

Hasim waved a dismissive hand. 'They'll die of exposure before then.'

'Not necessarily,' said Yablokov, 'accidentally' blowing smoke at him. 'They might have cached supplies on the glacier for emergencies, and while a crevasse isn't cosy, you can survive there, because it's out of the wind. I read that online as well.'

Hasim stared at him. 'You do realise what will happen if we fail to silence these people? They'll tell everyone what they saw and we'll be arrested. Strings will be pulled to get me released, but you . . . Well, I doubt you'll see your wife and kids again.'

He did not wait for a response, but leaned forward to whisper in Garik's ear. Yablokov watched with disapproval, wondering what impractical plan was being hatched now. Sure enough, when Hasim had finished, Garik cleared his throat and made an announcement.

'I've decided to optimise our resources. The crew will help Hasim's team hunt for the scientists.'

'But they're flensing the whale,' Yablokov pointed out. 'Not to mention dealing with the cargo.'

'Then they'll have to pull double shifts,' said Hasim. 'Zurin and Nikos can go, for a start

– there's no need for a helmsman or an engineer while the ship's anchored. You have to deal with the cargo yourself, Mr Yablokov. It is, after all, why we're here.'

Sarah scanned the horizon carefully before striking out in the opposite direction to the one taken by Berrister and Graham. Her plan was to walk north across the glacier, then double back to the camp. She could hide in another crevasse if she was spotted, although she was confident that she would not be – the whalers would not expect anyone to come from that direction. With Joshi in tow, she made good time across the ice, and then trudged west, towards the sea.

It worked perfectly. Within an hour, she and Joshi lay on their stomachs, looking down on the camp from the north. Nothing moved and there was no sign of a boat. There was no sign of Berrister and Graham either, but she tried not to let her concern show.

Carefully, they descended the cliff and crept towards the camp. It was a mess. The tents were sticky masses of burned synthetic, and their supplies and belongings had been scattered all over the place. Some were salvageable, but most were not.

'Look for sleeping bags and food only,' she instructed Joshi. 'Ignore everything else.'

They fared better than she had feared. Three sleeping bags were only singed, and the box containing Mortimer's stash of treats had survived. She shoved them in two servicable rucksacks, along with a small saucepan, three packets of

79

stock cubes and some tins of food with the labels burned off.

They were on the verge of abandoning the remains of the place that had been their home for the last three months when they heard the roar of an engine.

Berrister lost track of the time that the two men laughed and smoked above him. Once or twice, the pressure of the ice on his chest was so great that he was tempted to give himself up, but he gritted his teeth and endured it stoically, concentrating on breathing in and out, in and out. He wondered how Graham was faring.

He began to lose all sensation in his body. If he could have moved, he might have kept the circulation going, but afraid that the slightest twitch would give them away, he lay as still as a corpse, increasingly aware that he might soon become one.

Just when he thought the men could surely skive no longer, there was another waft of cheap tobacco and slightly raised voices, suggesting a debate was in progress. His mind began to wander, and at one point, he thought he was at home. He opened his eyes expecting to see his bedroom ceiling, but there was nothing but whiteness.

He almost leapt out of his skin when someone tapped him on the shoulder, but it was only Graham, kneeling next to him and glancing around anxiously.

'That was close,' the Scot muttered. 'I really thought we'd had it. God only knows how you managed to sleep through it – I was on tenter-hooks the whole time.'

Berrister did not explain that it had been more a case of his brain shutting down to survive than a comfortable nap. He began the agonising process of squirming out of his hiding place, so cold that he could barely feel his legs, while his chest ached abominably. He staggered to where Graham was watching the two men walk towards their boat. Its driver was waiting for them, while another man was slumped on the ground. When the other two arrived, they had to lift him into the little craft.

'He must be one of the ones we knocked down the hill or shot at,' whispered Graham. 'He was lucky – the other two must be under that sheet of canvas.'

He pointed, and Berrister saw a green tarpaulin draped over an irregularly shaped pile. Something white poked from under it: a human hand. Berrister felt sick. He saw no reason to suppose the enemy's dead had been dumped so unceremo-niously there, and felt it was more likely to be Wells and Freddy.

Graham misunderstood his despair. 'It was them or us, so don't feel bad about killing one with the flare. Besides, their friends don't seem bothered – they're not even taking them back to the ship.'

He was right – whoever lay under the tarpaulin was being left behind. It convinced Berrister more than ever that it was his friends, and that the whalers' own dead had been treated with more respect. Meanwhile, the two smokers went

81

through an elaborate pantomime with their hands, trying to convey that the scientists had fallen down a crevasse.

'They don't all speak the same language,' Berrister surmised.

'So?' asked Graham.

'So it tells us a bit more about them. The two who sat on us were quite happy to skive, which means that vengeance for the ones we killed isn't a priority – which suggests in turn that they don't know each other very well. I suspect they're mercenaries, hired for the season.'

'If I were their leader, I'd put a bounty on our heads,' said Graham. 'If these men are driven by cash, then what better way to ensure success?'

'Then let's hope he isn't a Scot,' muttered Berrister fervently.

They watched the boat skim towards the ship, after which they hiked back across the ice until they could look down on their camp. Two tiny figures were there, moving through the wreckage. Berrister trained his binoculars on them, but they were too far away to let him see anything other than that they were searching.

'Now what?' asked Graham dejectedly. 'We can't go down there, obviously. Or do you think we should launch a surprise attack?'

'Not really,' said Berrister, regarding him askance. 'They have guns, remember?'

'True.' Graham slumped in despair. 'It makes no sense. Why steal our food and bugger up our radios? Why not just kill us while we slept? I don't understand any of it. But I *do* think we're going to die.'

'We're not,' said Berrister firmly. 'We've evaded them so far. We can do it again.'

'For nine days?' asked Graham, unconvinced. 'Or longer, if *Worsley*'s late?'

'Yes, if necessary, but it won't be that long. Noddy Taylor will raise the alarm when he can't reach us, and the Chileans will send a plane. They'll see the whaler and all hell will break loose. We're going to make it.'

'I don't see how you can be so sure,' whispered Graham.

'Because I've done it before,' said Berrister, although it was not something he was eager to discuss. 'Survived inside a glacier, I mean. For days. It's a question of attitude. You'll live if you want to.'

Graham regarded him intently. 'When this happened, did *everyone* get out alive?'

'I was alone.'

'Alone? But that's not—'

'We can't go to the camp as long as the whalers are there,' interrupted Berrister, not about to confide anything else about an experience he would rather forget. 'And it doesn't look as though there will be much to salvage anyway.'

'No,' conceded Graham. 'So what do we do? Go back to the others empty-handed? Or do you have another idea?'

'I do,' said Berrister. 'Just not a very nice one.'

Sarah and Joshi froze at the distant roar of the engine, but no boats bounced towards them, and the sound grew softer rather than louder. Hearts pounding, they watched the end of the point, waiting for the splash of colour that would herald the next contingent of killers.

'It must've been on the other side of the ridge,' Sarah said eventually, forcing herself to relax. 'Perhaps they've decided to call off the search. It'll be dark in an hour, and it's already getting colder.'

Joshi shuddered. 'We've been here too long. Let's go.'

They began to slog up the slope. Halfway, Sarah was seized by a wave of giddiness. She had eaten virtually nothing all day, and the cold and constant tension were finally taking their toll.

'We have to eat,' she said tersely.

Joshi was pale and there was a sheen of sweat on his face. 'What about the others?'

'We'll be doing them no favours if we collapse.'

They sheltered behind a rock and opened a packet of water biscuits, which they smeared with honey. It tasted like nectar, and Sarah felt her strength return.

'Come on,' she said eventually. 'If you feel faint, tell me and we'll stop again. We're going to be relying on each other heavily until we're rescued, and we need to respect what our bodies are telling us. So if you feel weak, we rest. OK?'

Joshi nodded. Some of his pallor had faded, but perspiration had soaked his underclothes, and he was now shivering. They clearly needed to move more slowly – fast enough to stay warm, but not so fast as to work up a sweat. To take her mind off the ache in her arms and shoulders, she pondered a paper she planned to write when she got back, wondering if the memory stick in her pocket had enough data. When had she last backed up her data from the laptop? Two days ago? Three? She couldn't remember.

By the time they reached the ice, the roaring ache in her upper body was almost unbearable. They rested again, after which there followed an agitated hour in fading daylight trying to find their crevasse. Why didn't Mortimer or Lisa see them coming and give them a signal? Or had they been caught and killed in the interim?

They found the opening eventually, thanks to Joshi, who recognised a distinctive ice ridge. Sarah was unimpressed to slide down inside the crevasse, only to find Mortimer and Lisa asleep.

'One of you should have been on watch,' she snapped angrily.

Mortimer blinked blankly and with shock, Sarah recognised the first signs of hypothermia. Lisa was little better, although at least able to pull herself to her feet and help sort through their finds. She and Joshi prepared some food while Sarah wrapped Mortimer in the sleeping bags.

'Where are the others?' she asked. 'It's past nine o'clock.'

'Perhaps they're not coming back,' said Lisa in a low, strained voice.

'Of course they are,' said Sarah brusquely, although she suspected Lisa was right. Berrister and Graham should have returned ages before, and the fear that something dreadful had happened to them had been with her since she had gone out herself.

Joshi opened a tin. It contained peaches, which they ate with more crackers and a 'soup' of cold water and stock cubes – despite the chill in the crevasse, water still dripped down the sides, and Mortimer had been canny enough to scrape out a hollow to catch some.

'You did well to get all this stuff,' said Mortimer when they had finished. He looked better, the dullness gone from his eyes. 'We might make it out of this mess yet.'

'We will,' averred Sarah with conviction. 'But not by being careless. I'll take the first watch, and you can have the second. Andrew and Graham will never find us in the dark – they'll need us to guide them.'

'Yes,' said Mortimer, although it was clear that she and Lisa were not the only ones who thought their friends were dead.

'Wait a minute,' exclaimed Graham, shocked. 'You want to loot the gunmen's bodies?'

'Not loot,' said Berrister, still sure it was Wells and Freddy they would find, and eager to know, one way or the other. 'But we could take their coats and backpacks. There might be food in them.'

'That's disgusting!' Graham began to move away, glancing irritably over his shoulder as he did so. 'Well, come on then. Let's get it over with.'

The beach was deserted, and nothing moved except three terns that dipped and dived along the surf. Somewhere an elephant seal roared, producing short, staccato bursts of sound that went on for several minutes. As they descended, Berrister could not help but notice the stark

86

difference between the clean splendour of the icy mountains and the ship with its ugly tail of blood and half-butchered body. He felt a sudden wave of fury towards the whalers, and wondered how many more magnificent beasts lay in clumsily cut chunks in its stinking holds.

Graham chose a convoluted route to shield them from sight, so it took some time to reach the beach. Berrister glanced at his watch and saw it was approaching nine o'clock – they had been playing hide-and-seek for hours. He was tired and hungry, and his head ached from the constant tension. It was also nearly dark.

They approached the tarpaulin, where the dead white hand still curled from beneath it. Heart thudding, Berrister lifted a corner of the canvas and peered underneath. With relief, he saw the body belonged to a stranger – a circular burn on his jacket suggested he was the one hit with the flare. His head was twisted at an impossible angle – he had broken his neck in the fall.

Berrister forced himself to pull more of the cover away. There was one more corpse, and it, too, was unfamiliar. It lay face down with a red stain on the back of its hood. There was no sign of Wells or Freddy.

'Take what you want, while I keep watch,' said Graham softly. 'But hurry. I don't like it here.'

Nor did Berrister, and stripping bodies was a distasteful task, which he wished he had never suggested. He began with the coats, which weren't of nearly such good quality as his own – the mercenaries' employers had provided them with sub-standard gear. Underneath were woollen

87

sweaters, so he hauled those off, too. Then there seemed no point in squeamishness, so he removed their plastic trousers, woollen socks, and a collection of shirts and sweatshirts. Each had a daypack, so he stuffed some of the clothes into them, rolled the rest in the tarpaulin, and called Graham to say he had finished.

The Scot looked at the near-naked corpses in revulsion. 'You were thorough.'

'Waste not, want not. Now let's get back before it gets too dark to see.'

Without a word, Graham led the way back across the beach, selfishly leaving Berrister to carry both daypacks and the clothes-filled tarpaulin by himself. They retraced their steps up to the glacier, after which Berrister was so tired he could barely stand.

'You can't stop here,' hissed Graham, as Berrister slumped to his knees. He nodded towards the ship, where a boat could just be seen through the gloom. It was heading for shore. 'We need to get back to the crevasse before the light goes completely.'

'Help me, then,' gasped Berrister crossly. 'I can't carry all this on my own.'

Reluctantly, Graham took a corner of the bundle and hefted it up. 'Crikey! It's heavier than it looks.'

'I know,' said Berrister dryly. 'Oh, shit! I think they've seen us.'

Down on the beach, the boat had landed, and small figures were gesticulating towards them with stabbing fingers.

'Run!' cried Graham, dropping the bundle. 'Forget the clothes.'

88

'No,' snapped Berrister. 'We need them. Take one of the daypacks and I'll—'

He faltered when a sharp report rang out.

'Gunfire,' shrieked Graham. 'No, don't stand there gaping – keep moving! I bet this is what happened to Freddy.'

'And Dan,' gasped Berrister, refusing to relinquish what they had been to so much trouble to win.

'Not Dan,' spat Graham bitterly. 'Not him.'

'What are you talking about?'

A second shot rang out, and Berrister saw a puff of snow to his right. The third thumped into the bundle. Graham promptly raced away, leaving Berrister behind. The biologist was more tired than he had ever been, and hunger and cold were beginning to impair his judgement. With the absurd notion that the bundle might protect him from bullets, he gathered it up and hefted it over his shoulder. It seemed heavier than before, and it was an effort to keep moving. And then he was past the steepest climb, heading for the more gentle rise of the summit. He was out of the killers' sight – for now, at least.

Graham was a good way in front – barely visible in the dying light. Berrister closed his mind to the possibility of crevasses, and concentrated on forging forward as fast as he could. Then his foot caught in a dip and sent him sprawling. From his hands and knees, he could just make out Graham running hard in the distance. He staggered to his feet, but when he next looked up, Graham had disappeared.

He strained his eyes in the near darkness. Had

89

Graham reached the others or fallen down a new crevasse? Berrister stumbled again, and this time, it was more difficult to stand. He thought he could hear voices on the wind, and glanced behind him, expecting to see the killers, but there was nothing but ice.

He staggered forward with his bundle and daypacks, trying to gauge where Graham had gone. He set a course for one area, only to swerve away when he saw rocks poking through it – there had been no rocks near their hiding place. He looked around hopelessly, frantically searching for a clue that might help, but the ice was as hard as stone, and there were no tell-tale tracks. He was lost. In desperation, he struck out to his right, but the ice began to slope down, suggesting he was heading for the glacier's edge, rather than the middle. He veered left, only to see the sea again. He had been running in circles!

The voices were louder now, and he knew he was going to be caught. He thought he glimpsed the first of his pursuers, but as he started to run, still doggedly clutching his finds, the snow under him gave way and he plunged downward.

Sarah was standing watch at the crevasse when she heard the gunfire. She poked her head up warily, and a few minutes later, she saw Graham lurching towards her, almost invisible in the gloom. She waved frantically to attract his attention, not wanting to shout in case the wrong people heard. He stumbled towards her and almost pitched headfirst past her in his desperation to escape. She checked the horizon to ensure no one had seen him, then followed him inside.

'Where's Andrew?' she demanded, motioning Joshi to take over guard duty.

Graham wouldn't meet her eyes. 'I don't know.'

Above them, Joshi gave a strangled gasp before scrambling back down. 'They're coming this way. Six or seven, all armed to the teeth.'

'They've got rifles this time,' said Graham hoarsely. 'The range of those things . . .'

'Did they shoot Andrew?' asked Mortimer tersely.

'Yes, I think so,' replied Graham wretchedly. 'He was behind me, and when they started firing, I just ran. When I looked back . . . well, I'd have seen him if he'd done what I'd said . . .'

'Hush!' hissed Lisa, casting a fearful glance upwards. 'They'll hear.'

'Grab as much as you can carry and go deeper into the glacier,' ordered Sarah. 'Now they know roughly where we are, they're going to search more carefully. The darkness will help – hopefully it'll slow them down and give us more time.'

The others scurried to take what they could, then set off, Graham in the lead. Joshi followed, holding Lisa's hand, while Sarah and Mortimer were last. After a few metres, the tunnel became wider, deeper and much darker. Fortunately, Joshi had a pocket torch, and a little light went a long way in a place that was almost pitch black.

It was impossible to run. The bottom of the fissure was littered with ice, slick and uneven. Sarah fell once, wrenching her ankle painfully, but forced herself to keep moving.

'Brace yourself against the walls with your hands,' advised Mortimer.

Lisa stifled a scream as the ice under her foot collapsed, opening up a sinister black hole. For a moment, she was paralysed with fear, but Joshi hauled her forward. Then their crevasse forked, two equally unappealing tunnels of ice leading away in different directions. At the same time, they heard something behind them. Voices! The hunters had found the gear they had abandoned.

'Drop anything that'll slow you down,' ordered Sarah. 'We'll have to split up – it's our only chance. Geoff and I will take the left one, you three take the right. Go!'

She was away before they could argue, aware of Mortimer puffing behind her. He was more likely to slow her down than the others, but there was something about Graham's brazen selfishness that repelled her – she disliked the fact that he had abandoned Berrister so readily – and she realised she didn't want him with her. He wasn't a team player.

She could hear the enemy's voices behind her, getting ever closer. It was easier for them – they had torches, whereas she and Mortimer were obliged to stumble along in the pitch dark. She tried to move faster, conscious of Mortimer's rasping breath as he fought to keep up. She grabbed his hand, and pulled him on.

Suddenly, the tunnel narrowed to a slit. Sarah managed to fight her way through it sideways, but Mortimer was too big, even without his bulky clothing. Desperately, Sarah glanced up, assessing their chances of climbing out, but the sides of the fissure were too sheer. With anger and dismay, she saw it was over.

'Go,' urged Mortimer. 'I'll hold them here for as long as I can.'

'No,' said Sarah tightly. 'We'll meet them together.'

'Like hell we will! Now run, for God's sake. Someone has to tell everyone what happened.'

'I can't,' she said softly, thinking it was better to die with someone who cared enough to cover her escape than be gunned down like an animal.

'You can. Please do this for me.'

She looked at him in the gloom. He was pale, but calm. She reached out and touched his cheek gently, before turning to sprint down the narrow tunnel.

Chief engineer Nikos had been put in charge of the hunters, and he had divided his party in half when the fissure had split: he and two sailors had gone left, while Zurin and three other crewmen had gone right. Nikos was the first to catch his quarry. He found a very large man jammed in a crack that was far too narrow to accommodate him. The Greek watched him struggle for a moment, then went to help him extricate himself.

Shortly afterwards, Zurin's party caught up with the others. The right-hand tunnel ended abruptly when it met another, far deeper crevasse that sliced diagonally across it. It was of undetermined depth, and a good ten metres across. Graham, Lisa and Joshi had only just avoided plunging down it, and now stood at its edge, backs towards it as they faced their pursuers with a mixture of fear and dismay.

They had seen it before, because Wells had discovered it back in December, and had brought everyone to see it – or everyone except Berrister who had declined with a shudder. Joshi had dubbed it the Big Crevasse, a name that had stuck, despite the others' scathing remarks about his lack of imagination. Mortimer thought it reached bedrock, some two hundred metres or more below, although he could not be sure. One thing they did know, however, was that it led nowhere but down.

Zurin also stopped, alert for tricks. Then he moved forward slowly, and what happened next was a blur. With a terrified scream, Lisa was gone – although whether she had slipped, the ice had collapsed beneath her feet or she had jumped was impossible to say. For several moments, no one moved, then a soggy thump sounded faintly as her body hit something a long way below.

With a wail of anguish, Joshi peered down into the blackness. Zurin's habitually impassive face crumpled with shock, and he was unable to tear his eyes away from the yawning chasm. Graham said something, but Zurin couldn't understand him, and only shook his head.

Lisa's plunge to death had badly unsettled the helmsman, and he desperately wanted to leave the ice tunnels and their sinister blue gloom. He wanted to be back on *Lena*, with the familiar heave of the ocean beneath his feet, and he wanted Hasim and his nasty team to disappear into oblivion. Like Yablokov, he was having serious second thoughts about what he had got himself into. Indeed, he'd only signed up because Yablokov had, loyally assuming that the first officer knew what he was doing. Well, they had both learned the hard way that he didn't.

Eventually, he gestured for Graham and Joshi to follow him back up the tunnel. He had been surprised when Hasim had ordered him to take them alive, but vastly relieved. He was no killer, particularly now he had seen the intended victims – they were kids, and the younger one was regarding him with such fear that Zurin experienced a disconcerting wave of self-loathing.

'He wants us to go with him,' said Graham, trying to pull Joshi away from the crevasse.

'Then he can go to hell,' sobbed Joshi, tugging away from him.

'We have to,' urged Graham. 'They'll kill us otherwise.'

'They'll kill us anyway,' wept Joshi. 'And Lisa . . . I'm not going anywhere with them.'

But a few minutes later, he and Graham were stumbling back the way they had come, confused and dejected. Joshi was still crying, and the only sounds other than their footsteps were his sobs. They waited several minutes at the fork, and then Nikos' group emerged with Mortimer.

'Bit of a tight squeeze,' said Mortimer to Graham and Joshi, indicating his ripped jacket. 'Stopped me dead in my tracks. Good thing you weren't behind me.'

He smiled but his eyes held a warning. Fortunately, it had not occurred to Nikos to look for anyone else, which was lucky, because the

Big Crevasse sliced across the left-hand tunnel, too. Sarah had crouched at its edge in an agony of tension, listening to Mortimer being prised loose, and expecting at any moment for someone to come and nab her, too.

When Lisa's scream had come, she had covered her ears and huddled into a tight ball. It took a long time for her grief-numbed mind to accept that no one was coming to get her, by which time she was so cold that she could barely move. She stood unsteadily, and forced herself to stumble along the tunnel to the fork. The abandoned supplies still lay there. Mechanically, she gathered them up and continued towards their first hiding place.

By the time she reached it, the dull, helpless feeling had receded somewhat. The effort of clambering along the crevasse had warmed her, and her customary confidence was beginning to return. The fact that the killers hadn't looked for her suggested that they didn't know she was still alive – or even that she existed. As long as the others kept quiet, she might yet be able to tell their story when rescue came.

She advanced on the hiding place warily, anticipating that the whalers might have left a guard. But no such precautions had been considered necessary, and the place was deserted. She climbed up to the surface, and crept across the now-dark ice to where she could look down on South Bay. Torches lit Mortimer, Joshi and Graham on the beach, surrounded by men with guns, while two boats buzzed from the ship to collect them.

With a piercing sense of loss, she saw them clamber slowly aboard. As she watched them go, she had never felt more alone. Of her seven companions, three were being spirited away by pirates, while Berrister, Lisa, Wells and Freddy were dead. As the boats drew further away, she was assailed by the terrifying conviction that it was the last time she would ever see Mortimer, Joshi and Graham alive. The tears that had been threatening to overwhelm her ever since Mortimer had helped her escape burst, and she sank into the snow to weep.

Five

As the snow bridge gave way, Berrister plunged straight down to land with a bone-jarring thump on a ledge about the size of a kitchen table. It knocked the breath out of him, although the bundle of clothes saved him from serious harm by cushioning his fall. Warily, he sat up. It was too dark to see anything, but he recalled a torch in one of the daypacks. He rummaged for it and then clicked it on. What it illuminated made him turn cold with horror.

He had fallen down the fissure the others had dubbed the Big Crevasse. Shakily, he pointed the torch over the edge, and saw only inky blackness. Although he did not know it, his friends were doing exactly the same – Graham, Lisa and Joshi at one point, and Sarah nearby.

The ledge on which he had landed was just an irregularity in the wall, although he sensed it was not an especially secure one – he could see shards of ice breaking off it and spiralling into nothingness. As he looked, a scream ripped through the air, making him start so violently that he had to clutch at the wall to stop himself from falling. He experienced a stab of despair. It had sounded like Lisa.

He fought the urge to leap to his feet and scale the wall above him as fast as he could – sudden movements might send the ledge crashing down, taking him with it. And anyway, what awaited him on the surface was not necessarily any improvement on his current situation.

He glanced up. The sky was a dark blue smear about five metres above his head. He tried to look at his watch, but it was broken. Taking several deep breaths to calm himself, he stood, staying as close to the wall as possible. More ice clattered downward as he twisted around to shine the torch up. The crevasse was ancient, and its walls had melted and refrozen over many summers, so they were slick and as shiny as glass. Climbing them would be impossible.

Struggling to quell his rising panic, he held the torch in his mouth and began to untie the canvas bundle. Perhaps one of the dead men had pitons or ice-screws in his pockets. These specially designed pins used by mountaineers would be his best hope – he could drive them into the ice to form a ladder.

The coats yielded a variety of items, including a wallet stuffed with American dollars and a sausage in waxy paper. The daypacks brought forth a length of thin rope, a computer game, a knife coated with fish scales and a box of matches.

He fingered the knife, wondering if he could cut toeholds. He tried one, but quickly found it was impossible with such hard ice. He shone the torch to the opposite wall. It was too far to jump, and, if anything, was even more slick than the one above him. Then he shone the beam to the sides, and felt his spirits rise.

To the right was nothing but sheer ice, but to the left was another ledge, perhaps two metres away. Beyond that was a third one, and above it, the ice was rougher, perhaps enough to allow him to climb. He could not do it in the dark – he would fall for certain – but he could try in the morning. Resolutely quelling the horror he felt at spending six hours on an unstable platform over a bottomless chasm, he sat on the canvas bundle and huddled deeper into his coat to wait for dawn.

As they drew closer to *Lena*, Mortimer squinted up at the hull that towered above them, noting that the anchor chain was thick with rust and seaweed, and that some of the rivets were missing. The air around her was thick with the rank stench of blood, while skuas and other gulls bobbed on the waves, resting after a day of feasting on titbits of whale.

Zurin steered the Zodiac to the loading hatch and tied it off, indicating that the prisoners were to go up the rope ladder that dangled down the side. It was badly frayed and the two bottom rungs were missing.

'Crikey!' muttered Mortimer, regarding it apprehensively. 'Up that?'

Zurin's only reply was a firmly pointing finger. Mortimer stood carefully and reached for the ladder, but it was not an easy ascent for a man his size, and it took Zurin pushing from below and two seamen hauling from above to get him up. Joshi and Graham followed more agilely, after which the three of them stood looking around uncertainly.

They were in a loading bay that ran the width of the ship, a shabby, beige area that reeked of dead whale, sweating bodies and oil. Opposite, the starboard hatch was also open, and slabs of meat were still being manhandled through it, even though it was dark outside. A line of barrels stood against one wall, large black ones with no identifying markings. Two crewmen grabbed one and rolled it towards the port-side hatch, where they struggled to heave it out. It appeared to be very heavy.

Zurin poked them and nodded to some stairs to the right. They clambered up them and emerged into a mess hall. It was thick with cigarette smoke, and half a dozen men sat there, one watching a subtitled video, while the others played cards.

They were directed along a narrow corridor that someone had tried to brighten up with pages torn from calendars. Miss July lounged seductively between a pensive kitten and a dinosaur wearing a bow tie. At the end of the corridor was a row of doors with numbers.

100

Zurin opened one and gestured that his prisoners were to enter. When Mortimer started to demur, Zurin gave him a hefty shove that sent him staggering inside. Graham and Joshi were pushed in after him, and the door was slammed shut. Then came the snap of a key being turned in a lock.

The room was tiny, with two sets of bunks, a metal table and two chairs, all bolted down against rough weather. The blankets were threadbare and the lino on the floor was old and peppered with cigarette burns. Even so, the cabin was cleaner than Mortimer would have expected for such a vessel, and the covers on the bed seemed to be freshly laundered: someone still cared about standards, even though *Lena* was a miserable old tub.

Joshi was doing his best not to show his fear, but his voice still cracked when he spoke. 'What do they want with us?'

'I don't know,' replied Mortimer. 'But when they come, let me do the talking. Look at the door and the porthole – see if they can be forced open.'

Glad to have something to do, Joshi went to the door, tapping it to test its thickness and strength. Graham was intelligent enough to know it was a waste of time, and only slumped on one of the beds. His hands shook and his face was grey, and Mortimer knew he would easily be intimidated into telling their captors that Sarah was still free – which was something he aimed to prevent at all costs. He knew the three of them were doomed, but he was determined that Sarah would live to see their killers prosecuted.

Moments later, the door opened to admit two men. One was unmistakably Russian – big, bear-like and clad in cheap trousers and an old blue sweater. A gold tooth glinted in his mouth when he spoke, and his English was hesitant, as if he used it rarely. The other was smaller, neatly dressed and had a large black moustache. He appeared to be Middle Eastern, and spoke with a French accent.

'Welcome to our ship, gentlemen,' he said politely. 'I trust the ride was not too uncomfortable?'

'Who are you?' asked Mortimer curtly.

'Imad Hasim, the captain's adviser. And this is the first mate, Evgeny Yablokov.'

Mortimer introduced himself, Graham and Joshi, then added, 'We're scientists with promising careers and families who love us. I hope you bear this in mind when you consider our fate.'

Hasim made a reassuring gesture, although Yablokov stared at his feet. The Russian had not expected the prisoners to be so young – the one called Joshi was little more than a boy, with downy cheeks and tousled hair. Yet again, he wished he had never left the north. He should have known that the pay was high for a damn good reason.

'You're our guests, so we'll make your stay here as pleasant as possible,' said Hasim smoothly. 'Some food will arrive shortly, and Mr Yablokov has found you a few books in English.'

Mortimer glanced at them – a dog-eared dictionary, a first aid manual, several issues of *National Geographic* and a lurid-looking paperback entitled *Olga's Lovers*.

'Thank you,' said Mortimer. 'But what we really want is to contact our base. They'll be preparing a rescue mission as we speak, so we should tell them where we are.'

Hasim and Yablokov exchanged a quick glance.

'Later,' said Hasim. 'But in the meantime, another storm is brewing and it looks bad – falling temperatures, snow, high winds. You must see that your friends will be better off here than on shore. Tell us where to find them, so we can send out a search party.'

'Of course,' said Mortimer. 'They're at the bottom of crevasses, buried under ice falls or shot by your men. We were eight, but Andrew Berrister, Sarah Henshaw, Dan Wells, Freddy Fredericks and Lisa White are dead. We're all that's left.'

'If that were the case,' said Hasim coldly, 'we'd have found their bodies. You're lying.'

'It was my fault,' whispered Graham. Mortimer glared at him, willing him to silence, but the Scot mumbled on. 'I left Andrew. When you started shooting, I just ran, and when I looked back he was gone. He's dead – and it was my fault.'

'It was not,' countered Mortimer sharply. 'You weren't chasing him, were you? Nor did you push poor Lisa to her death.'

'That was an accident,' put in Yablokov quickly. 'I spoke to the crew – they didn't *push* her.'

Hasim ignored him, and glared at the prisoners. 'Please don't lie. It will be better for everyone if you tell me where your friends are hiding.'

'Freddy and Dan are under an ice fall and have been since yesterday,' replied Mortimer coolly.

'We were going to dig their bodies out today, but you came and . . . we had to revise our plans. Lisa and Sarah are in the Big Crevasse. I don't know which fissure Andrew was hounded down, but it was one close to where we were found.'

Hasim made an irritable sound at the back of his throat. 'Very well – play games if you must. Tell the guard outside the door when you come to your senses and decide to cooperate.'

'Guard?' pounced Mortimer. 'Why do you need one of those for "guests"?'

Hasim smiled thinly. 'We're just simple sailors, and my colleagues are foolishly shy of strangers. It's for your own safety.'

'Right,' said Mortimer. 'Incidentally, how many whales have you slaughtered so far?'

'Just the one,' replied Hasim. 'It's a small, but lucrative, sideline for us.'

He smiled at Yablokov, who did not smile back.

Mortimer frowned. 'So why else are you down here?'

'We'll answer your questions when you answer ours,' said Hasim. 'But it's getting late and we could all do with a good night's sleep. Rest well, gentlemen. We'll talk again in the morning.'

He gave a neat bow and left. The first mate followed, his face impassive but his eyes anxious.

'I could break the lock with a single kick, and there are two armed guards outside,' reported Joshi, the moment they had gone.

'Good lad,' said Mortimer approvingly, although he doubted the information would be of any use. 'Now, help me off with these boots. It's warm in here.'

While Joshi obliged, Graham went to one of the beds and flung himself down, turning his face to the wall. Mortimer watched him uneasily – he never imagined Graham would be the first to crack under pressure. He only hoped the Scot would rally in the morning.

Six

The night was the longest Berrister could ever remember, and with no watch, it was impossible to keep track of the time. It was bitterly cold in the crevasse, and he dared not sleep lest he moved and sent himself spinning down into oblivion. His arms and legs grew cramped; his ears, nose, toes and fingers throbbed from the chill; and he could not recall when he had last eaten. He took a bite of the sausage, but it was oily and rank, and he felt his gorge rise. He pushed it away, unwilling to risk throwing up.

But eventually tendrils of early-morning light filtered down to his ledge. When they did, and he could see clearly for the first time, it made his predicament seem worse than ever. Moving slowly and stiffly, he began to make preparations for his escape.

He repacked his canvas bundle so it included both daypacks. He attached one end of the thin rope to it, then tied the other around his waist, looping the excess over his shoulder. He ate another bite of sausage, although fear blunted his appetite again, and he tried to flex some of the stiffness out of his fingers. And then he was ready. It was now fully light, and he could see as well as he was going to.

He took three steps back, and made a running leap towards the second ledge. It was almost too far, and he had to grab at the wall to stop himself sliding off the other side. The new ice was also not as stable, and he felt it flex under his feet. He tried to get closer to the wall, where it was less likely to snap off, but something was in his way. He kicked at it impatiently, then gaped in horror. Under a frosting of snow was a body.

Reluctantly, he touched it. It was frozen solid and undeniably dead. Was it one of the whalers? He tried to scour away some of the ice, although he dared not turn the body over, lest the movement cause the ledge to collapse. Then he spotted something red, and he caught his breath when he recognised Freddy's distinctive bandanna. Stomach churning, he swept away more snow, but the face was a mask of frozen blood. Berrister had lost colleagues down crevasses before, and knew the damage ice could do. There was more blood on the body's arm, which had oozed from a dark, round hole, slightly charred at the edges. He had been shot.

Berrister felt rage burn inside him. Freddy had been cut down in his prime, just so a few criminals could kill whales. He wanted to kill *them* – see how *they* liked being shot and terrorized over money. What he actually did was touch the body in a brief gesture of farewell, and murmur a promise that he would do all in his power to

106

see the killers brought to justice, even if it meant spending the next eight days hiding inside the glacier. Resolve filled him, and he determined to escape.

The canvas bundle was still on the first ledge, so he tugged until he had taken up the rope's slack, then eased it towards him. The bundle slid over the edge and all but took him with it as it fell. His arms cracked with the tension as it swung back and forth. Swearing under his breath, he hauled it up, then considered his next move. The third ledge was further than the second, and not as big. There was a very real possibility that it was not strong enough to bear his weight.

Then he took one last look at his dead friend, and launched himself into the abyss.

He judged the distance well, but as his feet touched, the ledge began to collapse underneath him. He scrabbled desperately as chunks of it started to fall away, trying to throw himself forward. A large piece hurtled away into the darkness, then he, too, began to fall. He snatched at the walls in a futile effort to save himself, and then was dropping in earnest.

With a sickening jolt he was jerked to a halt. At first he thought he had hit the bottom, and the pain in his side was stoved-in ribs. Then he realised that the rope had snagged, and that he was suspended mid-air. He clawed at the wall, trying to gain a handhold, but it was too slick.

He looked around wildly, knowing the rope would not hold him for long. It was tight around his chest, making it difficult to breathe, and dizziness already nagged at the edges of his brain. Then he saw that the wall underneath the third ledge was rough, and should be possible to climb. The only problem was that he could not reach it.

The rope felt as though it would sever him in two. He reached up to grab it with one hand, feeling some of the pressure ease, and pushed against the wall with the other. He began to swing back and forth, higher with each new shove. Ice shards clattered around him. How long would it be before he spiralled after them? Then his fumbling fingers managed to lock into a fissure in the wall. He stopped swinging, and scrabbled with his feet until they encountered a shallow rim. Once he was standing, the pressure on his chest disappeared and he could breathe easily again.

He pressed his face against the wall, feeling its chill against his cheek. For a while, he could do nothing but cling there, waiting for his breathing to return to normal and the pain in his ribs to subside.

Eventually, he started to climb, inching upward until his head was level with the second ledge. He looked across at it, wondering what had arrested his fall. It was the body – the rope had caught on one of its legs, and as it was frozen into the wall, it provided an anchor. The ledge now tilted at a precarious angle, and Berrister saw that a few more moments of swinging would have brought the whole thing down, taking rope, Freddy and him with it. The notion turned his limbs to jelly again, and for several minutes he was unable to move.

He took a deep breath, and through a massive effort of will, forced himself to start climbing again. Then he heard voices and saw a silhouette peering down. The gunmen had found him.

Yablokov also slept badly that night, and when he woke from an uneasy drowse the following morning, the first thing he did was splash cold water over his face, trying to wash Joshi's frightened face from his mind. There was a rap on his door, but he ignored it. The handle turned as someone tried it, and Yablokov was glad it was locked. He heard Hasim calling softly, secretively, but he was not interested in what the man had to say. He stood stock-still, waiting for him to leave.

But he could not skulk forever. After a slug of vodka, taken straight from the bottle, he went to the bridge. His watch was due to start, and he didn't want to emulate the captain by being late. He felt in his pocket for his cigarettes – he didn't want to imitate him by reeking of alcohol first thing in the morning either.

Zurin was there, gazing sullenly across the grey sea, while Nikos leaned on the charts chest.

'I don't like this,' said Zurin. Yablokov blinked, startled to hear the taciturn helmsman speak. 'I want no further part in it. That girl . . .' He looked away.

'She fell,' said Yablokov. 'You already told us it was an accident.'

'Or she jumped,' countered Zurin, 'because she was so scared. I'm done with Hasim – I'm not hunting any more scientists.'

Silently, Yablokov agreed: he would have given his right arm to be home, warming his feet by the fire while his wife made cod and onions, his favourite dish. But there would be nothing for her to cook if he didn't earn some money. He rubbed his eyes wearily. What was a man to do when the fish stocks continued to dwindle year after year? He had to provide for his family somehow.

'How's our cargo?'

Yablokov started in shock: Hasim was so close that he could feel the man's breath on the back of his neck. How he hated his sneaky ways! Hasim looked smart and chipper in clean clothes, and he smelled of expensive aftershave. He made Yablokov feel grubby and inferior.

'Fine,' he answered shortly. 'We're still behind schedule, but making progress.'

'Well we can't afford to be behind schedule,' Hasim snapped irritably. 'Our timetable isn't flexible, you know.'

'And whose fault is that?' flashed Yablokov, irked enough to respond, although he knew he should hold his tongue. 'We lost hours while you sent the crew after the scientists. Speaking of which, when can I have my people back?'

'As soon as all the witnesses are accounted for – or you may as well step into a prison cell right now. Or can I assume that you'd rather go home to your family with a fat pay packet?'

Yablokov was spared from replying by Garik, who reeled onto the bridge. His eyes were glazed, his sweater was inside out, and he was wearing his shoes on the wrong feet. When the ship rolled a little, he had to clutch at Zurin to steady

110

himself. Then he walked to the captain's chair with the calculated care of the very drunk and slumped into it. Hasim immediately went to murmur in his ear. Moments later, Garik's eyes closed. The Arab whispered on, blithely unaware that Garik was asleep. A snore eventually gave the game away, and Hasim left in disgust.

'Can you make the door creak?' Yablokov asked Nikos. 'Or he's going to catch me bad-mouthing him soon.'

The Greek smiled grimly. 'Consider it done. You don't want him as an enemy, Evgeny – a powerful man with powerful friends. We should all watch ourselves around him.'

It was good advice, although not necessarily easy to follow.

'You did well yesterday, Nikos,' said Yablokov. 'Hasim's team spent hours hunting the scientists, but you caught them in a few minutes.'

Nikos winced. 'I'm not proud of it – and I was scared shitless. Did you hear that they killed two of Hasim's people, then stripped their bodies? I kept thinking that they'd do the same to us if we fell into their hands.'

'Well, we started it,' shrugged Yablokov. 'They lost five to our two. Of course, Hasim thinks there are more of them out there, although I believe they were telling the truth when they said there aren't. Christ! What a nightmare! If we come out of this in one piece, I'll never do anything like it ever again.'

'No? You'd turn down a year's pay for six weeks' work?'

Yablokov nodded vehemently. 'At least eight

people are going to die for this business – ten if you include Hasim's pair, plus one who is touch and go. I never signed on for that.'

Shouts echoed in Berrister's ears as he hung on the icy wall. He closed his eyes in despair. Why did he have to be caught now, after all his efforts and one of the most miserable nights of his life? It was several moments before he realised that the voice was female and was calling his name. He squinted up and gaped in disbelief as he recognised the distinctive profile of Sarah's furred hood.

'Come on,' she was urging. 'You can make it – just don't look down.'

Taking a deep breath, Berrister began to climb. It was not a difficult ascent, but he was exhausted, and his fingers and feet were numb with cold. All the while, Sarah clamoured encouragement at him.

'Not that way – keep right. No, *my* right. That's it. Now, grab that piece of ice by your left hand. Not much further now.'

Inch by inch, he scaled the wall, trying not to think about what lay below, while above Sarah clenched her fists so hard that they hurt. As he came nearer, she reached down and grabbed his hood, pulling so hard she risked making him lose his balance. He found another two footholds, and heaved himself over the lip of the crevasse, where he lay gazing up at the pale grey sky. Sarah hauled up his canvas bundle, then sat next to him, hugging her knees.

The wind had dropped, and for a while the only

sounds were Berrister's ragged breathing and the cry of a gull. She was about to ask him what had happened when there was a groan, followed by the sound of falling ice: the fragile ledge had finally collapsed.

'I heard you climbing,' said Sarah in the silence that followed. 'To be honest, I assumed it was one of *them*, and I was going to make sure he didn't make it to the top. I can't tell you how glad I was when I saw it was you.'

'Freddy's dead,' said Berrister in a low voice. 'They shot him, and he's down the crevasse.' He didn't say the field hand was frozen to the ice wall by his own blood – it was too grisly and not something she needed to hear. Then he added, somewhat irrelevantly, 'He was wearing his red bandanna, but not his lucky brown hat. Obviously.'

Sarah swallowed hard. 'And Dan?'

'The blood Graham saw on the beach must've been his. He didn't die under the ice – they must've shot him, too, and taken his body away. The sample pouch we found . . . Dan must've dropped it before all this horror began.'

They were silent again, then Sarah gave a disjointed, chaotic account of what had happened after he and Graham had left, including her own terrible night, huddled in the sleeping bags and expecting at any moment to hear footsteps coming for her. He regarded her in horror when she told him about Lisa – he had known the scream meant nothing good, but it wasn't pleasant to have his fears confirmed.

'We have to help her,' he said, rising unsteadily

to his feet. 'She might be caught on a ledge, like I was.'

'She isn't.' Sarah looked away. 'I heard her land on the bottom.'

'But we *have* to look. We can't just leave her. She might have survived.'

'I'll show you where it happened, but there's nothing you can do now, Andrew, believe me. I only wish there were.'

They began to walk, carrying the bundle between them. Berrister tested each step before putting his full weight upon it, and Sarah, realising that she had been somewhat reckless until now, did likewise.

'Freddy loved it up here,' said Sarah softly. 'During the last couple of weeks, he climbed the scarp two or three times a day.'

Berrister blinked; he hadn't known. 'Did he? Alone?'

Sarah nodded. 'None of us told you, because you'd have stopped him – said it was too dangerous. But he used to enjoy sitting on the crest with his binoculars, looking out to sea. Perhaps he saw the ship coming and ran down to greet them, only to be shot for his efforts.'

'Then ran all the way back up here to fall down the Big Crevasse?'

'Why not? We did.'

Berrister grimaced bitterly as he gazed westwards. 'He was desperate to trek over to the Byers Peninsula. If only I'd agreed – then we'd be safely over there, and he'd still be alive.'

'We can't start thinking like that,' said Sarah,

114

briskly practical. 'How were we to know that gun-toting maniacs would arrive?'

'So what are we going to do about them?'

'Do?' Sarah regarded him askance. 'Nothing – other than survive until help arrives. That's what Geoff asked me to do – live to tell everyone what happened.'

'No,' said Berrister, shaking his head firmly. 'We can't skulk here while they murder him and the others. We can't!'

'But they might be dead already,' argued Sarah. She saw the despair in his eyes and touched his arm in a gesture of sympathy. 'We'll think of something, but not right now. First, we need to rest and get our strength back – I'll be able to sleep if I know you're standing guard, and vice versa.'

Berrister nodded. 'When we've looked for Lisa.'

Sarah regarded him soberly. 'The Big Crevasse goes right down to the bedrock, you know. We won't see her. It's too deep.'

'Just let me shout to her for a while,' said Berrister tiredly. 'I need to be sure she's not still alive. When I fell three years ago . . . well, it's what I'd want someone to do for me.'

Sarah could see there was no point in arguing, so she led the way to the spot where Lisa had fallen. Berrister knelt and yelled her name until he was hoarse, but no sound came back from its black depths.

Eventually, he conceded there was nothing more they could do. He refused point blank to rest inside the glacier, so they gathered as much as they could carry, from his bundle and what had been salvaged from the camp, and set off across the ice. As they walked, he pondered the chain of events that had led them to this pass. There had been three shots: one had hit Freddy, while the others had killed Wells and probably caused the ice fall that they had so pathetically tried to excavate.

But what had Graham said? That Wells would not be dead? Berrister frowned. What had he meant? And was it his imagination, or had Graham behaved oddly since the gunfire? He struggled to think clearly, but it was too cold and he was too tired.

There was a rocky outcrop near the edge of the glacier. Its top afforded a fine view of the ship in South Bay, although she could not see them. At its foot was a hollow, where the ice had melted away to leave a gap. While Sarah did an inventory of their supplies, Berrister took the knife and began to cut large 'bricks' from the snow. Fortunately, the blade was sharp, and he soon had enough blocks to build a wall. Then, using a technique Wells had taught him, he sculpted an igloo-like roof that arched over the hollow to the rock beyond. He packed the gaps with more snow, and when Sarah glanced up, she saw he had created a shelter that would not only protect them from the weather, but hide them as well. She smiled tiredly. She would certainly rest easier in it than anywhere else on the island.

They ate tinned peas, crackers and a packet of peanuts, then wrapped themselves in smoke-tainted sleeping bags. Huddled together for warmth, they rested at last, one sleeping while the other listened for marauding gunmen.

Yablokov was supervising the flensing. It was snowing, so conditions were treacherous. He had asked the captain to suspend work until the blizzard abated, and Garik had agreed, but an hour later Nikos came to report that the men were out again – Hasim had persuaded the captain to change his mind. Wearily, Yablokov had gone to oversee the operation himself, fearing there would be serious accidents otherwise.

The whale looked as though a bomb had hit it. Uneven gashes scored its back, where lumps of meat and blubber had been hacked away, very different from the neat cuts Yablokov had seen in the historical photographs online. Earlier that day he had seen a black fin slicing through the water nearby. Alarmed, he had recalled the crew, but the orca had not come any closer, and Hasim had been there to order everyone back to work.

Eventually the snow came down so thickly that it was impossible to see, and even Hasim did not argue when Yablokov ordered everyone back on board. When he was sure all were accounted for, he went to the bridge, where Hasim was talking to the Norwegians. They fell silent when Yablokov came in. Hasim glanced at the clock.

'Time to feed our guests,' he said. 'Again.'

'How much longer will you keep them here?' asked Yablokov, finally putting the question that had been at the forefront of his mind ever since Hasim had made the peculiar decision that the

117

scientists were not to be shot, but brought back to *Lena*.

'As long as it takes,' replied Hasim, picking up a chart and studying it with aggravating insouciance.

'As long as *what* takes?' persisted Yablokov.

'As long as it takes to learn a few things I need to know. Only then will we resolve the problem they've become. How's the cargo, by the way? Do you have a progress report for me?'

'I have one for the captain,' retorted Yablokov.

'As you wish.' Hasim's smug smile did not slip one bit.

The first thing that penetrated Berrister's sleep-befuddled mind when he woke an hour later was that he was cold and hungry. He sat up. Sarah was kneeling at the entrance to their shelter, struggling to open a can with the knife. It contained tomatoes. She ate half and handed the rest to Berrister.

'Geoff was right, you know,' she said. 'He warned me that going out might interfere with what you and Graham were doing, and it did – you saw two people poking about the camp, so went to raid the corpses instead. Well, I suspect those two people were Joshi and me.'

'Probably.' Berrister nodded at the supplies laid out on the floor of their shelter. 'But if we hadn't gone there, we'd be minus the torch, the rope that saved my life, and the long knife for cutting snow, not to mention bread and sausage. It worked out OK.'

Sarah stared at their meagre haul. 'Can we last for seven days on this?'

118

Berrister did not answer. 'I want to go to the camp in a minute, to look at the long-wave radios.'

'Why? The generators are kaput, and the radios won't work without them.'

'The batteries might have enough residual power for an emergency transmission. I also want to watch that ship, see how we might help the others.'

'We can't do much without food. I think we'd be better sitting here, conserving our energy. Rothera will already be worried, and when we don't transmit tonight, Vince'll raise the alarm. Help could be here as soon as tomorrow. And even if he lets us down, *Worsley* should be here in a week.'

Berrister was thoughtful. 'We often catch fish in the krill nets – there'll almost certainly be a couple there now, given that they haven't been emptied for three days. Of course, it means one of us going out onto the point, and then we'd really be exposed if the whalers came . . .'

'I could keep watch – call you back if I see them coming.'

Berrister nodded. 'Alright then – we'll see about the radios first, then visit the krill nets. OK?'

Outside, it was snowing heavily. He donned a third jersey beneath his coat, while Sarah dragged on two more pairs of socks. They took the bread and sausage with them and set off. Snow swirled and within moments, they had lost sight of their shelter, so well hidden was it.

They reached the edge of the glacier, and

looked down. They could just make out the ship. Berrister was glad to see it, choosing to interpret it as evidence that their friends were still alive, although it also meant that he and Sarah would need to stay vigilant. He strained his eyes trying to see if there was any activity on board, but the snow was too thick. Cautiously, they made their way down the scarp to the camp. It was devoid of killers, and walking around its broken remains in the silent, floating snow was eerie.

A large bull fur seal had moved in, and was sprawled on what was left of the cook tent. Fur seals were aggressive, and Berrister was disinclined to do battle with it to get to the radios.

'Let's get the fish first instead,' he suggested. 'Maybe it'll have moved by the time we come back.'

They followed the curve of the beach to where rocks jutted out into the sea in a tapering finger. While Sarah kept guard, Berrister clambered out alone, moving confidently as it was a journey he had made daily for the past three months. The nets were at the very end of the point. He released the krill, kept the three fish that were with them, and made his way back to Sarah. As he went, he noticed that the wind was picking up, snow slanting directly into his face.

With no fuel, they had to eat the fish raw, which they did quickly and without pleasure, although both felt better afterwards. When they returned to the camp, it was to find the fur seal still in residence. It eyed them challengingly as they approached.

'If that were a penguin, I'd deal with it,' said Sarah. 'But seals are your department.'

Berrister picked up a piece of driftwood and advanced warily, hoping to drive it off without a major confrontation. The animal glared at him, and made a furious chuffing sound. It tried to back away, but something was stopping it.

'Damn!' he muttered. 'One of the guy ropes is caught around its neck. It's not going anywhere – and it's right where the radios are.'

'Can you cut it loose?' Sarah cast an anxious glance over her shoulder. 'We should try the radios and get out of here, because the longer we hang around . . .'

'The quickest option will be to sedate it,' said Berrister, reluctantly dismissing the one where they waited for it to fall asleep naturally. It might stay awake for hours and Sarah was right – they couldn't risk dallying too long. 'Wait here.'

He went to fetch the necessary equipment, glad to find his cache of ketamine had survived. He returned moments later with a syringe on a pole. He estimated the seal's weight and drew up the correct dosage. Just in case there was a mishap, he handed Sarah a second ampule and a spare syringe. She watched his preparations anxiously. Fur seals were fast and dangerous, and they could not afford for him to be savaged.

'Wave your arms at it,' he directed, 'to distract it while I sneak up from behind.'

Sarah obliged, so Berrister darted forward and inserted the needle into the seal's hind flipper. With a bark of outrage, it whipped around, and

121

he only just avoided a nip from its powerful jaws. He retreated hastily.

'How long will it take to work?' asked Sarah anxiously.

'Not long. But stay back – if we agitate it, we might have problems bringing it round. The last time I used ketamine on a fur seal, I had to resuscitate it.'

'You mean you gave it the kiss of life?' asked Sarah, regarding him askance.

'I used an air bag,' said Berrister, wondering what sort of man she thought he was. 'Yes – it's going under now. I'll see to it while you hunt for some wire and the battery from the weather station.'

'That won't work,' she said anxiously. 'It's not powerful enough.'

'No,' he acknowledged. 'But we might be able to jury-rig it, so it lets us send a brief transmission. Hurry – we've been here too long already.'

Sarah began to poke through the rubble, while Berrister crouched near the seal. He cut it free of the rope, then rolled it away from the tent, positioning it so it wouldn't choke. When he had finished, he retrieved the radios.

The primary one was a hopelessly charred mess, but the spare had survived relatively intact, although it was greasy with smoke. He had no screwdriver to remove panels, so had to resort to smashing them with a rock. He was forced to remove his gloves to wire it to the battery Sarah had found, and the wind made him pay for doing so. An elephant seal roared in the distance, but otherwise silence reigned.

'It's odd, isn't it?' mused Sarah, watching him tinker. 'That the whalers would bother to destroy our food, radios and fuel when they planned to kill us all anyway.'

'Yes and no – maybe they're just thorough. But Graham said something yesterday . . . he seems to think that Dan is still alive.'

'I know. He told me the same.' Sarah hesitated, but then forged on. 'He's been acting weird for days – long before all this started. I hate to say it, but I think he knows more than he's letting on.'

Berrister blinked his astonishment. 'What are you talking about?'

She bit her lip in an uncharacteristic gesture of uncertainty. 'He was furious when you vetoed Freddy's notion of a hike to Byers – you weren't there when we discussed it after, but he was *really* pissed off. With hindsight, it occurs to me that he had an inkling of what was going to happen, and the trek was an excuse to get us out of the way. And ever since Freddy and Dan disappeared . . . well, he's not been himself.'

'None of us have,' Berrister pointed out sharply. 'And I can't believe we're even having this discussion. Of course Graham isn't in league with them!'

'I didn't say he was *in league*—'

'You did if you think he knew they were coming,' he flashed back angrily. 'Or is the villain Freddy, because he suggested we go on the hike? Or Dan, perhaps? None of us know he's dead for certain, after all, and you know what these elderly botanists are like – villains to a man.'

'Stop it,' snapped Sarah, irked in her turn. 'And Graham . . . well, there's definitely something awry about him. For a start, he was drunk yesterday morning, when we all came out of our tents.'

'So? I might have had a drink myself if I'd had any. It proves nothing.'

'It proves he doesn't care enough about the rest of us to share. And think about how he was when you were running across the glacier – he abandoned you very readily.'

'Someone was shooting at us. Of course he ran for his life. I was doing the same.'

'Then what about his behaviour when Joshi fell down the scarp? He was very quick to assure us that Joshi was dead, and not very quick to stop throwing the rocks that might have hit him.'

'So he's selfish,' shrugged Berrister. 'It doesn't mean he's in league with criminals. What could he possibly gain from such an arrangement?'

'Money – maybe there's some kind of reward for reporting whale sightings to the wrong people. And neither of us really knows him. He's not like the others – Lisa and Joshi are students who've been with us years, while Freddy came recommended by colleagues from the Polish station. But Graham – well, he's just someone who applied for a job.'

'Then why are they trying to kill him as well?' asked Berrister archly, thinking that what she was suggesting was outrageous.

'But he *hasn't* been killed, has he? He's been taken to their ship. And who was it who ran

124

straight to where we were hiding, which told them where we were?'

'You think he did it on purpose?' asked Berrister incredulously.

'He might. And maybe it was *him* who stole the food as well, doing it bit by bit over time, so we wouldn't notice.'

Berrister blew on his frozen fingers. 'I suppose he put sugar in the generators, too?' he said caustically. 'To make sure we couldn't call for help.'

'It's a definite possibility, because whoever did it knew that we had *two* generators and *two* radios. How would anyone else know that?'

'Because it's standard practice.'

Considering the discussion over, Berrister turned his attention back to his tinkering, while Sarah crouched next to him, tucking her hands under her arms to keep them warm. Snow continued to fall, coating their shoulders in white. He finished quickly and glanced at her.

'You do realise that the ship is probably listening,' he said. 'If we transmit, they'll know we're not dead, and may come back to look for us.'

'Just get on with it,' she said tersely, irked by his unwillingness to accept that she might have a point about Graham. 'They'll find us anyway if we take much longer.'

He switched the set on with unsteady hands. Lights gleamed under the dials, and the speaker crackled. It worked!

'You won't get much more off that carcass,' announced Hasim in the mess room. 'It's time to cut it loose and find another.'

'Bullshit!' blurted Nikos, startled. 'We've barely started, and we can sell everything – intestines, cartilage, skin. It all has a market in the Far East.'

'But meat fetches the highest price,' argued Hasim, 'so why bother with the rest of it? How is the cargo coming along, by the way?'

Yablokov shrugged. 'The weather isn't helping. But we're doing alright.'

'We have a rendezvous tomorrow,' said Hasim, dabbing fastidiously at his moustache with a napkin. 'So you had better up your game.'

'A rendezvous?' Yablokov frowned. 'You haven't mentioned this before. With whom? And where?'

'I'll tell you when you need to know,' replied Hasim. 'Until then, Nikos must return to the island. One of the scientists is still at large.'

'How do you know?' asked Yablokov suspiciously. 'Did his friends tell you?'

Hasim smiled enigmatically and did not reply, while Yablokov fought down the temptation to punch the smirk off his arrogant face. With each passing day, he felt more like a puppet – things happened over which he had no control, and information wasn't being shared. Hasim had spent an hour in the radio room that morning with the door locked. Despite Yablokov later cajoling, pleading and finally threatening, the communications officer refused to say what he had been doing – Hasim was clearly a greater source of terror than Yablokov could ever hope to be.

Nikos gestured to the window. 'No point going now. We won't see a thing.'

126

'And I'm going to bring the crew in if it gets any worse,' warned Yablokov, looking at Hasim. 'It's already too dangerous out there.'

'They'll stay out until I say so,' said Hasim quietly.

'It's Garik's decision, not yours,' retorted Yablokov.

'Is it now?' said Hasim flatly, and stood to leave.

Yablokov fumed. Garik was now worse than a drunk on the bridge – he had let himself slide completely under Hasim's thumb, and Hasim neither knew nor cared what was safe. Yablokov wondered what would happen if he declared Garik unfit for duty. Would the crew agree to a mutiny? The Norwegians would not, and nor would the communications officer. And there was Hasim's team to consider – there was little he could do against men with guns.

Garik entered the mess as Hasim left. He flopped into a chair and called for the cook to bring him food. He reeked of vodka, and his hands shook as he picked up a fork.

'The snow,' said Yablokov, watching him with growing disdain. 'It's making the whale too slippery. We need to bring the crew in until it stops.'

'What does Hasim say?' asked Garik.

'Why should that matter?' demanded Nikos belligerently. 'He's not a sailor, so why is his opinion important? Personally, I think he has too much say in what goes on—'

'You dare tell *me* how to run my ship?' roared Garik, surging unsteadily to his feet, his eyes hot with anger. 'Yablokov? Place this man under arrest.'

Yablokov gaped at him. 'I hardly think—'

'Do it, or you'll be in the brig with him,' yelled Garik furiously.

Bright, challenging eyes held Yablokov's until he stood and put his hand on Nikos' shoulder. Without a word, Nikos rose and stalked out. Yablokov followed.

'What are you going to do, Evgeny?' asked the Greek tightly. 'Obey him? Or trust your instincts and toss Hasim over the side?'

'I'm going to join you in your cabin for a Scotch,' replied Yablokov calmly. 'And I'll talk to Garik about the situation when he's cooled off.'

'When he's sober, you mean,' retorted Nikos. 'But you'll be waiting a while. I can't recall the last time he didn't reek of booze. We must be mad, taking orders from him.'

'Well, we'll be home in three weeks. Then you can collect your pay and never set foot on *Lena* again.'

'And that would be too bloody soon!' Nikos opened his cabin door. 'How does Hasim know a scientist is still at large? And what's all this about a rendezvous? It isn't in our itinerary – which was to come here, deliver the cargo, grab a couple of whales and go home. No one was to see us, and certainly no one was to meet us. This whole affair stinks.'

'Yes,' agreed Yablokov worriedly. 'It does.'

'It works!' cried Sarah, as the lights glowed and the radio hissed softly. 'Start talking, quick.'

Berrister shook his head, feeling disappointment

bite. 'I can't – there's not enough power to transmit, only to receive.'

'Just do it,' begged Sarah. 'It's worth a try.'

Berrister obliged, but the button that should have lit when he spoke remained dark. Nothing was happening, but Sarah was fiercely hopeful, and he did not have the heart to disillusion her.

'We can listen,' he said, not meeting her eyes. 'See if we can hear anything about *Worsley*. And Rothera might be worried now that it's been two nights since our last check-in.'

'I'm more inclined to put my faith in Noddy Taylor. When he doesn't get his krill data, he'll go apeshit. Rothera will request a search plane just to calm him down.'

Berrister began to search the short-wave frequencies that were most often used by shipping, although not with much hope of success – the chances of anyone transmitting at that precise moment were slim, to say the least. There was nothing, so he moved to the less popular ones, feeling hope fade with every push of the button. Then suddenly, distant voices hissed through the receiver.

'What are they saying?' demanded Sarah. 'I can't understand. Is it Russian? Is it *them*?'

'It's Polish – a geological team at Villard Point. That's on the Byers Peninsula, Sarah – just along the coast. One is telling his ship – *Jacek* – that he's finished his work, and he's ready to be picked up.'

'You speak Polish?'

'I spent a couple of seasons at Arctowski – the Polish base – and picked up enough to get by.'

129

Berrister put his ear to the radio again, struggling to understand. '*Jacek* can't launch a Zodiac – it's too windy.'

There was a pause in the transmission.

'The Byers Peninsula is a Specially Protected Area,' said Sarah. 'Permits sure as hell aren't going to be issued to geologists. Are you sure you've got it right?'

Berrister nodded. 'Which is why they're transmitting on this particular frequency – they've landed illegally and don't want anyone else to know.'

The radio crackled again.

'Well?' demanded Sarah after a brief flurry of messages.

'*Jacek*'s dragging her anchor, so the captain wants to move somewhere safer. The geologist and his assistant have agreed to hole up in an old sealer's hut, and wait until *Jacek* can come back. He says it's worth it for the *Coniopteris*.'

'The what?'

'A fossil fern from the Triassic. I think . . . shit!'

The voices had started up again, but then faded. He jabbed at the scan button, then gave the radio a hefty thump. There was a brief crackle, then nothing. The battery was finally dead. He sat back on his heels.

'What's the time?' he asked.

'Two o'clock. You think *Jacek* might come this way?'

He shook his head. 'The captain will just move further out into Barclay Bay. He says he'll ride out the storm and pick up the geologists at four o'clock tomorrow morning – fourteen hours' time. I'm going to walk across the island and be there when he does.'

'Walk across . . . but you can't, not in fourteen hours! When Freddy was planning his hike, he said it would take us four days. And that was to the *south* coast of Byers – Villard Point is in the north.'

'Then what do you suggest?'

'Waiting here and signalling *Jacek* when she sails past.'

'But she won't sail past – she's going to Arctowski next, and that's on King George. She won't come anywhere near us.'

'But we *can't* go,' Sarah protested, appalled. 'It must be thirty kilometres, almost all of it across ice. We'll never make it – not in fourteen hours.'

'I'm not asking you to come with me. In fact, it's better that you stay here. Then, if I fail, at least someone will be able to tell everyone what happened to us.'

'But that's even more stupid,' shouted Sarah, suddenly afraid. 'You can't go alone! What if you fall down a crevasse? And, even if you do make it over there, the chances are that you'll arrive too late.'

'Then, I'll come back.'

'No,' she said firmly. 'It can't be done. Look at the snow – it's coming down harder than ever, and it's windier now than an hour ago. The captain's right: another storm is coming. You wouldn't let poor Freddy take us on a hike because you said it was too dangerous, and you were right.'

131

'There's a big difference between a jaunt taken for fun and a trek that might save our friends' lives. I have to try, Sarah.'

'But you'll die out there, and where will that leave me? We have to stick together. It's our best chance.'

'Ours, perhaps, but what about the others? We have to do something to help them – we'll never live with ourselves if we don't.'

Sarah could see that arguing further was futile. 'Then what do you need? You can take the bread and sausage. What else? A sleeping bag in case you get stuck?'

He shook his head. 'It'll slow me down. I've got a compass and a torch, so the only other thing I need is a watch. Mine broke yesterday.'

Sarah fumbled with her wrist strap. 'I want that back in one piece, Berrister. It was a gift from someone very important to me.'

He took it, and she trailed him up to the glacier. They walked in silence, she wondering if she should jab him with ketamine to stop him from undertaking such a suicidal mission, while he began mapping out his route in his mind, mentally sketching the geography of the island. He needed to avoid the heavily crevassed Verila Glacier near the coast of Walker Bay, so he would head more or less straight north, inland towards the island's higher peaks. Then he would strike off west, crossing a smooth cap of ice that rose to about 360 metres, but staying north of its highest point, Rotch Dome. That way, he would reach the sea near Ivanov Beach, and he could then follow the coast past Robbery Beaches to Villard Point.

132

When they reached the glacier, he turned and gave Sarah a hug. She opened her mouth to speak, but then closed it again, and they parted without a word.

He set his boot on the first of the ice so full of misgivings that he almost turned back. Every objection Sarah had raised was justified. Even if he were at the peak of physical fitness – which he wasn't – hiking thirty kilometres over such inhospitable terrain in fourteen hours would pose a challenge, and if he didn't fall down a crevasse, he might well die of exposure. And the weather *was* deteriorating by the minute. He glanced behind him, wanting one last look at the burned camp, to give him the incentive to continue, but there was nothing to see but swirling snow.

Seven

Joshi paced back and forth, restless, frightened and agitated. Mortimer watched him from one of the bunk beds, while Graham slumped in a chair near the porthole. The radio was on, because Joshi thought the cabin was bugged, and he was determined that their conversations would not be overheard. For some inexplicable reason, the only station available was one that played nothing but Latin American dance music.

'There must be something we can do,' said Joshi, going to the door and rattling the handle yet again. 'I'll go mad in here.'

133

'Stop,' warned Mortimer. 'Or you'll have the guards in here, irked because you're annoying them. And look on the bright side – at least we're warm, dry and fed.'

'Can we open the porthole?' asked Joshi. 'Then we might be able to slip out.'

'Slip out to what? If you think you can swim from here to the shore before you freeze to death, then be my guest.'

'The porthole's rusted shut,' said Graham gloomily. 'That doesn't surprise me on this tub – I've seen better maintained wrecks.'

'Is she very old, then?' asked Mortimer, more to initiate a conversation than to elicit information. Ever since their capture, the Scot had settled into a mood of black despair, and Mortimer didn't know how to jolt him out of it.

'Not *very* old,' replied Graham with a shrug. 'Just poorly built. I wouldn't want to be in a storm in her.'

'You think she might sink?' asked Joshi worriedly.

'She might. Rivets are missing, the steel on the hull looks sub-standard, and she hasn't been painted in years. The crew have done their best to keep her tidy, but poor old *Lena* is a dog – she should have been scrapped yonks ago.'

'Call me a bigot if you will,' said Mortimer, 'but there's something about this dingy decor that just screams ex-Soviet Union. I've been in hotel rooms this colour in Russia.'

'Probably part of the Barents Sea fishing fleet,' said Graham. 'Hired to come south while the north is closed by ice.'

They fell silent when the door opened and a crewman entered with a tray. Outside, Mortimer glimpsed the two guards, both armed and wary. Wordlessly, the sailor set the tray on the table and left, locking the door behind him.

'Two o'clock on the dot,' said Mortimer, consulting his watch. 'And breakfast was precisely at eight. At least they do something efficiently.'

When the first meal had been brought the previous day, Mortimer's inclination had been to wolf it down at once, but then it had occurred to him that it might be poisoned. He knew Hasim was going to kill them in the end, and administering a toxin was a lot less messy than shooting. Thus he had inspected each item carefully before deciding what was safe and what was not.

The bread had probably been baked as a batch for the whole crew, so he decided that was alright, as was the fruit – wrinkled apples and wizened oranges. But the potato and meat stew went down a gap between the floor and the wall. The three bottles of beer had all been opened, and a single, careful sip had revealed a suspicious metallic aftertaste that Mortimer had not trusted at all, so they were poured down the sink.

At lunch that day, he went through a similar ritual. Again, there was an unpleasant tang to the beer, and he was not about to trust the fish soup. They were left with black bread, fruit and three bars of chocolate. He directed Joshi to throw the rest away, while he rubbed his hands gluttonously above the remainder.

'Do you think Sarah will try to help us?' asked Joshi, speaking in a low voice, although the music was blaring. He ate a piece of chocolate without enthusiasm.

'What can she do?' asked Graham. 'She doesn't even have a way of getting to the ship, let alone dealing single-handedly with however many crew there are.'

'She might not have to do it alone,' whispered Joshi. 'Andrew might be with her. We don't know he's dead – not for certain.'

Graham immediately assumed the miserable expression he adopted whenever Berrister's name was mentioned. He set down the apple he had been eating.

'No one blames you for what happened,' said Mortimer, not for the first time since they had been caught. 'It was just—'

'But I left him! I ran away and left him.'

'Not so,' countered Mortimer briskly, wondering if guilt or self-pity raged more strongly in the morose Scot. Either way, his gloom was hardly healthy, and was beginning to be taxing. 'He just happened to be behind you.'

'I was so scared,' whispered Graham, almost to himself. 'These people . . . they're so dangerous.'

Mortimer nodded. 'Quite. Besides, he may be with Sarah as we speak, feasting on water biscuits and stock cubes.'

Joshi looked hopeful, Graham disbelieving. Personally, Mortimer was quite sure Berrister was dead – it seemed perfectly clear to him from Graham's account that he had either been shot or had fallen down a crevasse – but he refused to spend his last few hours on Earth wallowing in grief and anger. He decided he would rather fill Graham and Joshi with false hope than leave them with no hope at all.

Graham put his head in his hands. 'He didn't know the glacier as well as the rest of us, because he never went up there for fun. He didn't have a clue what he was doing.'

'Don't underestimate him,' argued Mortimer. 'He used to be a good mountaineer.'

'*Andrew* did?' asked Joshi in astonishment. Even Graham lifted his head to look at Mortimer askance. 'Are you sure?'

'I'd put money on him surviving a crevasse over either of you two,' said Mortimer. 'Now, eat this lovely food. If there's an opportunity to escape, I don't want you spoiling our chances by fainting from hunger.'

He made sure Graham ate, finished his own meal and went to stare out the porthole. Livingston was invisible, lost behind a waving curtain of snow. It was too windy to launch a boat, or he was sure the gunmen would be out looking for Sarah. All he could do was pray that the blizzard would last as long as possible, as every hour that passed would help her to dig herself into a place where the whalers wouldn't find her.

'I'm going to get this open,' said Joshi, prodding the porthole with a fork. 'I need something to do, and if they notice, I'll just say I wanted some fresh air.'

'Oh, they'll believe that,' said Graham scathingly. 'The notion of escape won't cross their minds.'

'Do it,' countered Mortimer. 'What harm can it do?'

Sarah watched Berrister disappear into the snow, still considering running after him and injecting him with ketamine before he realised what was happening. At least then he might survive. She knew he was walking to his death, and she could not help but think that she should have done more to stop him. She firmly believed that waiting for rescue was the best thing to do, although it would not be easy to sit tight and do nothing, especially now she was alone. She shoved her hands in her pockets and felt the syringe.

'Stupid man!' she muttered, becoming angrier the more she thought about it. 'Who does he think he is? Scott of the Antarctic?'

She ran a few steps through the snow, but Berrister had moved quickly and was already lost from sight. She shouted his name, but all she could hear was her own laboured breathing.

Miserably, she returned to the ice shelter. The snow was coming down harder than it had been, and was settling. She was now leaving footprints – and footprints could be followed. But when she looked behind her, she saw that the shallow depressions made by her boots were already filling. If the blizzard continued, they would soon be invisible.

She stuffed one sleeping bag in the entrance to keep out the wind, and began to inventory her supplies again, although she already knew by heart what she had. She picked up the video game that had been in one of the dead men's daypacks.

She switched it on, and to her surprise it bleeped, the power level showing at fifty per cent. She stared at it, before turning it over and pulling off the back. There were two 1.5-volt batteries. The radio handsets took those!

Heart pounding, she inserted them into the one that had been in her pocket since the nightmare had started, and switched it on. There was a sharp crackle and a low hiss. It worked! She changed the frequency, listening for voices, but there was nothing – it had been a stroke of luck to catch the Poles. Loath to run down the power, she turned it off and tucked it inside her coat to keep it warm – nothing drained batteries faster than the cold. She wrapped herself in the sleeping bags, and curled up to sleep.

When she woke, it was pitch dark. She fumbled for her watch before remembering that she had lent it to Berrister. She was puzzled. Even with the sleeping bag covering the entrance, some light should be filtering in. Then, with sudden, horrifying clarity, she realised what had happened: the snow had sealed her in, and what had been her refuge had now become her tomb. She was buried alive!

Falling snow enveloped Berrister as he trudged steadily upward. It was coming from the east, sometimes hitting the back of his hood, sometimes sending stinging needles into his face as he zigzagged up the slope. The storm was worsening. He glanced at Sarah's watch. It was just after five o'clock, which meant that he had been walking for almost three hours. His progress had been slow, because the trek had been one long ascent, but now, by his figuring, it was time to turn west.

The surface was smoother, although still somewhat up and down, and he began to make better time. At points, he felt he was moving too fast, not testing carefully enough for hidden fissures. The thought had scarcely crossed his mind, when ice beneath his foot gave way, sending him to his knees. It was not a crevasse, just an irregularity in the surface, but it warned him to take better care.

After a further three hours, the ground levelled, suggesting he had reached the plateau that ran between the central peaks and Rotch Dome. He checked the compass, and turned a few degrees south – a course that should take him directly to Ivanov Beach, but still keep him to the north of the steeply rising dome. The wind was blowing harder now, driving the snow horizontally. It was increasingly difficult to keep his balance, and even with the exertion of walking, he was growing colder.

He slogged on through the failing light, frequently checking the compass and then adjusting to a more south-westerly course. It was a longer route, but would allow him to stay on the level plateau. The soft snow made walking difficult, and his legs began to ache with the effort. He groped in his pocket for the food. The sausage was even more rancid than when he had taken a bite earlier, and he wondered if its previous owner had taken it from the garbage with some odd notion of feeding the wildlife.

The bread was frozen and stale, but he still wanted to eat it all. He forced himself to put half of it away. He might miss the Poles and end up walking back again, in which case he would need something to sustain him.

His progress slowed as he began to tire. Night fell, but the brightness of the snow kept the darkness at bay somewhat. He also had the torch for the places where it did not. He glanced at the watch again – almost midnight. He had roughly four hours left, but still had a long way to go – it was either further than he had figured, or he was moving more slowly than he had anticipated. Desperately, he tried to pick up the pace.

Eventually, he turned directly west again, which led him steadily downward – he was beyond the worst of the dome. He looked at the watch. Five past one. He had three hours to walk what he estimated would be about thirteen kilometres: five descending the snowfield to the sea, and eight along the coast. It was going to be tight.

As he increased his speed, he lost his footing. He fell, slithering helplessly down the slope, unable to break his fall. When he finally came to a rest, he was disorientated. He opened his eyes, but his world reeled and tipped. He was not sure how long he lay there before he was able to fumble for the watch. His pocket was empty. Horrified, he tore off his gloves and felt again, sighing with relief when he felt the metal strap.

He drew it out and saw with relief that it was only one-thirty. He had lost five minutes at the most. He climbed to his feet, staggering as the wind buffeted him. He checked the compass, found west, and began trudging forward again. After a kilometre or so, he checked the time again. The dial still read one-thirty. Silently, he cursed Sarah's 'someone important', who had not bought her a watch that was more robust.

Stomach churning, he continued to descend, stumbling and tripping, confused by the fact that there was no horizon in the white-out. Gradually, he became aware that the wind was dropping – the storm was blowing itself out. It was a mixed blessing. It made walking easier, but also meant that *Jacek* might collect the stranded geologists early. He forced himself to move faster, glad when the ice levelled off, then petered out completely. Suddenly he saw the sea in front of him – he had reached Ivanov Beach.

Byers Peninsula is joined to the rest of the island by a neck of land some four kilometres wide. Berrister was uncertain how far he was from the neck, but knew that if he followed the coast, he would reach Robbery Beaches and then Villard Point. Relief made him dizzy. He paused for a moment to rest, then forced himself to move, afraid he might be unable to start again if he left it too long.

He increased his speed now that he was off the ice and onto sand and gravel, but still could not move as fast as he wanted, and it felt like an age before he finally reached Robbery Beaches – a series of rugged bays lined with dark sand and outcrops of volcanic rock.

The area – in fact all Byers – was a different world from the glacier, with verdant beds of moss, although Berrister could see little of them in the gloom and snow. He wondered what time it was – after four, probably, given that he could now make out objects on the horizon, which meant he had to hurry. He tried to run, but fell almost immediately. It would be safer to keep walking. He ignored the burning exhaustion in his knees and hips, and ploughed on, step after step.

And then he saw Villard Point in the distance, a low headland that thrust out between two coves. He wanted to whoop with delight, but all that emerged was a croak. He made for the nearer cove, spirits rising, but it was empty. He broke into a lumbering trot to cross the point itself, hoping with every fibre of his being that he wasn't too late. There was a distinct lightening of the sky now, which meant it was probably nearer five than four.

Breath coming in gasps, he reached the second cove, and felt the bitter taste of disappointment when he found it was empty too. Gritting his teeth, he started to trot out to the end of the point – and then almost wept with relief when he saw what was there. *Jacek* was a tiny ship used for ferrying scientists on short trips from their base on King George Island. It was a good idea: it would be more economical with fuel than larger vessels like *Worsley*, and would reach places they could not.

But his exultation was short lived. *Jacek* was powering northward – he had missed her.

He stumbled to a small rise just above the beach, waving his arms and yelling as loudly as he could, but it was hopeless – the ship was already too far away. He dropped to his knees and watched her in despair. Every part of his body

143

ached, and he was not sure he had the strength to return to Hannah Point. Even if the weather was fair, he was simply too tired.

A dull boom was followed by a spout of water next to *Jacek*. At first he thought it was a whale but the 'blow' was the wrong shape. There was another boom, and *Jacek* lurched to one side, black smoke pouring from her stern. Berrister struggled to his feet. Was she having some kind of engine trouble? Then another ship nosed slowly into view, this one much larger and painted blue-grey. There was a flash of orange from her deck and a third boom. *Jacek* shuddered, her radio mast toppling to trail in the sea.

Berrister watched, appalled. There was another flash, another roar, and *Jacek* began to sink, her stern blasted away. Her bow lurched madly upwards, then, faster than he would have imagined possible, she was gone. All that remained was wreckage, an orange life-belt and a spreading smear of oil.

Feeling like a voyeur, Yablokov pushed his ear against the door to the scientists' cabin. After a few minutes, he gave up: he could hear nothing except music. He knew why they had the radio on, of course. What Russian born in the Soviet era would not? Even so, he was disappointed to return to Nikos' cabin, and report that they were no further forward.

Nikos was staring moodily out of the window.

'I heard Hasim tell the Norwegians that his "informer" let him know the position of our whales,' the engineer said. 'Which means that one of the prisoners is in his pay. I bet it's the youngster. Kids are the ones who can do clever stuff with communications these days.'

'No, it'll be the fat one,' argued Yablokov. 'He does all the talking when Hasim visits. The red-head's too scared, while the boy seems a bit simple. Still, it explains why Hasim brought them here, rather than killing them – he wants to spare the traitor's life.'

'But he *is* killing them,' whispered Nikos, his expression haggard. '*All* of them. I told you: he ordered me to give him the elemental mercury that I use in the sewage treatment plant. The bastard's poisoning the lot of them, the traitor included.'

Yablokov racked his brain, but could think of no reason why Hasim would prefer to poison his guests rather than shoot them. However, the man's ruthlessness made him fearful for himself and his crew. Would they meet the same fate once their work with him was done? Or was Yablokov allowing his imagination to get the better of him? After all, how could Hasim continue to operate year by year, if he murdered his associates after every mission?

'We need more information if we're going to understand what's happening,' Nikos was saying. 'I'm going to have a look around, talk to the crew.'

'You can't. You're confined to quarters, remember? My crew will look the other way, but the hired hands won't, and nor will Hasim's team.'

Nikos crashed his fist on the sill. 'Bloody Garik!

145

What's wrong with him? Can't he see he's losing control? All the crew think he's a joke, and some – like the Norwegians – only take orders from Hasim now. And you, me and Zurin are stuck in the middle, trying to keep everything going.'

Yablokov looked at the clock. 'I'm due on watch. Don't go out, or Garik might lock you somewhere more secure. Then I won't be able to visit.'

He headed for the bridge, noting that the corridor was filthy. He grimaced: Garik would never have tolerated such laxness in the north, even at the height of the cod season. *Lena* might not be the prettiest of vessels, but her crew had always kept her tidy, and he'd never had to remind them of their basic duties before. Nikos was right – Garik *was* losing control.

He was about to enter the bridge when he noticed that the door was closed to the communications room. As it was usually open, he could only surmise that Hasim was in there, either enjoying one of his secretive discussions with the Norwegians or communicating with his superiors. For the second time in an hour, he began to eavesdrop.

There was a murmur of voices from within, but they were too low for him to hear. He pushed his ear to the door harder, then almost toppled in when it was yanked open. Hasim gazed at him in astonishment, while the Norwegians smirked. Yablokov was torn between embarrassment and irritation, and felt his face grow hot.

'I was looking for you,' he mumbled lamely. 'The weather's clearing, so we can up the speed of the flensing.'

'No – concentrate on the cargo,' countered Hasim. 'That's why we're here, after all. Forget the whale – we're done with it.'

'We can do both.' Yablokov attempted a smile. 'We'll winch the whale over, which should make things easier for—'

'No time, I'm afraid. As soon as the last scientist is aboard, we're leaving this place. I want you to cut the whale loose.'

Yablokov thought of his family. His share of half a hold of meat would not save them if the cod industry crashed that year, as he sensed it would. They *had* to finish harvesting the whale, or the whole vile business would have been for nothing.

'Please,' he said, hating to beg, but seeing no alternative. 'Just a few more hours. We've only got half the meat and—'

'Then you should have worked faster,' retorted Hasim shortly. 'We have a schedule to meet, you know.'

'Yes,' said Yablokov stiffly, tired of hearing about it – and tired of not being told exactly what the schedule entailed. 'But at least let us continue flensing while you hunt for the scientist. After all, every new lump is a few more dollars.

Greed flowed into Hasim's eyes. 'Very well, but not a moment longer. You'll cut it loose the moment I give the order. Agreed?'

Yablokov nodded, aware that Hasim had finally dropped any pretence that Garik was in charge. Still, at least he knew where he stood. Or did he? What had Hasim been doing so secretly in the communications room?

* * *

147

Sarah scrabbled frantically at the walls of her shelter, trying to find the entrance. She could not breathe properly and the darkness was complete. Berrister's wall seemed to have hardened in the blizzard, and she might as well have tried to claw through concrete. Then she felt the sleeping bag she had used to block the entrance, and behind it was softer snow. She hauled it back, then scooped great handfuls of the stuff away, relieved beyond measure when she detected a glimmer of light. She dug harder, and cleared a hole the size of a tennis ball. Cold air rushed in, revealing how much the shelter had protected her during the storm. She was about to dig more when she heard voices.

The whalers! Heart thumping, she retreated to the back of the shelter and huddled against the rock wall. The voices came closer, and she cringed as one called from right above her head – he was climbing the outcrop against which her shelter leaned. Any minute now, and he would crash through the roof and land in her lap. She closed her eyes tightly, silently willing him to go away.

She leapt in alarm as something speared down close to her face. It was an aluminium probe. Above her, its owner was shouting to his cronies, laughing as he plunged the stick up and down, so close that she could see every blemish on its surface. A hot prickle of sweat broke out on the back of her neck. This was it, she thought – they had found her. She waited for Berrister's snow blocks to be hauled away.

Incredibly, though, she heard a scrape of a boot on stone, and the voices moved away. What was happening? Scarcely daring to breathe, she waited until she could no longer hear them, then peered out of the hole she had made. No one was there. She made it larger, then waited again, head tipped to one side as she listened intently. All was silent.

She crawled out through the hole and listened a third time. Still nothing. Warily, she took a few steps up the rock and saw the men fanning out across the glacier, poking the surface with their probes. She felt weak with relief. The man who had scaled the pinnacle had just been using it like she was – as a vantage point to scan his surroundings. She jumped down and crawled back into her shelter, surprised at how much warmer it was inside. It would have been cosier still with two, and she cursed Berrister for leaving her.

Shovelling snow back over the opening to hide it, she wondered where he was. Enjoying a hot breakfast on *Jacek*, happy in the knowledge that help was on its way? Or dead on the glacier? Although not a natural pessimist, she knew it was the latter. She did not have enough faith in his fitness or ability as an outdoorsman to imagine otherwise. She considered going to find him, but the chances were that he was buried under a snowdrift. Her hunt for him would be as futile as the whalers' was for her.

For something to do, she picked up the handset and switched it on. A woman was rattling off a long list of numbers in Spanish, while a late-season tourist ship was chatting to a shore party. She knew she should conserve power, but the cheerful banter between tourists and ship heartened her, and she was loath to break contact. The ship, she learned, was *Akademic Solzhenitsyn*, a Russian ice-breaker chartered by an American company. They were visiting Deception Island, a collapsed volcanic caldera some thirty-five kilometres south. It was still seismically active, and was popular with visitors, who liked to bathe in its thermally heated pools, an intriguing experience when the ground around them was dusted with snow.

The tourists were enjoying themselves, and Sarah could hear shrieks of delight as they wallowed in the hot springs. She scowled at the radio. How could people be having fun while she was in a hole being hunted by armed killers? She snapped off the sound angrily. On a clear day, Deception was visible from Hannah Point, a grey smudge on the horizon. It was ironic that Berrister had tried to walk thirty kilometres across ice to rescue their friends, while tourists frolicked about the same distance in the opposite direction.

But listening to the radio had told her one thing: no one at Rothera was worried about them, or *Solzhenitsyn* would have been morally obliged to make a detour. As far as the base was concerned, all was well and no help was coming in a hurry. So much for Noddy Taylor and his krill!

Sarah had never felt so helpless. At least Berrister had tried to help the others. If she survived, she knew she would spend the rest of her life wondering if she should have done the same, and at that point, she realised that no matter what it took, she *had* to transmit a mayday. Maybe she could combine parts from the two generators

150

and get one to work. It was worth a try, she decided, so she crawled out of her shelter and scaled the rock to look down to the camp.

Damn! The whalers were there. A couple were shoving the burned remains of tents into refuse sacks, while others were loading the empty food boxes onto a Zodiac. She frowned. Surely they couldn't imagine that eradicating every trace of the camp would mean that no questions would be asked? It would only serve to deepen the mystery of the eight missing scientists.

Then she heard a sound behind her. She spun round in alarm, only to find herself staring down the barrel of a gun.

'You haven't been honest with me,' said Hasim, eyeing Mortimer reproachfully. 'You claimed that all your colleagues were dead.'

'They are,' said Mortimer. 'You were horribly thorough.'

It was just after six in the morning, and none of the prisoners had slept well. Joshi complained of stomach cramps, while Graham refused to speak at all. Mortimer had a vicious headache, which he attributed to strain.

'You say two died before our ship arrived, two fell down crevasses, and we have you three. But that leaves one: the penguin woman.'

Mortimer tried to keep the dismay from his face. Had Hasim overheard them talking, despite the blaring music? But that did not explain how he knew Sarah was an expert on penguins. There was no toilet in the cabin, so they had to ask to use the one at the end of the corridor. Had Graham or Joshi betrayed Sarah to the guards once they were out of earshot? Surely not. Hasim must've found out some other way.

'The last time I saw her was at the Big Crevasse,' he replied truthfully. 'We separated to escape from you lot. But even if she didn't fall down it, do you think she could have survived last night's storm with no shelter?'

'What are you going to do with us?' blurted Joshi before Hasim could reply. He looked frightened, and his fingers were bleeding from his efforts to open the porthole. Graham sat beneath it, to hide the rust and paint chippings that were scattered on the floor. He was pretending to read, but held the first aid manual upside-down.

Hasim gave a pained smile. 'You'll be put ashore near one of the bases on King George Island. You might have a little walk, to allow us time to put some distance between us, but nothing too arduous.'

Mortimer knew he was lying, and wished he understood why they were being kept alive. If the plan was to dump their bodies at sea, why not kill them now, rather than go to the trouble of keeping them under guard? And why were they being poisoned? To see if his theory was right, Mortimer pressed a hand to his stomach, as if it hurt, and had his proof in the gleam of triumph that flared in Hasim's eyes. Of course, it didn't tell him *why* the whalers preferred one mode of execution over another.

'Tell me about your research,' said Hasim, perching on a chair and indicating that Mortimer

152

should sit too. 'I've always been fascinated by biology.'

'Our biologists are dead,' replied Mortimer flatly. 'I'm just a glaciologist. Young Joshi had notions of a career in polar botany, but the season's finale has put him off.'

'Pity,' said Hasim smoothly. 'But I'm more interested in krill. Tell me about that.'

'Krill?' blurted Mortimer, startled. 'Why?'

'Because they fascinate me. Don't you find it remarkable that so many of them live in this near-freezing ocean? What a resource! It could end world hunger at the drop of a hat.'

'It couldn't,' countered Mortimer. 'They aren't limitless, and if we start hoovering them up, then the stocks will go the same way as the Atlantic cod. And without food, the seabirds will die and so will the seals. Not to mention what's left of the whales.' He gave Hasim a look of disgust.

'How many krill live here, around Livingston?'

'Don't have a clue,' replied Mortimer, racking his brain for a reason as to why Hasim should want to know. 'Enough to feed a few penguins and a rapidly dwindling pod of whales.'

Hasim stood abruptly. 'Think about it, Dr Mortimer. It's in your interests to cooperate.'

'Why?' pounced Mortimer. 'You said you meant us no harm.'

Hasim gave a tight smile. 'And nor do we. Incidentally, we have plenty of beer, so ask if you want more. And now you must excuse me – we leave soon, and I have a lot to do.'

'Really?' Mortimer was astonished and uneasy to hear it. 'But your whale can only be half-flensed.'

153

'Perhaps so, but it's easier to catch another than scrape about with this one.'

'But you could spend days looking for a second animal,' said Mortimer, bemused. 'These things don't grow on trees.'

Hasim's smile was unpleasant. 'We took the precaution of attaching a tracking device to one of its friends, so we know exactly where they went. They're a couple of hours away, near the Byers Peninsula.'

Disgusted, Mortimer struggled for a way to dissuade him. 'If you're boarded on your way north – and lots of countries have ships that do nothing but hunt illegal fishing boats – you'll have trouble explaining why your holds are full of whale meat.'

'They all turn a blind eye to the odd minke – for a price.'

'But you don't have "the odd minke". You have a blue – and those are protected.'

Hasim laughed. 'Can *you* tell that from a lump of flesh? In a hold that stinks of fish, and in which the lights don't work very well?'

'No, but *they* might. Besides, these aren't easily corruptible officials – they're dedicated men and women who want the Antarctic to be safe from criminals like you.'

Hasim sneered. 'Everyone has his price. But we'll never be boarded – our radar is the best money can buy, and we'll see them coming long before they spot us. We'll never be caught – too much is at stake.'

'If that's true, why come down here? Your chances of getting away with slaughtering endangered species are much better further north.'

Hasim smiled slyly. 'You assume that whaling is our prime objective. Well, it isn't. We needed to be in the Antarctic regardless, and as we were here, we decided to see what the captain could snag with his harpoon.'

'So, what *is* your "prime objective"?' asked Mortimer, wondering what could be worse than whaling.

Hasim opened his mouth to reply, but a crewman entered the room and whispered in his ear. He nodded in satisfaction, then turned to Mortimer.

'My men have found your biologist. You'll have company, gentlemen.'

Berrister watched in horror as the rogue ship launched an inflatable to nose about in the debris from the sunken *Jacek*. The ship dropped an anchor, and he saw a smear of red down her starboard side as the wind turned her towards him – at some point, she had been involved in butchering some hapless whale.

Although her identifying markings had been painted over, her name had not, so he could just make it out on her side – *Galtieri*. He was no expert, but she looked like a warship – there were turrets where more big guns could be mounted, and she had the sleek, predatory appearance of a medium-sized naval vessel. He wondered where the crew were going to store the meat, given that military vessels tended not to be equipped for carrying bulky cargo.

So how many ships did these criminals have? Just the two, or had an entire fleet been dispatched to pillage what should have been a safe haven for cetaceans? He supposed a fleet made sense. Then, if one ship was caught, the profits from the others would pay for any losses. Of course, if they blew witnesses out of the water with heavy artillery and hunted down others with guns, the chances of getting caught weren't going to be very high . . .

As he watched, the men on the inflatable pulled individual pieces of wreckage from the water and examined them. Some they kept and some they tossed back into the sea. He understood at once what they were doing: removing anything that was suggestive of foul play. Clearly, they wanted any investigators to believe that the hapless *Jacek* had suffered a catastrophic accident, rather than an attack by a warship.

Berrister watched for a while, then stood on unsteady legs. Glaring at the vile ship was doing no good – he needed to find somewhere to rest before attempting the return journey. He could see the hut that the Poles had used, so he began to stumble towards it. At the very least, he could sit out of the wind for a few hours, and it might even contain something to help him – blankets, perhaps, or emergency supplies.

He was almost there, when he heard voices. He ducked behind it quickly, angry with himself for not being more cautious. When he peered around the corner, he saw four people there – three with their hands raised and another with a gun. Near the surf – visible now he was closer to it – two more men were busy with a pair of boats. One was *Jacek*'s, and the other was newer, with a larger engine. It did not take

Berrister long to grasp what was happening: *Jacek* had been destroyed while the two geologists and their driver were still ashore. *Galtieri*'s crew were now tinkering with *Jacek*'s Zodiac, and Berrister could only suppose that they aimed to make *that* look as though it had had an accident as well.

The geologists and the driver – two men and one woman – were white with shock and confusion, and Berrister knew they were about to be executed. Without considering the consequences, he picked up a stone and leapt towards the guard, hitting him from behind as hard as he could. The man crumpled, and the three Poles blinked their astonishment.

'The gun,' Berrister croaked, aware of the two men by the water's edge beginning to turn towards them. 'Get his gun.'

He had spoken English, but the woman understood. She darted forward, grabbed the weapon and promptly shot the two *Galtieri* men, even as they were reaching for their weapons. Then she aimed at him.

'Put your hands up,' she ordered sharply in heavily accented English. 'Or I'll kill you.'

Berrister did not doubt it, given that she had not hesitated to dispatch the whalers. He did as he was told, trying to explain at the same time. He did not blame her for being suspicious, but he *had* just saved her life, so he thought she could afford to be a little less hostile.

'I've come from Hannah Point,' he began hoarsely. 'There's another—'

'Hannah Point?' interrupted an elderly man

157

with a neat white beard. 'But that's more than thirty kilometres away. You can't have done.'

'Please!' said Berrister exhaustedly. 'We can't stay here. The gunfire will have been heard on that ship and—'

He stopped when the woman took a firmer hold on her weapon. 'You're one of them.'

'No! I'll explain everything later. First, we should go—'

'You'll explain now,' said the woman. 'Or die.'

Without a choice, he told his story, aware even as he spoke that it was a fantastic one. Indeed, had not *Jacek* just been obliterated before their eyes, he wouldn't have blamed them for thinking him a lunatic. Much to his agitation – he was sure *Galtieri* was preparing to send more killers – they kept interrupting with questions that underlined their own shocked incredulity. They argued with each other, too, so he learned that the white-haired man was Professor Drecki – the person ultimately responsible for the tragedy, as he was the geologist who had insisted on making an unofficial and illegitimate stop. His assistant was Maria, and the driver Tadek.

'I know Freddy Fredericks,' said Maria sharply. 'He's the Australian who worked at our base for the last three years. He's a cook.'

'That's right,' said Berrister, hopes rising.

She regarded him in icy triumph. 'You say he was killed on Wednesday, but I heard him on the radio yesterday – Friday. He was telling Rothera that all was well. And that means your tale is an elaborate and unconvincing lie.'

'I saw his body,' said Berrister desperately,

glancing at *Galtieri* and alert for the sound of trouble on the way. Why couldn't they argue about it later? 'What you heard was someone impersonating him. Australian accents aren't difficult to mimic.'

'Shoot him,' hissed Tadek in Polish. 'He invented this wild story to keep us busy until they rescue him. Kill the bastard – for what he did to *Jacek*, if nothing else.'

'I had nothing to do with—' began Berrister.

'And now he speaks Polish all of a sudden?' interrupted Maria. 'Hah!'

Berrister hadn't realised that he had changed languages. He rubbed his head and glanced towards *Galtieri* again. 'It doesn't make me one of them. Please. You *have* to believe me.'

'I do,' said Drecki softly, and inserted himself between Maria and Berrister. 'He brained that guard to save us. Therefore, he can't be with them. He—'

'A sly ploy to gain our trust,' said Maria, and took aim again. 'I've had enough of this crap. Get out of my way, Professor. It's time for him to die.'

Eight

'Get your filthy hands off me!'

Mortimer exchanged a wry smile with Joshi as Sarah's furious voice echoed down the corridor. There was a series of thumps and a man howled

159

with pain before the door was opened and Sarah stalked in, contemptuously throwing off her captors' grip. The door closed behind her, leaving them alone. Before she could speak, Mortimer put his finger to his lips and switched on the radio.

Sarah looked at each of the three in turn. All were pale and hollow-eyed, but Graham was by far the worst. His hair was matted and dirty, and his skin was sallow. She wondered if remorse was responsible for his decline – that he regretted throwing in his lot with criminals, and had come to the realisation that whatever he had gained from the agreement was not worth it. She considered confronting him with his betrayal there and then, but decided that keeping the knowledge to herself was the only advantage she had over him.

'Sorry,' she said to Mortimer. 'I did my best, but it wasn't good enough.'

'You did better than I would've done,' he replied consolingly.

'Who are these people? Russians?'

Mortimer raised his hands in a shrug. 'Russians, Greeks, Scandinavians, Arabs – and those are just the ones we've met. I think some are *Lena*'s regular crew, while others have been brought on board for . . . whatever it is that they're doing down here.'

She hauled off her coat. 'Well, at least it's warm. Do they feed you?' She pounded on the door. 'Bring me something to eat, you pigs!'

'Easy,' said Mortimer mildly. 'Let's not antagonise them needlessly. Now tell me what you've been up to since we last met.'

160

'I hid in the crevasse, but they caught me,' she replied tersely, and because she was loath to say more in front of Graham, she indicated that the two younger men were to move away. 'I want a word with Geoff – privately. Go over to the window and talk about tyres or whatever it is that boys chat about when they're together.'

'Why?' demanded Graham immediately. 'We have a right to hear anything you've managed to learn.'

Sarah forced a smile. 'I haven't learned anything – I just want to talk to Geoff for a moment. It's personal. Do you mind?'

Graham clearly did, but Joshi pulled him away to work on the porthole, leaving her and Mortimer to sit on the bed. In low voices, they exchanged news.

'Don't tell them Andrew's alive, Geoff,' she whispered when she had finished. 'What they don't know, they can't blurt out. Besides, he probably *is* dead. It was a stupid thing to have attempted.'

'Don't underestimate him. He was very good at that sort of thing before his accident, and it's not something you forget – especially when it's important.'

'I hope you're right, I really do. But even if he did make it, he probably missed *Jacek*. He only had fourteen hours to get there.'

'Fourteen hours – that would be tough. And that's our only hope?'

'Well, there's a tourist ship at Deception – *Akademic Solzhenitsyn*. Perhaps they'll stop at Hannah Point. Of course, they won't find much if they do – when I left, this lot were clearing up the mess they made.'

'There's Rothera – they must be worried about us, given that three days have passed without contact.'

'I've been thinking about that – they *should* be concerned, but nothing was mentioned on the radio. I suspect someone's been making the transmissions in our stead, telling Rothera that everything's fine.'

'Well, obviously it's none of us,' said Mortimer. 'So if you're right, it must be someone pretending to be us.'

'Do they keep you in here all the time?' Sarah asked carefully. 'Or do they let you out on occasion?'

Mortimer gave her a hard look, understanding exactly what she was asking. 'They let us use the bathroom, obviously, but I assure you, none of us three has been helping these people.'

Sarah changed the subject, sensing that now was not the time to voice her suspicions about Graham. Perhaps she would confide them later, after she'd watched how the Scot behaved for a while. 'So why are we still alive? Surely it would be easier – safer – to kill us?'

'I think they aim to use our corpses to "prove" some kind of accident,' explained Mortimer. He had thought of little else since his last encounter with Hasim. 'They don't want the attention that eight murders would generate, so they plan to make everyone think we died in some sort of mishap instead. They claim they'll leave us on King George, but I don't believe it. Joshi does, so please don't disillusion him.'

'Poor Joshi.'

'I'm fairly sure they're poisoning our food,' Mortimer continued. 'Or rather, the beer. It has a nasty metallic flavour that I don't like at all, and Hasim said we can have as much of it as we like. We pour it away, but let him think we're drinking it, lest he takes it into his head to tamper with something else.'

Sarah raised her eyebrows. 'Do they seriously expect anyone to believe that eight people can be fatally poisoned by accident? It'll be obvious that foul play is involved.'

Mortimer shrugged again. 'I could be wrong – it's only a guess.'

'So what are we going to do? I'm not sitting here in this filthy tub, waiting to be murdered on the sly.'

'Joshi's been trying to get the porthole open with a fork. He has a fanciful notion of escaping through it.'

'Don't mock it,' said Sarah. 'It's better than doing nothing.'

'I suppose so,' said Mortimer, unconvinced. 'But—'

They were interrupted by Graham, who flung down the fork he had been using and stepped towards them.

'You have to tell us if you know anything,' he said sulkily. 'We've got a right to know.'

'Very well,' said Sarah coolly, thinking perhaps he *should* be told what his treachery had brought about. 'Freddy's dead. I found his body.'

'I bet you didn't find Dan's, though,' muttered Graham. 'Oh, no. Of course you didn't.'

163

'What do you mean by that?' she demanded.

'Just what I say. Dan's out there somewhere, doing what he's always done – pleasing himself. He's never been one of us, and I don't know why Andrew brought him along in the first place. He flouts all the rules, and goes where he likes, when he likes.'

She stared at him. Could he be right? It would explain why they had found no sign of Dan – because he had been collected by his criminal accomplices, and was relaxing happily somewhere else on *Lena*. Or was Graham merely trying to shift the blame away from himself? She leaned back on the bed, no longer sure what to think.

'Get out of my way,' ordered Maria, after Drecki had stepped in front of Berrister a second time to prevent her shooting him. 'You're wasting time with this nonsense.'

Drecki regarded her coolly for a moment, then did as he was told. Berrister cringed as her finger tightened on the trigger.

'However,' the old man said coldly, 'bear in mind that I *will* report his murder to the authorities, both on the base and in Poland.'

'Oh, screw it,' Maria spat in exasperation, throwing the gun in front of him. 'He's all yours then. *You* can make sure he doesn't turn on us. Tadek, start up the boat. We've got to get back to Arctowski and tell them what's happened here.'

The pair began to sprint down the beach, where the two inflatables undulated in the surf.

'But Arctowski is more than a hundred and

164

fifty kilometres away,' Drecki shouted after them. 'We'll never make it.'

'Not in our boat,' Tadek called back. 'But we will in theirs. Come *on*, Professor – hurry!'

'They'll blow us out of the water,' argued Drecki, although he put on a decent spurt of speed to join them. 'You saw what they did to *Jacek*.'

'We'll be a smaller target and moving very fast,' replied Tadek grimly. 'They won't catch us, believe me. Not the way *I* drive.'

Berrister could only stand and watch as Tadek and Maria pushed the larger craft into the waves and leapt in. But Drecki still had some way to go when another Zodiac suddenly appeared from behind the ship. It carried four men, all armed. Tadek turned his boat around, while Maria screamed for Drecki to run.

The new boat powered towards them, and Tadek, evidently deciding that Drecki wouldn't make it in time, gunned the engine and roared directly towards the whalers, on a collision course. Maria was flung backwards as the boat accelerated.

It was the gunmen who blinked. At the last second, they veered away, leaving Tadek to fly past them and aim for the open sea. The whalers turned to follow, but Tadek had a good lead and was the better driver. He began to pull away. Silently, Berrister urged them on.

'You! Quick!'

It took a moment for Berrister to realise that Drecki was speaking to him.

'We'll take the other boat and slip away while

165

their attention is elsewhere. Well, don't just stand there, man – move!'

Berrister forced his stiff legs into action, and hobbled down the beach, expecting at any moment to see a second enemy boat racing towards them. Drecki clambered into a little inflatable that had definitely seen better days, while Berrister shoved it into the surf. He didn't think his feet could be any colder, but the seawater chilled him to the bone, making him gasp with the shock of it. He climbed in awkwardly and looked for the ignition button. The engine was so ancient that it didn't have one – just a pull-cord, like an old-fashioned lawnmower. He hauled at it with all his strength. Nothing happened.

'Again!' hissed Drecki. 'Harder!'

Berrister did, and the antiquated motor chugged briefly before clattering into silence. He glanced up, expecting to see gun-toting killers racing towards them, and yanked the cord again. This time, the engine caught, so he jammed it in gear and aimed for deeper water.

'Head for the iceberg,' shouted Drecki, pointing at a great blue-white monster that had grounded in the bay. It was a good idea – the iceberg lay between the cove and the ship, so would shield them from view for a while. They began bouncing across the waves towards it, spray flying into their faces. A wave caught them head on and the bows jerked into the air. Drecki moved forward in an effort to weight them down, although he was too light to make much difference.

Meanwhile, the other two craft had already travelled some distance. Tadek was still well in the lead and Berrister felt his hopes rise. Maybe they *would* reach Arctowski and raise the alarm, and he and his friends might be saved yet.

Then there was a vivid flash and a dull thump. *Galtieri* was firing at them, as she had done at *Jacek*. The gunmen's driver swerved away fast – wisely so, as the missile had landed closer to him than to Maria and Tadek. Clearly, someone on *Galtieri* was more interested in stopping the Poles than in the safety of his own men.

Berrister cut his speed when he was as near to the berg as he thought was safe – they were notoriously unstable, and anyone getting too close ran the risk of them collapsing or tipping over. As he sat on the pontoon, he silently cursed himself for not having grabbed one of the dead men's guns from the beach. Hopefully he wouldn't need it – *Galtieri* would head for the open sea once they thought no one was left at Villard Point – but it would have been comforting to have one.

Galtieri was still firing at Tadek. There was another thump, and a fountain of spray appeared off the inflatable's starboard side. The little craft zigzagged to avoid the seething water, then picked up speed again. The third shot also missed, but sent a huge column of water shooting up directly in front of it. The boat jerked and flipped, landing upside down and hurling its occupants out. The gunmen moved in on them like sharks.

Sarah prowled restlessly, pausing every so often to watch Joshi scraping at the bolts that sealed the porthole. Mortimer lay on his bed reading

Olga's Lovers, shaking his head from time to time in amused disbelief.

Earlier, she had hammered on the door, and had demanded – and was provided with – clean clothes. She now wore baggy twill trousers, thick sea socks and a sweatshirt with a leering Donald Duck. Her own clothes had been rinsed and were hanging up to dry. She had also eaten bread, four apples and a lump of the same kind of spicy sausage that Berrister had found in the dead man's pocket. It came with beer. She took a tiny sip, and concurred with Mortimer that there was definitely something amiss with its flavour. She also did not like the fact that the bottle was open.

She had been impressed to note that Joshi had started work on the screws that were hidden by the curtains. When their guards came, he simply let the material fall back into place, as if he had been innocently looking out of the window. He had managed to loosen some nuts, and it looked as though he might get the porthole open yet. When his efforts flagged, she took a turn, sawing and poking so vigorously that Mortimer had to raise the volume on the radio lest she was heard. Graham's spirits had improved since she had arrived, and when she stopped for a respite, he took her place.

'You do know it's a waste of time,' whispered Mortimer, so Graham and Joshi wouldn't hear. 'Jumping out into the sea would kill us for certain.'

She nodded. 'But I'll go crazy, just sitting here waiting for them to kill us. Besides, you never

168

know – maybe those tourists will sail past, and we can hang an SOS out the window.'

Mortimer raised sardonic eyebrows. 'I'll make one then, shall I?'

'Use one of the sheets,' said Sarah, taking him at his word. 'I've got a pen somewhere.'

At that moment, there was an almost imperceptible judder.

'We're off,' said Mortimer, cocking his head. 'That was the bow thrusters starting up.'

He elbowed Graham away from the window and looked out. The ship was turning, providing a panoramic view of Hannah Point as it went. Their camp, which should have shown up as a bright splash of green and yellow, was gone, and anything that might have been left was smothered under a blanket of snow.

He saw something dark in the water – the dead whale had been cut loose and was slowly beginning to sink. Gulls wheeled around it, fighting for scraps.

'Now where? King George?' asked Joshi hopefully.

'That's east,' said Mortimer, flatly. 'We're heading west.'

A few minutes later, the door opened and Hasim entered, Yablokov at his heels. Hasim regarded Sarah with interest, while Yablokov stared at Joshi. Mortimer was uneasy. Had the burly first mate guessed what was happening to his porthole?

'Charmed to meet you, Dr Henshaw,' said Hasim with an exaggerated bow. 'Welcome aboard *Lena*. Do you have everything you need?'

'No,' replied Sarah coldly. 'Because what we *need* is our freedom.'

'All in good time,' said Hasim. 'We'll be at King George soon, where you'll be released.'

'Do you know the way?' asked Mortimer. 'Because you're sailing in the wrong direction.'

'Ice,' replied Hasim blandly. 'We have to set a course to avoid it. Don't worry – the captain knows his business.'

If only that were true, thought Yablokov bitterly.

'So, who *are* you?' demanded Sarah. 'And what do you think you're doing down here, besides slaughtering endangered species and kidnapping scientists?'

Hasim perched on the edge of the table and ran a hand through his thick black hair. Now we shall see, thought Yablokov, watching him. If Hasim tells them the truth, they're dead for certain and the promise of safe passage to a research base was a cruel lie.

'My employers have chartered *Lena* for a few weeks,' Hasim replied. 'We're an organisation called the Southern Exploring Company.'

So the scientists were to die, surmised Yablokov. He glanced at Joshi. Holy Mother! The boy was only a child – not much older than his own son. How had he let himself become involved in such a filthy business? Yet again, he wished he'd had the sense to refuse Garik's invitation to make some quick and easy cash.

'A suitably ambiguous name,' Mortimer was saying. 'Explores for whale meat, does it?'

'We don't really explore very much at all,'

170

replied Hasim. 'We're more in the transport business.'

'And who buys the illegal whale meat you "transport"?' asked Sarah, eyeing first him and then Yablokov with such disdain that the first mate winced.

'The Far East, mostly,' replied Hasim, unperturbed by her hostility. 'Although, as I've said, whaling isn't our sole purpose. Now I've a proposition for you. I'd like to know about the krill at Hannah Point. In return for your cooperation, I'm prepared to be a little more . . . protective.'

'Protective?' echoed Sarah, suspiciously.

'About your lives. I want to put you ashore near one of the scientific bases, but not everyone thinks this is the right thing to do. I'm afraid the captain wants to kill you.'

Yablokov stifled a gasp of disbelief. Garik barely knew the scientists were on board, and would certainly not offer an opinion that was in the remotest way contrary to that of his adviser. Hasim shot him a quick warning glance before continuing.

'If you cooperate, I stand a good chance of persuading him to spare you. Of course, if you are obstructive, who can say what'll happen?'

'I see,' said Sarah. 'Well, you can go to hell.'

Hasim looked at the others. 'Does she speak for you all? Will you let her stupid obstinacy cost you your lives?'

No one spoke.

'Why do you want to know about krill?' asked Mortimer eventually.

Yablokov was keen to hear the answer to that, too.

'Let's just say that I'm interested,' replied Hasim. 'All I want to know is how many krill are in the area. The figure doesn't have to be precise – a guess will do. What was the figure this time last week?'

Mortimer regarded him coldly. 'The only man who could've told you that was Andrew Berrister. Unfortunately, you killed him – your louts chased him down a crevasse.'

'I know about krill,' said Graham, standing abruptly. 'I'll tell you.'

'No, he doesn't,' said Sarah quickly. 'He's a field hand, not a biologist.'

'I do,' insisted Graham. 'I always checked the nets with Andrew. I can tell you what you need to know.'

Sarah wanted to grab him by his treacherous throat, and prevent him from ever speaking again, but Hasim took Graham's arm and bundled him outside before she could move. Yablokov hesitated uncertainly for a moment, then followed. The door closed behind them. Mortimer looked stricken at the turn of events, while Joshi gaped his disbelief.

'Thank God you didn't tell him about Andrew and the Poles,' murmured Mortimer. 'I have a bad feeling Hasim would have had it out of him.'

'I'm sure of it,' said Sarah bitterly. 'Just as I'm sure that someone has been betraying us all along. You were wrong to claim it was none of you three.'

'I hardly think . . . I don't believe . . .' Mortimer trailed off unhappily.

'Of course, it doesn't make any difference

whether he knows about Andrew or not,' she went on softly. 'Not when Andrew is almost certainly dead, and the Poles are sailing back to their base in blissful ignorance.'

Galtieri's crew circled the upended boat for an age before someone was retrieved from the sea. Even from a distance, Berrister could see the person was either unconscious or dead – the latter, probably, given the amount of time that had passed. The gunmen searched for a while longer, then turned back towards their ship.

Berrister eased around the ice, careful to stay out of sight as the enemy craft buzzed past. In the bows, Drecki sat with his head in his hands, grieving for his lost friends. When the whalers had gone, Berrister cut the engine, uncertain what to do next. Tadek had had the benefit of a considerably faster boat, but he had still been blown out of the water, so trying to outrun *Galtieri* in *Jacek*'s little Zodiac with its puttering motor was clearly out of the question. Unfortunately, *Galtieri* was still at anchor and showed no indication that she was ready to leave. Thus Berrister and Drecki were trapped in the bay for as long as she stayed.

He squinted up at the sky. Two storm petrels soared and circled, performing an intricate ballet for each other. To his right, part of the iceberg had melted to form a small platform, and a crabeater seal had hauled out on it, dozing contentedly. The scene was one of such peace and beauty that he found it hard to believe that people had met terrible ends nearby.

The iceberg itself was magnificent. It was a cathedral-sized lump that had once been a tabular berg – one of the great, flat-topped slabs, some the size of countries, that regularly broke off the Antarctic ice sheet. It had been battered by sea and wind for decades, growing ever smaller as parts broke away or melted, and had finally turned upside down as its weight had shifted. Its top was now a series of jagged pinnacles that stretched down like the columns of a Greek temple, simultaneously beautiful and deadly. Arches and caves in blue, violet and indigo had been carved near the water line.

'They're coming back,' he said, hearing the distant roar of an engine. 'Now what?'

Drecki raised a tear-stained face. 'Start the motor,' he ordered. 'And hide inside the ice.'

Berrister blinked. 'You want me to drive into an *iceberg*?'

He didn't need to tell the Pole that icebergs were treacherously unstable, especially once they were grounded and thus in their death throes, or that even the vibrations from his engine might cause it to tip or collapse. Drecki would already know.

'Hurry, before they see us,' urged Drecki.

Numbly, Berrister yanked the starter cord, glad when the engine caught the first time, and chugged closer to the great blue-white mass until he felt its cold breath on his face.

'There!' hissed Drecki, pointing to a turquoise-blue fissure near the water line that disappeared into darkness. 'Go in there.'

The roar of the other boat was audible over

their own now, so Berrister did as he was told quickly. The temperature immediately fell by several degrees.

'Further,' urged Drecki. 'Try to get out of sight.'

The icy walls closed around them, and Berrister cut the engine, afraid of what the throbbing vibrations would do. In the resulting hush, he heard the splatter of trickling water as ice melted within, along with the greedy slurp of waves. He used an oar to propel them further along the tunnel, until Drecki raised his hand, telling him to stop. They waited and listened.

For a while, there was no sound except waves sucking and slathering, and the tinkle of dripping water. Then they heard the other boat.

'They're looking for us,' surmised Drecki. 'They must've noticed our boat gone and guessed what happened.'

Berrister wished he'd been thinking more clearly, because with hindsight, taking to the sea had been a stupid thing to do.

'We should have stayed ashore,' he whispered. 'I know caves where we could have hidden.'

'They'd have found us. They're not—'

Drecki stopped speaking when the chug of the other engine was suddenly much louder. He and Berrister exchanged a glance of disbelief: the driver had followed them in! Berrister grabbed an oar and poled them even deeper into the berg, hoping the man would come to his senses before he brought the whole thing down on them all.

'What's he doing?' he whispered, frantically struggling to gain purchase on the slick walls. 'Doesn't he know it's dangerous in here?'

'Perhaps it's more dangerous *not* to find us,' murmured Drecki soberly, leaning over the side to paddle with his hands. 'Go left.'

Again Berrister did as he was told, easing into a cave that was so narrow there was barely enough room to clear the sides. The larger boat would be unable to follow. It was darker there, full of blue shadows. The roar of the other engine sounded horribly loud, and Berrister flinched when a large hunk of ice dropped from the roof and fell into the water behind them.

'Here they come!' hissed Drecki.

Holding his breath and expecting to be discovered at any moment, Berrister watched the gunmen pass the entrance to their tunnel. Incredibly, none of them looked left. Berrister and Drecki sagged in relief and exchanged a quick grin.

But they had celebrated too soon. The main cave had come to a dead end, so the driver began to reverse out. And this time, one of the men did glance in their direction. He gave a triumphant yell.

Even before Yablokov had closed the door of the scientists' cabin, Hasim had whisked Graham further down the corridor and was plying him with a barrage of questions. The Scot answered unsteadily, his voice low and secretive. Yablokov strained to hear, but both spoke softly, and Graham's thick Scots accent was difficult for a man whose English was no better than adequate.

'Return him to his friends, will you?' Hasim

said when he had finished. 'And inform them that his common sense has saved their lives.'

'So it's you, is it? said Yablokov to Graham in distaste, when Hasim had gone. 'I thought it was the fat man, but you're the one who's been helping us.'

'I don't know what you're talking about,' said Graham shortly.

He pushed past Yablokov, opened the door and shut it firmly behind him, leaving the first mate standing in the hallway. Yablokov watched the guards lock the door, and went to look for Hasim. He found him in the communications room. Hasim scowled when he walked in.

'I need to contact *Galtieri*,' Hasim said irritably. 'In private. Close the door on your way out, will you?'

'*Galtieri*?' asked Yablokov with a frown of his own, not moving. 'Why? She's miles away – nowhere near the Antarctic.'

Galtieri was a retired Argentine warship, and Yablokov had voiced reservations about an association with her when they had met 'by chance' off the coast near Buenos Aires. What they were doing was risky enough, and they certainly didn't need to compound the danger by consorting with a vessel like that. Hasim had assured him that she was no different from *Lena*, but Yablokov had known then that it was a lie. Perhaps *Galtieri*'s holds *had* been adapted to take special cargoes, but enough of her superstructure had been left to let her revert to her original purpose without too much trouble. Moreover, her crew weren't fishermen, but mercenaries like the ones that Hasim had brought aboard *Lena*. He saw he had been a fool to accept Hasim's smooth assurances that *Galtieri* would stay further north, well away from the area where *Lena* would be working.

'She had to come,' said Hasim. 'To solve a problem involving some Poles.'

'What kind of problem?' Yablokov felt sick. The situation was getting way out of hand.

'Don't worry – it has already been dealt with.' Hasim grimaced. 'For an uninhabited wilderness, this place is positively seething with people. It was supposed to be empty.'

'And *Galtieri* was *supposed* to stay up north,' said Yablokov accusingly. 'She has no business being down here.'

'Nor does *Lena*,' Hasim pointed out with impeccable, if annoying, logic. 'Now please excuse me. I'm busy.'

He propelled Yablokov through the door before slamming it in his face. Yablokov was aware of the Norwegians smirking at the insult, although Zurin kept his eyes fixed on the course he was steering. Yablokov clenched his fists. If it were not for his family, the money he would earn and the fact that Hasim had armed men at his command, he might consider quietly dispatching the man and taking *Lena* home, where she belonged.

Inside the iceberg, Berrister regarded the other boat with weary resignation. It was too bad, after all he'd been through, but at least he could die in the knowledge that he had done his utmost to escape and save his friends.

178

He watched the four men engage in a low-voiced, agitated discussion. He knew what their dilemma was: if they opened fire inside the cave, the chances were that the inevitable collapse would kill them as well as their victims. But it was not long before there were nods, as a consensus was reached. The driver began to turn his boat.

When he was facing the exit, he gave a mocking wave and drove out. Berrister and Drecki exchanged a glance of incomprehension as he disappeared from sight. But their bewilderment did not last long. There was a tremendous rattle of gunfire, and they saw ice flying off the cave roof.

'Clever,' murmured Drecki in the brief silence that followed. 'To leave before they collapse the ice on us.'

There was a moment when Berrister thought the ploy had failed, but then a huge lump of ceiling dropped so close to his stern that water slopped over it. There was a crack, and he saw a larger piece set to follow – one that would land right on top of them.

'Drive!' screamed Drecki, grabbing the oar and trying to propel them forward.

Berrister yanked the engine into life. He glanced back as they chugged away, and saw the ice plummet down, blocking the way they had come. There was no other direction to go but forward now. With the roof crumbling all around them, they began to speed down the narrow tunnel, walls flashing past them. Then it opened into a sizeable cavern, and Berrister saw daylight ahead. He hurtled towards it, flinching as an enormous icicle crashed into the boat, narrowly missing his leg.

Above them, a crack of sky had appeared, while the inside of the cavern was filled with a mass of ice flakes, like dust. The iceberg had split, and the two parts were slowly falling in opposite directions. Berrister twisted the throttle as far as it would go, desperately trying to coax just a little more speed out of the labouring engine.

Suddenly, there was a loud boom that momentarily drowned out the creaking and groaning of the splitting berg. It was the third time that day that *Galtieri* had launched missiles.

'They're firing at it, to make sure it collapses,' shouted Drecki – unnecessarily because Berrister understood exactly what was going on. 'They're crazy! Their own men will still be too close.'

Berrister had already seen that the commander of *Galtieri* did not care about his minions. There was another boom, and more ice fell. A piece struck Berrister's shoulder, and with horror, he saw that while the crack above them was growing wider, the arch of daylight ahead was shrinking – and they wouldn't survive if they were inside the berg when it came apart. He swerved to avoid a huge chunk that crashed down in front of him, almost flinging Drecki out.

The opening was getting smaller with every passing second, and the motor had no more power to give. Berrister urged it on, his eyes fixed ahead. Another boom tore at his ears, and the engine coughed as ice fouled the propeller.

'Duck!' he yelled, throwing himself down as

180

they reached the now-tiny arch at a speed that was far from safe.

The propeller hit ice, killing the engine, but they were going fast enough that they kept flying forward anyway. He was aware of the top of the opening skimming past his head. If they stopped now, they would drown, pressed under the water by the roof above. But then, incredibly, they spurted out of the gap and plopped into the frothing water beyond.

'We'll capsize!' screeched Drecki. 'Get us away!'

'The propeller's gone,' Berrister shouted back. 'Row!'

Drecki grabbed an oar and began to paddle, kayak fashion, from the bow. Berrister did the same from the stern, struggling to keep his balance as the boat pitched and tipped. Then the two halves of the berg finally broke apart with a great creaking hiss, bobbing and rolling until only their very tips protruded above the surface. Moments later came the waves – huge ones, caused by the displaced water.

'Hold on!' yelled Berrister, and grabbed a safety rope.

The first wave tossed their boat high into the air, then hurled it forward. The second spun them around and deluged them with icy water. Berrister felt his grip begin to slip as the little craft lurched one way and then the other. Water slopped everywhere, dashing into his face and drenching his clothes.

Just when he thought he could hold on no longer, the buffeting eased. He blinked water from his eyes. Where there had been one mammoth iceberg, there were now two, along with a great mat of smaller pieces that heaved up and down, hissing and chinking together.

'Look,' whispered Drecki, pointing. 'The other boat.'

He had been right to predict that it would not have enough time to reach safety. It undulated among the mass of bergy bits, but was empty, its occupants washed overboard.

'We can't see the ship, which means it can't see us.' Drecki pointed. 'If we can reach that beach undetected – by keeping the ice between them and us – we might escape yet.'

'How?' asked Berrister wearily. 'We don't have a propeller – and they'll certainly see us if we row, because it'll take too long.'

'Then we'll use *their* boat,' determined Drecki, beginning to paddle towards it with the oar he had somehow managed to keep hold of. Berrister's had been lost when the first wave had hit.

It did not take long to reach it, and they had soon clambered aboard, taking with them Tadek's spare fuel and a bag of emergency supplies. Careful to stay out of sight, they aimed for the little cove Drecki had chosen. It was impossible to move at speed through the litter of ice, but that was no bad thing – it would just make them more difficult to detect on radar. When they arrived, Berrister drove behind a rock and cut the engine.

'We made it,' crowed Drecki, although Berrister was too cold, numb and exhausted to feel any exhilaration. 'We fooled them. Now we have a better Zodiac and two spare tanks of fuel.'

He unscrewed the caps to see how much they had, while Berrister watched indifferently, his mind dull from shock and tiredness.

'Pity,' sighed the Pole. 'One tank is empty, one has just a dribble, and only the spare from *Jacek* is full. These men are stupid, driving around with virtually no fuel.'

The enemy had been stupid in several ways, telling Berrister that they were unfamiliar with the Antarctic or they would not have been so recklessly complacent. He wanted to say so, but the effort of speaking was simply too great. Drecki took a flask from his backpack.

'Drink some tea. It'll do you good.'

It did. It was black, strong, hot and sweet, and Berrister wished there was more. They exchanged some of their wet clothes for dry ones from Drecki's pack, after which he gave Berrister two soggy meat sandwiches and a hard-boiled egg. Berrister wolfed them down, and gradually his trembling exhaustion began to recede.

'So,' said Drecki, when he had finished. 'Do you know what's going on?'

Berrister told his story haltingly, including the details he had left off before, and his theories about the deadly ships and what he thought they were doing. Then Drecki explained why he had persuaded the captain of *Jacek* to land him illegally in a Specially Protected Area.

'Although my *Coniopteris* wasn't worth this,' he whispered wretchedly. 'Maria, Tadek, Captain Anders . . . so many good people.'

183

'Your base will be worried about you,' said Berrister, not sure he would describe Maria or Tadek as good, given that one had wanted to shoot him, while the other had driven off to save his own skin, leaving Drecki to fend for himself. 'They'll send someone to look, so all we have to do is sit tight until they arrive. I can't see *Galtieri* hanging around here after what happened. These men can't keep killing *everyone* they meet – they'll have to stop at some point.'

Drecki winced. '*Jacek* will be missed, but Arctowski won't look for her here. They think we're at Greenwich Island – which is where I told them we'd be.'

Berrister silently cursed the geologist's maverick antics, but remonstrating with him would do no good, so he decided to change the subject by asking what had happened by the hut.

'Why didn't they shoot you straight away when they caught you?' he asked. 'What were they waiting for?'

'I think they hoped to make our deaths look like accidents – to take us out to sea and sabotage the inflatable so that we'd drown. The same is true of *Jacek* – if wreckage is found now, everyone will assume there was an explosion in the engine room. It'll never cross anyone's mind that she was blown up deliberately.'

Once again, the whalers had proven themselves to be ruthlessly thorough in covering their tracks.

'Maybe the crew sent a message before *Jacek* went down,' suggested Berrister hopefully.

'They didn't,' said Drecki sombrely. 'I'd have

184

heard it on my handset. Whatever we decide to do, we're on our own.'

'How *could* you?' demanded Sarah accusingly when Graham re-joined them in the cabin. The Scot's face was flushed and his eyes were bright with defiance. 'You heard what he said – the captain wants to kill us, and he's the one running the ship. Hasim was lying – they have no intention of letting us go.'

'Maybe,' said Graham, and leaned towards her. 'But—'

'Get away from me!'

She snapped on the radio and grabbed a fork, intending to vent her rage on the porthole. Mortimer closed his eyes, while Joshi looked stricken at the bald declaration that their fate was sealed. Undeterred, Graham went to stand next to her again.

'Don't you understand?' he whispered. 'It was our chance!'

She glared at him. 'Our chance to what? Help those bastards in return for being murdered?'

Graham moved even nearer, to avoid being overheard. Sarah elbowed him back in distaste. Stoically ignoring her anger, he edged closer again.

'To escape.' Graham smiled at her immediate suspicion. 'I think I've just managed to alert Rothera – to send them a message that we're in trouble and need help.'

Nine

Berrister stared out across the ice-littered bay, trying to decide what to do. The nearest occupied base was too far to reach with the available fuel, and waiting for rescue was obviously out of the question – Drecki's people would be looking in the wrong place and his own still thought all was well, or there would have been a plane. He remembered *Worsley*, due to arrive in six days. Clearly, he had to warn her, lest she meet the same fate as *Jacek*.

'I have to help my friends at Hannah Point,' he said eventually. 'Assuming they're still alive, of course.'

'How?'

It was a perfectly reasonable question, but not one Berrister could answer. Any ideas he had were dependent on being able to contact a base – or having access to more fuel.

'Freddy,' he said eventually, when no amount of brain-racking brought a solution – or at least none that was sensible. 'Maria claimed she heard him talking to Rothera the day after he died. Why did she lie?'

'She didn't,' said Drecki. 'Because I heard him, too. However, all Australians sound alike to us, so I imagine he'd be easy for a native English speaker to imitate.'

He was, and Berrister had done it himself

several times to make the others laugh. It would have been easy for the whalers to listen to Freddy's brief daily broadcasts, then take over once he was murdered. Berrister had insisted that Freddy be concise, so Rothera would expect nothing more than a terse message saying that everything was fine.

Of course, there was another possibility: that the mimic was Graham or Wells, as Sarah believed. But that was an unpleasant thought, and one he was disinclined to share with anyone else.

'It couldn't be done for long,' he said. 'We know the guys at Rothera, and they know us.'

Drecki shrugged. 'Perhaps the mimic claimed there is something wrong with the radio, limiting him to short transmissions.'

'That wouldn't satisfy Noddy Taylor – I've been sending him regular reports on krill, and when he doesn't get one, he'll be clamouring to know why.'

'He can clamour all he likes – it won't mend a malfunctioning radio.' Drecki sighed. 'We're in a fix here – the two of us against warships and an undetermined number of armed killers. It doesn't look good.'

To Berrister it looked hopeless. 'I can't think,' he said wretchedly. 'I know I need to do something, but I can't think . . .'

'Then sleep for an hour,' suggested Drecki. 'We can't go anywhere, so why not? I'll keep guard, and who knows? Perhaps something will occur to you when you wake refreshed.'

Sleeping would take time away from helping

the others, but Berrister's weariness was crippling, so he curled up in the bottom of the boat, thinking a few minutes' rest would do no harm.

Some hours later, he jolted awake with a start. He had never been so stiff and cold in his life, and every joint ached from his trek across the glacier. He looked for Drecki. The Pole was atop the rocky bluff that hid them, watching *Galtieri*. He turned when he heard Berrister climbing towards him.

'I'm afraid we have a problem.'

Berrister lay beside him and looked into the bay. What he saw filled him with horror. Two dead minke whales floated there, tethered by ropes to *Galtieri*'s side. Men swarmed over them. But that was not the worst of it: two more ships had anchored nearby.

'I don't follow,' said Sarah, eyeing Graham coldly. '*How* have you warned Rothera by cooperating with these bastards? And you're in my way. Stand back, or you might find yourself stabbed with a fork.'

'I understand,' said Mortimer, hope surging. 'I see exactly what he's done.'

Sarah scowled angrily. 'Then explain.'

Mortimer smiled. 'If Rothera thought we were in trouble, they'd send help, right? There'd be ships, planes and all sorts coming. Even the tourists you heard over on Deception would have made a detour.'

'Right,' said Joshi. 'So?'

'So either Rothera suddenly got careless *or* they're still receiving messages from "us" – or

188

rather, someone pretending to be from our camp.'

'I'm not sure that would work,' said Joshi. 'Vince has been the communications officer all season – he'd recognise a different voice.'

'Not necessarily,' said Graham. 'He doesn't know me, you or Lisa, because we tend not to make the nightly broadcasts. But that's not to say that we never would. It'd be easy to fool him.'

Sarah continued to frown. 'Even so, I still don't see how you telling Hasim about krill has warned Rothera.'

'Think,' said Mortimer. 'Andrew sends reports to Noddy Taylor every three days—'

'And *that's* why Hasim wants to know about krill,' finished Graham triumphantly. 'It's something he *can't* invent without raising eyebrows, so to prolong the pretence, it's got to be done properly – well enough to satisfy Noddy.'

'And?' asked Sarah.

'And I gave Hasim figures that are six times higher than they should be,' said Graham with pride. 'Noddy will know they're wrong, and he'll demand an explanation. When he does, I'll give him more duff data. He'll want to talk to Andrew, and when that doesn't happen . . .'

'He'll *know* something's wrong and will raise the alarm,' finished Mortimer.

Sarah stared at Graham. He seemed sincere, but she had never been more uncertain of anything in her life. Had he really put a clever plan in motion, or simply used the opportunity to share more of their secrets – such as their attempt to prise open the porthole? She gave a stiff smile and nodded at him, deciding to reserve judgement. Of course, even if Graham was genuinely trying to help, it would do no good. Even Rothera would be powerless against men with guns.

Mortimer clapped Graham on the shoulder. He was hopeful, even if Sarah remained wary.

'We'll have to keep up a pretence of hostility towards you,' he said, 'or Hasim will get suspicious. From now on, you stay at one end of the room, and we'll take the other. And no helping Joshi at the porthole, in case they burst in and see you together.'

Graham retreated immediately. The other three looked out of the window, watching Hannah Point disappear as *Lena* picked up speed. After a while, Joshi and Sarah continued working on the porthole, while Mortimer lost himself in *Olga's Lovers* again, grateful for once that he was a slow reader.

It was not long before the ship began to lurch with sickening irregularity – they were heading out to sea. Lulled by the motion, they fell asleep. They woke when a meal was brought: the obligatory stew, fruit, chocolate, bread and beer, which was treated like all the rest. The gap between the wall and the floor was beginning to stink, and Mortimer hoped what they were doing wouldn't become too obvious. Afterwards, he went back to sleep. Sarah and Joshi returned to their scratching, and Graham leafed through old issues of *National Geographic*.

Suddenly, the ship began to move much faster, waking Mortimer, who looked around in confusion. Everything shook and rattled, and then *Lena* heeled sharply to starboard.

'We're turning,' said Mortimer, staggering from the bed to the window. 'Although most ships don't do it at this speed without good reason.'

'They have one,' said Sarah grimly. 'Whales.'

'They're blues,' cried Joshi.

'Hasim said he'd attached a tracking device to one,' said Mortimer. 'Look! There goes the harpoon.'

They crowded around the window to watch the missile with its cable and exploding head snake across the water. When it missed, they cheered. Minutes later, a second was fired.

'Dive!' screamed Joshi, as though the whale could hear. '*Dive!*'

They cheered again when the harpoon went wide. The great whale dipped under the surface and was gone.

'But it'll come up again,' said Sarah bitterly, 'and then they'll get it.'

'Maybe not,' countered Joshi hopefully. 'They keep missing.'

At that moment, another whale blew close to their window, sending a spume of spray high into the air. There was a sharp bang as the harpoon gun sounded again. The animal was so close that it was impossible to miss, and there was an explosion that splattered red. The whale jerked and showed its back as it dived. It took too long, and a second head exploded in it before it could disappear.

'Go deep,' urged Mortimer. 'Break the lines.'

They could see the rope being played out as the animal swam away, and fancied they could hear winches screaming. Then there was silence. The engines had stopped, and *Lena* rocked gently from side to side. No one spoke, and the only other sound was water slapping against the sides of the ship.

'Maybe they lost it,' whispered Joshi. 'Maybe it escaped.'

Sarah shook her head. 'It's gone deep. Frightened, probably.'

'And injured,' added Mortimer. 'Exploding grenades are supposed to kill more humanely – meaning in minutes, rather than hours. Of course, that's if you have an experienced gunner. I'm not sure this tosser knows what he's doing.'

It was almost half an hour before the whale blew again. There were shouts from the deck and the thud of running footsteps. The engines started up and winches took up the slack on the lines. Another crack signalled the firing of the harpoon. There was a fountain of red, and the whale rolled before diving again. This time it surfaced after a few minutes, and there was blood in its blow.

'This is awful,' said Joshi shakily. 'The *bastards*!'

'Why do they need another one anyway?' asked Mortimer, unable to watch any more and turning away. 'They didn't finish chopping up the first. It's completely unnecessary. Graham – get away from the window. You're supposed to be in disgrace, remember?'

Sarah went to sit next to Mortimer on the bed, although Joshi continued to gaze out of the porthole, wiping the glass with his sleeve when his breath fogged it. Graham retreated to a chair near the door.

192

'Hasim keeps talking about "other business" that's more important than whaling,' said Mortimer in a low voice. 'What can it be, do you think?'

'God knows,' muttered Sarah. 'Minerals? The Antarctic's supposed to be rich in them.'

'Yes, but no one knows for sure. Besides, they're all under the ice sheet, and thus out of reach.'

'Transport,' mused Sarah. 'Hasim said transport. Maybe he means those barrels they're dumping. But what could be in them to merit such a long and dangerous journey? If they just want rid of them, what's wrong with dropping them in the middle of the Atlantic?'

'We shouldn't put too much store in what Hasim says. Remember how much whale meat costs? That would be incentive enough.'

Outside, the whale surfaced again, spurting blood. There was a rattle as the winches tightened the cables, and then nothing but the hollow rasp of the whale struggling to breathe.

On deck, Yablokov wrested the harpoon gun away from Garik before he hurt himself with it. He had suspected that the quick kill in South Bay had been more luck than skill, and was appalled by the length of time it had taken to secure the second animal. Garik was jubilant, though, and strutted around seeking the adulation of his crew.

'This'll put a few coins in our pockets,' he crowed. 'We'll be rich!'

Hasim agreed gleefully, and leaned over the side to watch the dying whale thrash. He started backwards when a flick of its tail sent a deluge of water over him, and Yablokov was sure he was not the only one who wished it had washed him overboard.

'I thought exploding heads were supposed to kill quickly,' muttered Nikos. He was no longer under arrest – *Lena* could not manage long without a chief engineer.

'Only if the harpooner knows what he's doing,' replied Yablokov. 'And if he's sober.'

He went to dismantle the gun, hoping they would not have to use it again. The kill had appalled him, not because of the animal's suffering – he was a fisherman, after all, and so used to seeing creatures flailing around trying to breathe – but because the frantic battle had put the crew at risk. A Swede had been badly burned by a hot winch, and an Estonian had almost been dragged overboard when his foot caught in poorly coiled rope.

'You'd better go aft,' said Nikos. 'Hasim's trying to direct the tethering operation himself.'

It was true, and as Hasim had no idea how it was done, the result was chaos. Even the usually deadpan Zurin was exasperated. Yablokov hurried to take over, struggling to undo the harm Hasim had done with crossed and tangled lines. He had the situation under control eventually, but then realised that Garik had neglected to drop anchor, so they had drifted dangerously close to the shore.

'Mr Hasim told us not to bother,' explained one of the Norwegians when Yablokov demanded to know why one of them hadn't used his common sense. 'In case we need to leave in a hurry.'

'And what did the captain say?' asked Yablokov, sure that even Garik would have pointed out the folly of that asinine instruction.

'He's . . . not here,' replied the officer, which Yablokov interpreted to mean that Garik was probably insensible in his quarters.

'And Hasim?'

'He went to lie down for a while as well. I don't think he appreciated you showing him up when he was trying to help.'

The officer's expression was bland, but Yablokov knew the remark was a direct challenge to his authority. He barked some orders that would keep the man busy for the rest of his watch, then saw *Lena* safely anchored. When he had finished, he went to find Garik, steaming with anger. It was unconscionable to have left the ship in the hands of such inept officers – another ten minutes would have seen them run aground.

Garik had not managed to reach his cabin before passing out, and was sprawled on the stairs halfway down. For a moment, Yablokov thought he might be dead, but a tentative poke resulted in blearily opened eyes.

'Things aren't good, Evgeny,' Garik whispered hoarsely.

'No,' agreed Yablokov sourly. 'They were better when we were in the Arctic.'

'The cargo?' asked Garik, as Yablokov hauled him to his feet. 'Is it offloaded yet?'

'The forward hold is clear, but the afterdeck hold is still full – as I told you when you asked two hours ago.'

'You need to be careful with it, Eysha.'

'I know.' Yablokov struggled to keep Garik upright while he opened the cabin door.

'You've no idea what it is, have you?' said Garik with a laugh that ended in a hiccup.

'Phosphorus,' replied Yablokov shortly. 'Hasim told me. A by-product of strong fertilisers, which can't be dumped anywhere else, because it reacts with warm water – causes algal blooms or something. The Southern Ocean is the only place cold enough to render it inert.'

Garik sniggered and flung a heavy arm around Yablokov's shoulders. 'It's not phosphorus! Do you think the Southern Exploring Company would pay all this money to bring phosphorus down here? Idiot!'

'Need a hand?' It was Nikos who asked, on his way to the engine room. He looked amused at the sight of the captain embracing his first mate so fondly.

'Yes, please,' said Yablokov coolly, seeing nothing to grin about.

'Phosphorus,' murmured Garik as they manoeuvred him towards his bed. 'Glows in the dark.'

So would his few remaining brain cells if he kept up that level of drinking, thought Yablokov acidly, letting him fall face down on the bed and half hoping he would suffocate himself.

'Did I hear him say that the cargo isn't phosphorus?' asked Nikos, as they left him snoring wetly into his pillow. 'Because if he did, he should've mentioned it sooner – it might have made a difference to how we stored it.'

'Well, it doesn't matter now,' said Yablokov. 'It'll all be gone soon.'

'Incidentally, Hasim was on the radio to *Galtieri* again while you were on deck. I eavesdropped, and learned why he's so interested in krill.'

'Yes?' asked Yablokov curtly. He needed to get back to the flensing before there was another accident. The riddles of the Southern Exploring Company could wait.

'So the information can be relayed to Rothera. Apparently, one of the scientists has been measuring the things, and Rothera is demanding to know why the reports have dried up. Hasim doesn't want their planes or ships coming to nose around.'

Yablokov regarded Nikos in horror, flensing forgotten. 'Rothera? You mean there are yet more of these scientists? I thought they were down here alone.'

'No one's alone down here these days, Evgeny – they all contact each other regularly. If ours miss a certain number of scheduled transmissions, someone will come to check on them. Fortunately for us, *Galtieri* has been communicating on their behalf. I know you don't like *Galtieri*, but her intervention has certainly saved our bacon.'

'Rothera can't tell the difference between their own scientists and someone from *Galtieri*?' asked Yablokov incredulously. 'That sounds unlikely.'

'It's worked so far, the only problem being the krill – hence Hasim's peculiar interest.'

'Then why could he not just tell us so? Why all the secrecy?'

Nikos shrugged. 'Knowledge is power. Wasn't that the motto of your KGB?'

'Hardly! But Hasim's supposed to be on the

same side as us. How can we work together if we can't trust each other?'

'Presumably because what you don't know can't hurt Hasim, should the unthinkable happen and we get caught. However, if we are, I'm not taking the blame for the murders. I'm going to make it clear that *he's* the one who put elemental mercury in their beer.'

Yablokov lowered his voice. 'They don't drink the beer – they pour it down the sink. I know because that particular basin leaks, and half of it's dripping down my cabin wall.'

'Then Hasim hasn't realised it yet, or he'd put it in something else.'

Yablokov hesitated, but then plunged on. 'I'm going to help them escape.'

Nikos raised his eyebrows. 'In exchange for what? Clemency when we're all arrested for hunting endangered species and killing four scientists?'

'Why not? Besides, it's not *four* scientists – it's more. *Galtieri* killed some Poles on the other side of the island. It's all getting out of hand, Nikos, and I've had enough.'

'Me too, but there's nothing we can do about it now. My advice is to keep your head down and your mouth closed, and maybe we'll get out of this alive.'

'The prisoners won't.'

'No,' agreed Nikos. 'They won't.'

'Just a little further, then we'll use the engine,' said Drecki, kneeling in the bow and glancing at Berrister behind him. 'Are you alright?'

Berrister nodded; he had no breath for talking. He hauled as hard as he could on the oars, hoping that Drecki's 'a little further' was not too different from his own.

'Stop!' hissed Drecki suddenly. 'Don't move.'

Berrister froze obediently, sufficiently exhausted to be grateful for the respite. It was the fourth time the Pole had done it. The first had been because he had spotted a leopard seal – large, aggressive animals known to attack and puncture Zodiacs. The second and third were because he thought he could hear engines, although it had only been his imagination.

They had watched the three ships for some time before finally agreeing on a plan. Unfortunately, hiking away to hide in the interior of the island was not an option, because *Galtieri* had put a number of people ashore, so their only real choice was to try to escape by sea. It was Drecki who had devised a way to do it. His idea was simple, but had worked so far – to hide behind a screen of ice and row to freedom. Rowing was a good idea for two reasons: it eliminated engine noise, and it meant they would not move quickly enough to be spotted on radar. The downside was that it entailed tying their boat to a lump of ice large enough to conceal them. It was heavy, and it was fortunate that the tide was with them, or the task would have been all but impossible.

'What's wrong?' whispered Berrister as time ticked past and the Pole made no signal for him to resume rowing.

'I saw that leopard seal again,' replied Drecki.

199

'Dangerous things, leopard seals. But I think it's gone now. Alright – off you go.'

Berrister began to haul on the oars once more, trying to distract himself from the burning exhaustion in his arms and back by thinking about what he would do when they reached Hannah Point. Drecki had agreed to go there with him, to find Sarah in the ice shelter, but neither had any idea what they would do if they arrived to find *Lena* still there. Berrister wasn't sure of the time, but the light was beginning to fade, and it would be dark by the time they got there, which was one thing in their favour.

'They're lowering a Zodiac,' whispered Drecki urgently. 'They must've seen us.'

Berrister stopped in alarm. 'Then we should cut loose and make a dash to the headland while we have a good lead.'

At that point, they realised that neither of them had a knife.

'Matches!' gulped Berrister. 'We'll burn the rope through.'

While Drecki continued to struggle ineffectively with the knots, Berrister frantically rifled through his pockets, hunting for the box he had taken from the bodies. Or had he left them with Sarah back at the ice shelter?

'Oh, it's alright,' said Drecki. 'They're not coming this way – they're just using the inflatable to manoeuvre the whales for flensing.'

Berrister felt sick with relief. He raised a shaking hand to his head, wondering how much more he could stand before he finally snapped from the tension.

'You can start rowing again,' said Drecki cheerily. 'We'll make it easily now all their attention is on the whales.'

Berrister did as he was told, and there followed a long, hard pull until they eased around a rocky bluff and *Galtieri* and her consorts were lost from sight.

Drecki clapped his hands in childlike delight. 'We did it. We're home and dry!'

They were nowhere near anything that could remotely be described as home, and Berrister was certainly not dry. He flopped backward, breathing hard, and felt the little boat vibrate as Drecki started the engine. The sea was fairly calm near the coast, but once in more open waters, it was rough. He climbed into the bow, hoping his weight would hold it down and give them an easier ride, but it made little difference. He was forced to cling on for dear life to avoid being pitched overboard, and it was not long before he grew even more tired. He gestured to Drecki to slow down.

'I thought you wanted to reach your friend as soon as possible.'

'I do, but I want to be in a condition to help her when we get there. I couldn't make her a cup of tea at the moment.'

Drecki reduced speed, and the Zodiac stopped bouncing like a wild animal. Instead, it rolled up and down in a way that made Berrister feel queasy. He was not sure which was worse.

They were soon around the end of the Byers Peninsula, passing Rugged Island with its great jagged cliffs. They turned south, to the area of treacherous rocks and stacks called Devil's Point. And then they hit more trouble. Drecki killed the engine abruptly.

'Two more ships,' he breathed, appalled. 'How many of these damned things are there?'

Once the dead whale had been secured, the grisly business of gathering meat began. The prisoners' dinner was late, because the crew was busy, and when it arrived, the sight of grey meat and overcooked potatoes made Sarah feel sick.

'I hope this isn't whale,' said Joshi, eyeing it in distaste.

'As a biologist,' said Mortimer drily, 'you should be able to tell the difference between a whale and a pig, even when dead and served on a plate.'

'There's another ship!' whispered Graham from the window suddenly. 'It's coming this way.'

'Where?' demanded Sarah, leaping to her feet and elbowing him away so she could see for herself. 'Perhaps the krill—'

She only just stopped herself from blurting out that the krill plan might have worked. She closed her eyes, disgusted with herself for almost betraying them to the people she was sure were monitoring their every word. Mortimer switched on the radio.

'I can't see it very well,' Graham said, wiping the window with his sleeve.

'It could be *Worsley*,' said Joshi, and looked at Mortimer with such an expression of hope that the glaciologist was unable to meet his eyes.

'Possibly,' he said briskly. 'Let's just wait and see what happens.'

'I hope these whalers don't . . .' began Joshi uncertainly. '*Worsley* isn't very big . . .'

'If *Lena* was going to attack her, she'd have done it by now,' said Sarah. 'Besides, eliminating a whole ship is a lot more difficult than getting rid of eight people and a few tents.'

'They could sink it,' said Joshi fearfully.

'With what?' asked Graham sneeringly. 'A harpoon?'

'Enough,' said Sarah sharply. 'Here's a ship and we're in need of rescue. How can we turn the situation to our advantage?'

'By hanging a sheet saying "HELP" out of the porthole,' replied Joshi promptly.

'How do we do that?' asked Sarah. 'We haven't got it open yet.'

'Then how about a flashing light?' suggested Joshi. 'We could signal SOS in code.'

'Another good idea,' said Sarah. 'But we don't have a torch.'

'I do,' said Joshi, 'on my mobile.'

'Wait,' cautioned Mortimer. '*Lena*'s made no effort to hide her whale, which I suspect she would have done if the new ship was indeed *Worsley*. Unfortunately, I bet that it's a sister ship, here for the same nasty purposes.'

'Perhaps,' said Sarah. 'But it's a chance we'll have to take. Besides, *Worsley* will be along sooner or later, and when she is, we want to be ready. From now on, we signal SOS constantly. We'll take it in turns.'

'The batteries will run out,' said Graham.

Sarah gestured to the overhead lights. 'Then we'll switch those on and off instead. Well? What are you waiting for?'

As Drecki hastily eased their boat behind a rock, Berrister looked at the scene ahead in horror. One of the two ships had already caught a blue whale and roped it to her side, while the remainder of the pod circled in confusion. The whale was still alive, because he could see a faint pink plume emerging from its blowhole every so often. And the ship was *Lena*.

The second vessel looked very similar, and he supposed it was another old bucket from the northern fishing fleet. As he watched, there was a flurry of activity in the bow, followed by a bang that echoed across the water. He held his breath, willing the missile to go wide, but blood splattered as it exploded in the whale's body, near the tail.

'Bastards!' he snarled, jumping to his feet. 'They've hit a calf! We've got to stop them or they'll slaughter the whole pod.'

'How?' asked Drecki quietly. 'They've got guns and torpedoes.'

'Get between them and the whales. Or drive the whales away – ram them, maybe.'

'When Greenpeace did it, they had the world's press looking on,' said Drecki in the same calmly reasonable voice. 'Here, there's nothing to stop those pirates from harpooning you. There's no way they'll let us get between them and their fortune, and if we try, we're going to get ourselves killed. And how will that help anyone?'

Berrister wanted to argue, but he knew the Pole was right. He felt despair wash over him. He had spent his whole adult life working to conserve marine mammals, and to watch precious blue whales slaughtered before his eyes was very hard to bear. Worse, the hunt meant that Mortimer, Graham and Joshi were almost certainly dead, because he was sure they wouldn't be permitted to witness such a spectacle.

He stared at *Lena*, wishing her to the bottom of the sea. Something winked from one of the windows, probably a malfunctioning light – which was no surprise from such a tub. He looked at the injured calf. She lay on her side, flipper waving pathetically, while the other whales rallied around her. She tried to dive, but surfaced within seconds, spouting blood through her blowhole.

Berrister turned away. Over the hiss and gurgle of water around the Zodiac, he could hear the distant shouts of men and the shallow puffing of the calf as she died. There was another deep, echoing thud as the next grenade was fired. Berrister only hoped it had put the hapless animal out of her misery.

Drecki was watching through his field glasses. 'There's a tracking device on the bigger animal – I can see it glinting in the light from the decks.'

'They probably attached it when they made their first kill,' said Berrister dully. 'So they'd know where to find the rest of the pod when they were ready. Evil sods!'

He and Drecki sat side by side with their backs to the grisly scene. Drecki produced a packet of crushed crackers and divided them in half – the last of their supplies. Berrister might have enjoyed them more if he had not been so thirsty.

'Do you think blue whales will survive as a species?' asked Drecki eventually, more to take his mind off their predicament than for information.

Berrister shook his head. 'It's too late: the ecological balance has already shifted, and the niche once occupied by them is now the domain of penguins and seals. Unfortunately, I suspect the blues are doomed.'

Drecki raised his eyebrows. 'Even though they're protected?'

'And we can see how helpful that is,' said Berrister in disgust. 'Besides, it's not enough just to stop killing them – we need to protect the areas where they feed and breed as well. There's no point in banning hunting if we're just going to pump crap into the seas and vacuum up all their food.'

When Drecki did not reply, Berrister twisted round to look at the two ships again. The faulty light was still winking on *Lena*, and both whales seemed to be dead, although it was difficult to tell, as not only was it getting dark, but a mist was rolling in from the sea. Livingston was prone to fog, and he wondered if they might be able to use it to creep past the ships, and head for Sarah at Hannah Point. He suggested it to Drecki, who shrugged to say it was as good an idea as any.

They secured the boat to a rock so it wouldn't drift, and tried to rest. It wasn't easy. It was cold on the water, and their breath plumed in the icy air. They sat close together for warmth, huddled under a survival sheet, hoping they would not have to wait too long.

Ten

Even Zurin broke his usual impassivity to gape at Garik's order to drop the starboard anchor. He looked at Yablokov for confirmation. Yablokov shook his head, so the taciturn helmsman silently turned his attention back to his duties at the radar screen.

'Is there a problem?' asked Hasim, puzzled and irritated by the refusal to comply.

'The port hook's already down,' replied Yablokov shortly.

He turned away, thinking no other explanation was necessary, and even drunken Garik had the grace to blush when he realised what had almost happened.

'So?' asked Hasim, still bemused. 'We're drifting in a current – a second anchor will stabilise us, and allow us to deal with the cargo more efficiently.'

So, it had been Hasim's idea, thought Yablokov in disgust. Well, at least the captain had not entirely taken leave of his senses. He sincerely wished they would both leave him to run the ship before they did some serious harm.

'The chains will get tangled up with each other,'

he explained curtly. 'And once they do, we won't be able to sail, so our only option will be to cut them loose. Will the Southern Exploring Company buy us some new ones? Because we couldn't sail again without them.'

'And anchors are expensive,' added Nikos. 'Not to mention the fact that it would be dangerous to be down here without one.'

'I was merely trying to improve efficiency,' said Hasim, equally taut. 'We're taking far too long. *Volga* finished offloading her cargo ages ago, and it's making us look bad.'

'We'd be a lot further ahead if *he* didn't meddle,' muttered Nikos to Yablokov. 'If we'd remained in South Bay, working on the whale we had, instead of charging over here to get a new one, the cargo would be gone, and our holds would be full of meat.'

Hasim came to look at the chart, although Yablokov knew he was just trying to eavesdrop.

'But *Volga* has a smaller whale than us,' Yablokov told him. 'She'll need to catch another if she doesn't want to go home half empty. We're ahead of her on that front.'

Hasim sniffed, unappeased. 'When will we finish unloading?'

Nikos raised his hands in a shrug. 'It depends on the weather. There's no easy way to raise the barrels from the hold without a proper crane, and rough seas slow us down.'

Lena was not equipped with a crane because her catch was usually unloaded in port. It meant the heavy barrels had to be lifted manually, which was a complicated and time-consuming business.

It was labour-intensive, too, especially when the sea was choppy.

'So what shall I tell *Galtieri*?' pressed Hasim. 'Mr Orlando wants a timetable.'

Nikos considered. 'Two days, maybe. Longer if there's a storm. We can't unload when the ship's bucking like a bronco.'

'That's too long. We'll have to dump as we sail north.'

'That would be unwise,' said Yablokov, suspecting the Arab was stupid enough to try it. 'It might foul the propeller, and I doubt the other ships would risk giving us a tow, so we'd be stuck down here. Unless you felt like asking the US Coast Guard to help?'

Hasim glowered. 'Mr Orlando says the longer we dally, the more likely we are to run into additional scientists. Rather too many have stayed later than they should have done.'

'We noticed,' said Yablokov drily. 'But you said everything would be under control once you'd broadcast those krill numbers. Were you wrong about that, too?'

Hasim flushed with annoyance. 'I wasn't "wrong" about anything – the situation is merely more complex than we anticipated. However, it's not my side of the operation that's the problem – it's yours. Mr Orlando is unimpressed by the time you're taking with the cargo. Rectify the matter or there'll be consequences.'

'So, the jackal is afraid of the crocodile,' mused Nikos as Hasim left the bridge. 'However, the "consequences" had better not mean docked pay. We have an agreement and we've done our part.

209

It's not our fault that the weather down here is terrible.'

Yablokov had a bad feeling that withheld wages would be the least of their problems.

'I suspect Hasim's been chatting to *Galtieri* several times a day all along,' he said, taking the unofficial log book from a drawer and running his finger down the columns of figures to see how much cargo was still on board. 'And I think these stupid ideas don't all come from him – he just jumps when Orlando cracks the whip.'

'I wonder what Orlando will say when he learns that *Volga* killed the whale with the transmitter,' said Nikos. 'What a fuck-up! It will make next year much more difficult – these beasties aren't exactly plentiful.'

Yablokov didn't care. There would be no next year for him, because he was done with the Southern Exploring Company.

'Are you sure it'll take two days to dump the rest of the phosphorus?' he asked. 'There's less of it left than I thought.'

Nikos waggled his eyebrows. 'Hasim will get it in the neck when he tells Orlando what I said, and that's no bad thing. But we should be done in a day – assuming the weather stays calm. Are you done up here, Evgeny? Then come to the mess with me. Neither of us has eaten much all day.'

'I daren't,' said Yablokov, nodding to where Garik slumped in his chair. 'I'll come when he's gone to bed.'

'Gone for a drink, you mean,' said Nikos, eyeing the captain with unveiled disgust. 'Did you know he had this problem when you signed up?'

Yablokov shook his head. 'He's always liked a drink, but it's never interfered with his work before. Maybe it's dealing with Hasim that's driven him to the bottle.'

Zurin caught his eye, and jerked a thumb towards the window. A mist was rolling in, thick and white. Yablokov made a note in the log and reached for his cigarettes, but found only an empty carton.

'Stay here and keep an eye on things, will you, Nikos?' He tossed the box into the waste bin. 'Back in a minute.'

His quarters were two floors below, and to reach them he had to walk past the prisoners' cabin. Hasim was in the hallway outside it, talking to Graham. Yablokov gave the red-haired Scot a disgusted look as he passed: he did not approve of men who betrayed their comrades. As usual, music blared from the cabin, and Yablokov pitied the mess crew who berthed next door. No wonder the ship's food was becoming progressively less palatable.

Anxiety meant he was smoking more than usual, and all he found in his cabin was another empty box. He removed some dollars from his sea chest and went to find the purser. It felt odd to be using American money, but it was the currency the Southern Exploring Company paid him in. He fingered the crisp green notes suspiciously. They lacked the greasy familiarity of rubles, and he did not like the fact that all the denominations were the same colour and size.

211

The purser, Mikhail Romanov, was not in his office. Like most of the crew, Romanov had been assigned extra duties, and his were to supervise the men in the hold. Conditions down there were grim – damp, cold, slippery and smelly. When the phosphorus had first been loaded, Yablokov had been astonished that such fine new containers should be used for something that was just going to be thrown into the sea. He could not imagine such wanton wastage in Russia. But the Southern Exploring Company was not an organisation that encouraged questions, so he had given it no further thought.

He considered it now, however, as he watched two crewmen struggle to manoeuvre a barrel into a sling, ready to be hauled up on deck. None of the canisters had escaped the journey unscathed: all were dented and many had cracked seals. He found one with a loose lid and peered inside.

In his mind, phosphorus glowed in the dark, but all he saw was a kind of grainy concrete. Perhaps water had seeped in and changed its consistency. But it didn't matter, given that it would all soon be at the bottom of the sea. He glanced towards the cargo hatch, where the whale meat was coming aboard, to be stacked in the place the barrels had vacated. That was likely to be battered by the journey, too, but it was delivered in such crudely hacked hunks that he supposed it did not really matter. It just went against his natural sailor's inclination for neatness.

'I've been wanting a word with you,' said

Romanov as Yablokov approached. 'A couple of the men are sick.'

Romanov was the only man aboard with a qualification in first aid, so had been designated *Lena*'s medical officer.

'What's wrong with them?'

'Vomiting, tiredness, headaches. Sort of thing that's a bit difficult to pin down. They've had enough of this lark, I suspect, and fancy a couple of days in bed.'

'What do you want me to do?'

'Nothing. A nip of the captain's vodka and a good night's sleep should set them right. Lazy buggers.'

'Alright, if you're sure.'

Romanov nodded. 'I only mentioned it so you could leave them off the duty rosters tonight. Now, what was it you wanted? Other than a dose of rat poison for the rodent on the bridge.'

'Garik?'

'Hasim.' The purser pulled Yablokov aside and lowered his voice. 'Should you decide to take this ship home a bit sooner than scheduled, the regular crew would be happy to go with you. The hired hands might be a bit difficult, but I think we can handle them.'

Yablokov gazed at him. 'Mutiny?'

'More like a decision to survive. Garik's a liability and no one likes Hasim. Did you hear that he wanted to take all the fire axes and use them for flensing? I know we sometimes have a casual approach to Health and Safety, but that was beyond the pale.'

'It's almost over,' said Yablokov. He had never liked the purser, who could be Hasim's spy for all he knew, sent to test his loyalty. 'Another three days and we'll be heading north.'

'If we survive another three days,' countered Romanov pointedly.

Drecki dozed and Berrister kept watch while they waited for the mist to thicken and the darkness to deepen. He untied the rope and eased the boat forward, to see if *Lena* and the other ship – *Volga* – were still visible. Lights gleamed dully through the fog, and distant voices suggested that work was continuing apace, despite the plummeting temperatures and poor visibility.

He also heard a splash as more rubbish was dropped from the open cargo door. For small ships, the whalers seemed to be generating rather a lot of it. He picked up the binoculars and swept them over *Lena*, trying to memorise every last detail of her, just in case he was ever in a position to report her to the relevant authorities. The faulty light was still flickering – it stopped briefly before starting up again. Berrister frowned. Was it tapping out a specific pattern? But it vanished at that point, and did not start again.

Time passed slowly, although he was distracted for a while by the spectacle of a large leopard seal hunting a few late-fledging penguins not far from the shore.

He yawned and looked back at *Lena*. She was little more than a grey silhouette now, although the light was flickering again. Absently, he watched it . . . three short, three long, three short, stop. Three short, three long, three short, stop. He

214

struggled to his knees. Shaking with excitement, he woke Drecki.

'But why would your friends be signalling to the other whaler?' the Pole asked, watching it through his binoculars. 'Although it's definitely spelling out SOS.'

'They wouldn't – Geoff must be trying to contact Sarah.'

'But you said she planned to stay at Hannah Point until she was rescued. We're many kilometres away from there – she's not going to see it.'

'Yes, but Geoff and the others don't know that. It's *got* to be them. Who else could it be?'

'Someone else who's fallen foul of these people? Someone who's bored and is messing about? Regardless, there's not much we can do about it – unless you plan to drive over there and rescue them.'

Berrister opened his mouth to reply, but then could think of nothing to say. Drecki was right – there was nothing they could do. Then Drecki raised his hands in the air, palms up.

'But why not? The mist is thickening nicely and it's dark. Why not sneak across and have a look? It's not on the side where the men are cutting up the whale, so we should be able to reach it undetected. We'll decide what to do when we get there. No point in making plans when we don't know what we'll find.'

Berrister regarded him in astonishment. 'For an old man, you live very dangerously.'

Drecki laughed softly. 'We'll give it another hour – it will be eleven o'clock by then – late enough that most of the crew should be asleep. You sleep and I'll wake you when it's time.'

But Berrister was far too fraught to close his eyes. The light continued to wink on and off, increasingly difficult to see as the fog closed in. Then it disappeared completely. Soon, they could not see the rocks behind which they hid, and Berrister estimated that visibility was less than ten metres. Even so, Drecki refused to leave until the allotted hour.

'No point in taking needless risks,' he said.

Berrister fretted at every passing minute, but eventually Drecki indicated that it was time to go. Berrister put the oars in the rowlocks, hoping he would have the strength to do what was needed – his hands were full of blisters and his arms ached horribly. Drecki took the compass, and began whispering directions.

The sea was millpond calm, and the fog encased them in a bubble of silent grey-white. It took less time to reach *Lena* than they anticipated – rowing across flat water was faster than doing it on choppy seas – and they almost collided with her before Drecki frantically gestured for Berrister to stop. All but spent, Berrister slumped forward, struggling to catch his breath without making a noise. The sweat that coursed down his back and drenched his clothes would chill him later.

'Which porthole had the flashing light?' whispered Drecki.

'Sixth along from the stern, bottom row.'

Drecki began to propel them along the side with his hands. The water was tinged red with blood, and the voices of the men who still worked on the carcass, despite the lateness of the hour, seemed uncannily loud in the still air. Why couldn't they have been in bed, like normal people? All it needed was for one to look over the side, and the game would be up.

Then Drecki froze in alarm. A man stood right above them, smoking. He could not miss them, lit as they were by the light that spilled from the portholes above. Silently, Berrister cursed himself. How could he have been so stupid as to come out to the ship? Now, not only had he squandered his own life, but Drecki's as well. He braced himself, waiting for the shout of alarm that would herald their capture.

Yablokov failed to understand why Hasim was laughing. What was funny about four frightened people desperately signalling for help?

'Because they think *Volga* will save them,' Hasim explained as he chuckled. 'I'd go down there and tell them that she's our sister ship, but it's too hilarious. I thought they were supposed to be intelligent people.'

'They are,' said Yablokov coldly. 'Which is why they know you've no intention of letting them go. They're trying anything they can think of to save themselves, because they don't trust you.'

'I know they don't trust us,' said Hasim. 'If they did, they wouldn't keep that awful music on so loud. They're doing it to prevent us from listening in on them.'

Yablokov didn't admit that he and Nikos had been doing the same. Hasim's nasty habit of eavesdropping on other people's conversations

217

was not confined to sneaking up behind them or installing bugs in their cabins: Yablokov had twice caught him with his ear to the captain's door and once to his own.

'Your spy would've told you what they were doing anyway,' he said, unable to keep the disapproval from his voice. 'Even if *Volga* hadn't sent you an email.'

'My spy?' asked Hasim mildly.

'Did he tell you about the blue whales being here, too?'

'I have my ways,' replied Hasim loftily. 'But they're not for discussing with the likes of you. And now, if you'll excuse me, I have work to do.'

He left abruptly, so Yablokov knew his growing suspicions were right – there was indeed a snake in the scientists' camp. Hasim would not have killed someone who was useful to him, which left the four in the cabin. Of those Joshi was too young, Sarah too angry and Mortimer too honourable – Yablokov's dealings with the portly glaciologist had made him revise his initial reservations, and now he rather liked him. In another life they might have been friends. Graham was the only one of the quartet who was left – a sly, shifty-eyed man who spoke to Hasim with an ingratiating eagerness that made Yablokov want to punch him.

Ever since his discussion with Nikos, Yablokov had been desperately trying to think of ways to help the other three scientists escape – Graham, he assumed, would prefer to stay on board. They would need a boat, supplies to last until they

218

were rescued and enough time to get well away. He knew what helping them would mean for him, but he was beginning to realise that it was not just the prisoners who would be executed to keep the Southern Exploring Company's business quiet. As soon as *Lena*'s work was done, Hasim's team would ensure that no one lived to reveal what had happened – so giving Mortimer, Sarah and Joshi a chance to tell their story to the world was revenge of sorts.

Outside, the mist swirled around the ship in dense, milky folds. He was tempted to bring the crew inside, but knew that Hasim would only countermand him, and it was not worth the confrontation that would follow. He glanced at Garik. The captain dozed fitfully in his chair, so he ordered the Norwegians to take him to rest in his quarters instead. Hasim went to help. As soon as they had gone, Zurin approached. The helmsman's normally impassive face was full of disgust.

'Garik ordered repairs,' he muttered. 'In fog!'

'What repairs?' Yablokov looked in the logbook, but there was nothing written about them. And Zurin was right – it was ridiculous to carry out that sort of task when visibility was poor.

'Two men inspecting the hull – saw them when I went for a smoke.'

'Who?' asked Yablokov, suspecting that Hasim would be irked when he found out what Garik had done. Six of the crew were now claiming to be ill, which meant fewer hands to work. No one could be spared for non-essential duties.

Zurin shrugged. 'Couldn't tell. Too misty.'

Yablokov was bemused. 'Well, let me know if he does it again – discreetly, though. We don't want trouble. Are they still out there?'

Zurin shook his head. 'Gone.'

Yablokov closed his eyes as a sudden wave of nausea drifted over him. The six crewmen were not the only ones beginning to suffer from Hasim's killing pace. Yablokov himself felt sick with exhaustion, but could not afford an early night, not with the captain unfit to command a rowboat and Hasim issuing asinine orders at every turn.

He glanced at the clock. Past midnight, and Nikos was late for his turn on the bridge. Chief engineers did not usually stand watch, but Hasim had decided to flout that particular rule, on the grounds that every man should pull his weight and more. Yablokov left Zurin in charge of the bridge, and went to find Nikos. He was so tired that he could barely walk, and every bone in his body ached. Friend or no friend, Nikos had some explaining to do.

The Greek was not in his cabin and not in the mess. Irked, Yablokov went to the engine room, where he learned that Nikos had failed to appear for the usual evening briefing, leaving his team uncertain what to do. They all looked exhausted, so Yablokov told them to go to bed. No one argued.

When they had gone, he leaned against the door, fighting off a wave of dizziness. *Lena* was not very big, and there were a limited number of places Nikos could be. Yablokov went to the scientists' cabin first, wondering if Nikos had taken it into his head to visit them, but the guards assured him that the engineer had been nowhere near it.

There was only one place left: the afterdeck hold. Nikos had never been happy with the way the phosphorus had been loaded, and had been appalled by the dents and broken seals caused by the stormy weather – the vapour was poisonous, he said. So it made sense that he had gone to inspect them before taking his turn on the bridge. Yablokov rubbed his throbbing temples. Were the fumes the reason why the crewmen were ill and he was developing the mother of all headaches? If so, then the faster they got rid of the stuff, the better.

He climbed down to the hold and looked around. Only about a third of the canisters remained, the rest having been 'delivered'. The purser was there, listlessly watching two teams of men struggle with the heavy canisters. No one was working very hard.

'I was about to come and see you,' Romanov said. His face was pale and sweaty. 'Steve Deng – he needs a doctor. You need to get the one from *Galtieri* to come over.'

'Why? What's wrong with him?'

'He's pissing blood. I feel like crap, too – I'll give this another hour, then I'm off to bed. I had to send Jusef and Rainier off early, as well – they were spewing all over the place. Nikos told me that phosphorus is dangerous, and nearly all the seals are faulty. The bloody stuff must be leaking out and poisoning us all.'

'We shouldn't be surprised,' said Yablokov. 'It's why the pay's so good – danger money.'

'Then let's hope we live to enjoy it,' said Romanov grimly.

'Have you seen Nikos? He's due on watch.'

'He probably overslept – Hasim is working us all too hard.'

Too weary to explain that he'd already checked Nikos' cabin, Yablokov headed for the forward hold. No one was in it. All the phosphorus had been dumped, and slabs of whale meat had taken its place. He gagged at the stench, and had to leave quickly to avoid throwing up. After a few moments in the cold air, the nausea passed, and he climbed back down the stairs, calling Nikos' name.

He skidded on the slick floor, and only saved himself from a tumble by bracing himself against the nearest pile of meat. It was soft and moist, and he drew his hand away in revulsion. There was something sinister and rotten about it: a dirty cargo for a dirty business.

He was about to give up when he saw a boot caught under one of the piles. Puzzled, he went to investigate. The boot was attached to a leg. In growing alarm, he began to haul lumps of slippery flesh away from the body that was buried beneath them. It was Nikos, as dead as the whale that had hidden him.

Eleven

In the cabin, Sarah fought an overwhelming sense of helplessness. Although Mortimer had sworn that the distant thumps they had heard were the other ship catching a whale, she refused to believe it. She had insisted on signalling until the fog became so thick that they could barely see the water under their window, let alone the other vessel across the bay. But the real blow came when they had finally undone all the screws from the porthole, only to find that it had rusted shut.

'No, don't give up,' said Mortimer, hating to see her despair. If she cracked, so would the other two, and he did not want to spend his last few days – or hours – in a pit of gloom. Anything they did would be a waste of time, he knew, but it was better than sitting around feeling sorry for themselves.

'But it's stuck fast,' said Joshi tearfully. 'It won't budge.'

'Just keep sawing at the edges,' urged Mortimer. 'Graham and I have almost finished the banner.'

But Sarah had had enough. Her fingers were blistered, and she knew she could do no more. She went to lie on the bed, one arm across her eyes to hide the hot tears of anger and frustration. Joshi continued to scrape and rasp alone.

'There's a boat in the water, right beneath us,' he said suddenly.

'So?' asked Mortimer. 'They've been around the ship all day.'

'Not since the mist came down,' said Joshi, standing on a chair for a better view. 'My God! It's Andrew!'

Sarah shot off the bed and elbowed him out of the way. 'It *is* him,' she breathed, a slow smile spreading over her face. 'He's come to rescue us.'

'It *can't* be him,' whispered Graham, stunned. 'He's dead . . . the crevasse.'

'He must've climbed out again,' crowed Joshi, and lowered his voice when Mortimer made an urgent gesture with his hand, reminding him that they might not be alone.

'He saw our signal and waited for night before coming to get us,' said Sarah excitedly. 'He's waving for us to come out.'

'And how does he expect us to do that?' asked Mortimer bleakly. 'Jump through the porthole?'

'I think so,' said Joshi. 'He doesn't know it's rusted shut.'

Sarah felt determination seize her. 'Get sawing, Joshi. Geoff, make a rope out of the bed sheets. Graham, start bundling up our outside clothes – we'll need them on the water, but we won't fit through the window if we put them on.'

'You mean *I* won't,' said Mortimer, not sure he'd make it through stark naked. It wasn't very big and he was a large man.

Joshi and Graham leapt to do as they were told, while Sarah grabbed a fork herself, making so much noise with her frantic scraping that Mortimer felt compelled to sing, to drown her out.

*   *   *

224

Berrister gazed at the porthole, wondering what was taking them so long. Then he glanced at the rail, expecting at any moment for the smoker to reappear and challenge them. He had been sure the game was up when they had been spotted, but with cool aplomb Drecki had given him a cheery wave and pretended to inspect the ship's side. The man had nodded back, finished his cigarette and moved away.

'Come on, come on,' he muttered, as time ticked by and nothing happened.

'They can't open the porthole,' whispered Drecki. 'The salt has probably corroded the metal and rusted it shut.'

'We can't sit here while they mess around with it,' muttered Berrister. 'Someone will see us.'

'Then we'll row away and come back in half an hour. We don't need to go far – not in this fog.'

It seemed the only practical solution, so Berrister stood and pointed behind him, following that by holding up both gloved hands, fingers apart. He clenched them into fists, and then spread his fingers again, and again. Sarah made the thumbs up sign, so Berrister took the oars and rowed into the mist. As he had no watch, he began counting off seconds and minutes in his mind.

'We've got half an hour,' said Sarah, glancing at the clock on the wall. 'We *must* be ready when he gets back, because we can't rely on the fog to last forever and we'll need it if we want to make a clean escape.'

She levered at the window with a strength born

of desperation. Something cracked. Encouraged, she did it again, this time with Joshi helping. There was another crack, and a broken fork cartwheeled across the room. Undeterred, Joshi snatched up a spoon, while Sarah stepped back to give him room.

She glanced at Graham. He had gnawed his lower lip so much that it was raw, and she wondered if he would choose to leave or stay when push came to shove. One thing was certain, though: he would not be leaving the cabin to natter secretly to Hasim again – which he'd done twice more since claiming he'd provided the man with duff krill data. She was not about to let him sabotage their one chance of freedom.

'Pack food,' she instructed Mortimer, careful not to let Graham hear. 'Just in case we have to return to the crevasses.'

Mortimer had already done it, sure they were not about to be transferred from one warm ship to another. Then he kicked his sheet rope under the bed, out of sight, along with the bundles of clothing, in case Hasim made one of his annoyingly unannounced visits.

'Five minutes left,' grunted Joshi, glancing at his watch in agitation. 'Damn this thing! It won't budge!'

Mortimer went to try, but the porthole remained resolutely sealed.

'We're levering from the wrong angle,' he said, after stepping back to inspect it. 'It's most firmly jammed at the bottom, so let's try from the sides and top simultaneously.'

'Two minutes,' announced Graham.

Sarah glanced at him sharply. He had spoken rather loudly. Was he trying to warn the guards? Suddenly Mortimer wheeled around and grabbed her by the waist. Confused, she tried to wriggle free, but his grip was firm.

'Then you move like this,' he said, swinging her away from him, but keeping a hold on her hand. She stumbled, and he hauled her back again. The door opened to reveal Hasim standing there.

'What are you doing?' he demanded.

'Teaching her to tango,' explained Mortimer. 'I've always enjoyed dancing. And music.'

Joshi glanced covertly at his watch. Berrister would be outside now, waiting on his boat. Hasim strolled casually towards the window, while Mortimer and Sarah exchanged an agonised glance. What would he notice first? The scratches around the porthole or Berrister?

Hasim noticed the scratches. He reached out to touch one with his finger, then roared with laughter.

'What are you going to do?' he asked, once he had his mirth under control. 'Swim back to your camp? Or do you think your flashing signal will save you?' He smirked at their dismay. 'Oh, yes, I know all about that. But open the window by all means – it's probably against some maritime law for it to be rusted shut anyway. In the meantime, I want another word with Mr Graham.'

'No,' said Sarah, stepping forward to prevent it, but the guards were inside in a trice. She was shoved back, Graham was whisked out, and she was powerless to do anything about it.

'He'll blab,' she whispered tearfully to Mortimer, barely able to contain her bitter disappointment. 'Joshi – signal Andrew to leave without us. Do it now!'

'I can't,' replied Joshi, bewilderment creasing his face. 'He's not there. D'you think he's already been caught?'

Mortimer pressed his ear to the door – their captors were not the only ones who could eavesdrop – but he could make out nothing of what was being said outside. However, whatever it was did not take long, because he only just had time to jerk back before it opened and Graham was ushered back inside. The Scot was pale, while Hasim looked pleased with himself.

'Jump out of the window, if you like,' he taunted. 'But bear in mind that you'll freeze to death long before you reach the shore. And even if you do manage it, then what? You'd be soaking wet on an uninhabited island with no food and no shelter. I assure you, you're much better off here.'

He turned on his heel before they could reply, shutting the door behind him. As the guards locked it, Joshi rushed to the porthole and peered out, while Sarah and Mortimer looked at Graham.

'He's not there,' whispered Joshi, distraught. 'And it's been forty minutes.'

'What did he want?' asked Sarah, ignoring Joshi to glare at Graham. 'And more importantly, what did you tell him?'

'Krill,' replied Graham in a low voice. 'He wanted more information about krill.' He swallowed hard. 'And he said he'd kill me if I told

228

him any more lies. I was scared . . . I didn't dare make up another wild number . . . I told him what Noddy would expect to hear.'

Sarah regarded him with contempt. 'And what did you tell him about Andrew? Because there must be some reason why he hasn't come back.'

Graham gaped at her. 'You think I'd . . . No! Hasim never asked about him, and I never mentioned it. What do you take me for?'

Sarah thought it best not to answer. She turned away abruptly and peered out at the empty sea herself.

'We'll work on the assumption that he's staying back because some of the crew are on deck,' she said briskly, not looking at Graham. 'And he's waiting for them to go back inside. Which means he could be here at any moment, so we need to be ready.'

Gamely, Mortimer picked up a spoon. 'I'll lever from the top, while you three take the sides. Ready?'

'An accident?' echoed Yablokov, regarding Hasim incredulously. 'His skull is smashed in!'

'Yes – because he slipped and fell.' Hasim was infuriatingly cool. 'You know how slick the steps can be. You should have detailed someone to hose them off.'

'But Nikos was *under* the meat.'

Yablokov knew he was shouting, and that half the ship was listening to the conversation, but he no longer cared. Nearby, Garik wept for his lost engineer, but Yablokov was unsympathetic.

The captain was a disgrace, and should never have let his adviser seize so much control.

'Then it collapsed on him when he skidded into it,' insisted Hasim, all smooth reason. 'Get a grip, Yablokov. Ranting in front of the crew is scarcely setting a good example.'

If Yablokov had been himself, Hasim would have died right then. He would have grabbed him by the throat and squeezed the life out of him with pleasure. But Yablokov's head throbbed, his vision was blurred and his legs were like jelly, which meant he was far from certain he would win such a battle. He willed the weakness to recede, silently seething at the reprimand.

'If it'll make you happy, I'll order an investigation when we get home,' Hasim continued. 'We can question everyone then, see if anyone saw Nikos go down to the hold.'

Yablokov turned away in disgust. Yeah, right! Question them at a point when all they would be thinking about was getting their money and seeing their families; and when enough time had passed that memories would blur and witnesses had been cajoled – or worse. But Yablokov had never been more certain of anything in his life: Nikos had been murdered. The location and shape of the wound were wholly inconsistent with a fall, and meat did not hide a body of its own accord.

Hasim would not have killed Nikos himself, of course, but Yablokov knew he had given the order – the Greek shouldn't have been so vocal in his criticism. He made a silent vow that Hasim would not get away with it, and would pay with his own life. But not yet. First, he had to contact *Galtieri*'s doctor, because it was obvious that the crew weren't malingering, but were genuinely unwell. Hopefully, it wouldn't take too long for the powerful warship to sail to them from the Byers Peninsula.

On the bridge, he picked up the handset and asked to speak to the medic while Hasim listened with brazen interest. The doctor came on air and asked Yablokov to describe the symptoms. Then there was such a long pause that he thought the connection had been lost.

'No, I heard you,' said the doctor shortly. 'But there's not a lot I can do, other than suggest giving them milk – it reduces the acidity in the gut.'

'They need more than milk,' snapped Yablokov, unable to keep the irritation from his voice. 'They're bleeding inside, for God's sake! Our medical officer thinks they've been contaminated by the cargo.'

'Unlikely.' There was another pause. 'Your medical officer's the purser, isn't he? Has a certificate in first aid?'

'The seals were broken on most of the barrels,' continued Yablokov, ignoring the implication that Romanov was an amateur who didn't know what he was talking about. 'Clearly, the phosphorus has leaked and poisoned the crew.'

'Phosphorus?' came the doctor's cautious voice after yet another pause.

Yablokov wondered if the man had been drinking, because he seemed remarkably slow on the uptake. 'It can cause symptoms similar to the

231

ones experienced by our men – he looked it up online. So we need an antidote – *now.*'

The radio hissed to itself as the doctor considered the problem. Or, thought Yablokov acidly, while he looked up what Wikipedia had to say about it. Eventually, the man spoke.

'It's not the phosphorus – it's more likely to be the food. Perhaps bad meat—'

'If it were bad meat, everyone would be sick,' interrupted Yablokov, 'but it's only the men who handle the cargo. Hasim's team is symptom free.'

'If you really think your diagnosis is right, then you need to dose them with calcium gluconate,' said the doctor. 'There should be some in your dispensary. Give each man two tablets every three hours, mixed with as much water as he can swallow. And they'll need to wash with warm, soapy water. Once it's off their skin, you should start to see an improvement. How much more of the cargo is still on board?'

'About fifteen per cent,' said Yablokov, thinking the remedy sounded worryingly mild for what seemed to be such a serious problem. He hoped it would work.

'Good. Mr Orlando is here with me. He wants me to assure you that there will be no long-term effects, but that you should direct the crew to wear gloves and masks from now on. And the faster you get the stuff off the ship, the faster they'll recover.'

Personally, Yablokov suspected there might be a good reason why the doctor had not offered to visit in person – he doubtless knew a good deal more about phosphorus than he was willing to admit, and was not about to expose himself just to tend the sick.

'Mr Orlando knows what he's doing,' said Hasim, when Yablokov broke the connection and dropped the microphone back in its cradle. 'Trust him.'

'Right.' Yablokov leaned back in the chair, fighting the dizziness that threatened to overwhelm him. The last thing he needed was to collapse – then no one would stand between the ship and disaster, what with Garik drunk and Nikos dead.

Hasim chuckled suddenly. 'Did I tell you that the scientists are trying to climb through their window? First the Morse code, and now an attempt to swim to shore. Fools!'

'*I'd* rather drown than drink your poisoned beer,' retorted Yablokov. 'And I see nothing funny in their terror.'

'Poisoned beer?' echoed Hasim, laughing again. 'Whatever are you talking about?'

Yablokov did not bother to argue. Black spots were niggling at the edges of his vision, and he no longer had the energy to spar with Hasim.

'I need to dig out some gloves and masks,' he said shortly. 'Zurin, come with me.'

He left the bridge, hearing the door screech on its hinges as he pulled it open. Nikos had done that, to prevent Hasim from sneaking up on them. Fat lot of good it had done, he thought sourly.

'Hasim killed Nikos,' growled Zurin, once they were out of earshot.

'I know,' said Yablokov. 'But he'll regret it – Nikos was the only man who could coax fifteen

233

knots out of *Lena,* so the rest of the fleet will leave us standing on the way home. He won't make it back by the date he wanted, and it serves the bastard right.'

'He killed him because Nikos searched his cabin,' said Zurin.

Yablokov stared at him, and then bundled the helmsman inside the storeroom, so they would not be overheard. 'How do you know?'

'I saw him in there.'

'And?' demanded Yablokov. It was like drawing blood.

'Hasim caught him.'

'Clearly,' said Yablokov. 'But what did Nikos find? It must've been something important or Hasim wouldn't have felt the need to silence him.'

'Some papers regarding the cargo. Nikos threatened to tell you what they said. Then I heard the captain coming, so I hid.'

'What about the cargo?' asked Yablokov urgently.

Zurin shrugged. 'Nikos didn't say – just shook the papers at Hasim.'

'When did all this happen?'

'Few hours ago.'

'Why didn't you tell me sooner?' demanded Yablokov, exasperated.

'Thought Nikos would.'

Yablokov rubbed his head. Would Nikos still be alive if Zurin had come to him at once? And would it have made a difference if Nikos had managed to tell him whatever it was he had discovered? Or would it just have meant two bodies in the hold? He tried to think.

'I need to know what Nikos found,' he said. 'Will you help me?'

'It'll be dangerous.'

'Yes,' acknowledged Yablokov. 'But less so, if you keep watch while I go in.'

Zurin thought for a moment, then nodded, and together they crept to Hasim's quarters. The door was locked, but Yablokov's master key opened it. While Zurin hovered at the end of the corridor, Yablokov stepped inside.

Hasim liked his creature comforts. Ship-issue blankets had been replaced by a duvet, and the worn leather chairs were enlivened with pretty batiks. Japanese prints hung on the wall, while under the table were several crates of vodka. As Hasim did not touch alcohol, Yablokov could only assume it was for Garik. There was something else, too – phials of sedative and evidence that Hasim had been adding it to the bottles. No wonder Garik was asleep half the time and drunk the rest.

Nikos' supply of elemental mercury was there, too, along with several bottle tops, suggesting that Hasim had indeed been poisoning the scientists' beer.

There was a desk with two drawers by the window. They were also locked, but Yablokov had a key for them as well. Inside were printouts of emails from *Galtieri* and *Volga*, urging Hasim to speed up the dumping of the cargo. There was also an inventory of the cargo itself. When Yablokov read what was in the barrels in his holds, he thought he was mistaken. He rubbed his eyes and looked again. Then his jaw dropped in horror.

* * *

235

Berrister had finished counting thirty minutes and looked at Drecki. The Pole consulted his watch, nodded briefly and pulled out the compass. Berrister began to row, trying not to let the oars splash in the water. As time ticked by, he glanced questioningly at Drecki. Surely they should be there by now?

'Skull to the left a bit,' directed Drecki tersely.

Berrister did, glancing over his shoulder for the looming shape of the ship, but there was nothing but fog. With a pang of dismay, he realised what had happened.

'We must have drifted while we were waiting, which means we've overshot the thing.'

'Yes, but drifted which way?' asked Drecki worriedly. 'How can we compensate?'

Berrister felt wretched when he realised the answer to that. 'We can't – not unless we know how far we've gone and in which direction. Which we don't.'

Drecki consulted the compass. 'There seems to be a current moving west. Let's try going east for a while. We might be lucky.'

With no better idea, Berrister rowed in the direction of the geologist's pointing finger, listening intently for a sound that might guide them, but there was only silence. After a while, Drecki indicated that he was to change course again. And then again. Eventually, Berrister stopped and glanced up at the sky. It was still dark, but for how much longer?

'What's the time?' he whispered.

'Nearly three o'clock.'

Berrister was horrified. 'We should have been

236

there two hours ago – they'll think we're not coming.'

'Perhaps, but they're not going anywhere, are they? They have no choice but to wait. Now row in that direction. I think I heard voices.'

Berrister began to pull again, watching as Drecki listened intently, but after another fifteen minutes, he lifted the oars from the water and let the boat drift. 'We're totally lost, aren't we?'

Drecki nodded dejectedly. 'I'm afraid so.'

'What are we going to do?' Berrister hated to imagine how the others were feeling, and his head ached from the tension, a dull throb that pulsed in his temples.

'The only thing we can,' replied Drecki with a shrug. 'Keep looking until we find them. It can't be far.'

'I'm not sure how much longer I can keep this up.' Berrister flexed his cramped, aching shoulders, aware that the blisters on his hands had burst and were sticky inside his gloves.

'Then let me row for a bit.'

But Drecki was hopeless – not only did he splash too much, but his strokes squeaked in the rowlocks. Someone on *Lena* would hear him coming a mile away. Tiredly, Berrister indicated that they were to change places again. His muscles burned with exhaustion, but at the same time, he was cold. The moisture on his clothes had frozen, and his feet were so numb he was not even sure they were still attached to his legs.

After what seemed like an age, Drecki gave a soft hiss. Something loomed in the mist ahead of them. The sea was pink – they were near the

237

half-flensed whale. Berrister reversed quickly, catching a glimpse of a dark mound in the sea with its purple-red gashes. A dull yellow light oozed through the fog.

'It's the calf,' he whispered, 'which means it's not *Lena*, but the other one. I think we need to go that way.'

He nodded with his head. Drecki shrugged agreement and they were off again.

The mist was patchy now and the sky was definitely lighter in the east. And then they saw *Lena*. With relief, they eased along her until they reached Mortimer's porthole. He glanced up, but was too exhausted to answer Joshi's excited wave.

'He's here!' hissed Joshi.

'Good,' said Sarah. 'Now just one more heave and we're out of here. Ready? Push!'

With a protesting squeal, the porthole swung free and frozen air flooded into the cabin. Joshi shivered, partly from the chill, but mainly from exhilaration. Sarah quickly tied the rope to one of the beds, while Mortimer tossed the bundles of clothes out through the window for Berrister to catch. Graham stood and watched, his hands at his sides.

'Joshi – go,' ordered Sarah. 'Hurry!'

The student needed no second bidding. He went feet first through the hole, and shinned agilely down the knotted sheets. The bunk creaked and one knot tightened, but the rope held. When it went slack, Sarah turned to Mortimer.

'You next.'

Mortimer was just climbing onto a chair, when the door opened, and Hasim entered.

Yablokov had been in a state of shock ever since he had discovered that *Lena* was not carrying phosphorus, but something far more sinister. No wonder men like Hasim had been assigned to each of the six ships, he thought – to keep their crews from knowing the truth. All he could hope was that Hasim was contaminated too. Of course, Hasim had never been anywhere near the holds, so that was unlikely. Bitterly, Yablokov realised he should have guessed far sooner what was going on.

So now what? Nothing would be gained by confronting Hasim – indeed, Yablokov would likely end up with *his* brains bashed out. No, it was best to let Hasim remain in ignorance of their discovery – for now, at least. However, that didn't mean doing nothing, and Yablokov was resolved to help the scientists escape that day. Let them tell their story – and let the Southern Exploring Company pay for what it had done. He would recruit a few trusty crewmen to over-power the guards, then put the prisoners on a boat before Hasim and his team knew what was happening. The scientists could race back to the island and hide in the ice again until *Worsley* came to collect them.

He hurried to their cabin, intending to tell them his plan, but Hasim was already there, waiting for the guards to unlock the door. Shit! He'd have to come back later. He started to leave, but

Hasim's angry roar made him hurry back again. A quick glance inside the cabin told him exactly why Hasim had shouted: the porthole was open and Joshi had gone.

Sarah gazed at Hasim and Yablokov in dismay. No! It was five in the morning, for God's sake. Why were they up at such an hour? Then she frowned as the first mate planted a heavy hand in the middle of Hasim's back and firmly propelled him inside the cabin, before turning to say something to the guards. He stepped inside quickly, and shut the door behind him.

'Get them,' she hissed urgently, preferring to take the situation into her own hands than wait for the first mate to explain his curious behaviour.

She dived at Hasim, managing to grab him around the neck only because he was too startled by Yablokov's shove to duck out of her way. She shoved a fork to his throat to keep him still. Quick on the uptake, Mortimer seized Yablokov. The first mate didn't struggle.

'Please,' he said quickly in English. 'I want to help you.'

'Of course you do,' sneered Sarah, indicating that Graham was to help her subdue Hasim, who was continuing to thrash about. The Scot did so reluctantly.

'I told the guards to leave us,' Yablokov insisted. 'Look outside if you don't believe me.'

'Oh, sure,' said Sarah. 'And have them rush in with their guns?'

Hasim's face had gone from shock to contempt.

240

'Traitor,' he spat in Russian. 'I should've killed you when I got rid of that prying Nikos.'

Yablokov ignored him. 'I'm dying,' he told Sarah. 'Radiation sickness.' The scientists exchanged a quick glance, but didn't order him to shut up, so he continued. 'Radioactive waste in barrels of concrete, but the seals broke because the Southern Exploring Company didn't load them properly.'

'You got what you deserve,' spat Hasim, still in Russian. 'Treacherous scum! Now get the guards back or I'll personally make sure your family—'

'He's been trying to poison you,' Yablokov interrupted. Hasim's threats were irrelevant, because he wasn't going to leave the cabin alive – if Sarah didn't kill him with her fork, Yablokov would do it with the knife Hasim carried in his belt. 'The beer.'

'We know,' said Mortimer shortly. 'Sarah – leave Hasim to Graham and go. Now!'

'Yes, go – you won't get far,' taunted Hasim in English.

Sarah didn't move. 'Radioactive waste . . . is that what you've been dumping? For God's sake, why? *Why* here? The penguins and seals . . .'

Yablokov felt a stab of shame. She was right, of course – inert phosphorus was one thing, but barrels spewing radiation was another altogether.

'I know why,' said Mortimer.

He glanced at the door, not sure they could believe that the guards weren't there. He indicated the window with his eyes, imploring Sarah to go before it was too late. Yet he could see why she was unwilling to let go of Hasim – Graham's hold on him was very tenuous.

'Why?' asked Yablokov, more willing to believe what the scientists said than to trust anything coming from the glowering, spitting Hasim.

'Because it has to go where currents won't carry any leakage to places it can be detected,' explained Mortimer. 'There's a technique called isotope analysis, which can identify exactly where sources of radioactivity come from. Doubtless your Southern Exploring Company deals with some highly dubious regimes and organisations – ones that don't want anyone to know they have nuclear capability.'

It sounded plausible to Yablokov, but it was no time to be discussing such matters.

'Let me help you,' he whispered urgently. 'I can get you a good boat and supplies. I can send a message to your base as well – tell them you need help. It's too late for us, but you can tell everyone about the Southern Exploring Company – finish them for good.'

With a howl of rage, Hasim threw off Sarah – Graham started back of his own accord – and managed to draw his knife. Mortimer was the closest, so he lunged at him first. It would have been the end of the portly glaciologist had Yablokov not acted. He twisted, putting himself between blade and target. He felt a solid thump in his middle.

At first, he thought the wound was superficial, but then the room tipped, and he found himself on the floor. He heard the rasp of his own breathing and a blur of voices. Beneath him was a spreading stain of red. His senses returned gradually, along with a deep, aching pain that came with an awareness of his life ebbing away. Still, it was a cleaner fate than the one that faced his crew.

He looked up to see that Sarah and Mortimer had overpowered Hasim again in the interim – he lay on the floor, pinned down by Mortimer's considerable weight and with his own hat stuffed in his mouth. Sarah fumbled in her pocket and withdrew a bottle and a syringe. She quickly drew all the clear liquid into the needle and plunged it into Hasim's neck. Unable to howl, he gave a muffled snarl of anger.

'That's the stuff Andrew uses to sedate seals,' said Mortimer. 'And you've just given him enough to drop an elephant. He'll die – and so will we unless we get out of here *fast*.'

Yablokov was gratified to see Hasim's eyes grow wide with terror. The captain's adviser began to writhe, although whether it was in an effort to escape or as a result of the drug was difficult to tell. Meanwhile, Graham had not taken his eyes off Yablokov.

'He saved you, Geoff,' he whispered. 'He took the blade intended for you.'

'He probably did it by accident,' said Sarah dispassionately.

Yablokov fumbled in his pocket for the sheaf of printed emails he had taken from Hasim's cabin, along with the documents detailing the real nature of the cargo.

'Take these. Show them to everyone.'

Mortimer accepted them warily and Yablokov sagged in relief. The geologist would see the Southern Exploring Company pay for its dirty business. It wouldn't help his family, of course, but . . .

'He's dead,' said Sarah, pulling Mortimer away. 'Now come on!'

Mortimer stowed the papers inside his shirt and aimed for the window, where Sarah and Graham were obliged to help him wriggle through a hole that was not nearly big enough.

'He's stuck,' gulped Graham in alarm. 'We should've gone first.'

'We couldn't,' panted Sarah, shoving with all her might. 'He'd never have got out on his own.'

'So we die, just because he's fat?' demanded Graham. 'That's not fair.'

'None of this is fair,' retorted Sarah. 'And it wouldn't have happened if *someone* hadn't collaborated.' She glared at him. 'Now push, you little shit.'

'I *had* to tell Hasim what he wanted to know,' snapped Graham defensively. 'He would've killed me if I'd given him another unbelievable krill report.'

'I'm not talking about the krill,' said Sarah coldly. 'I'm talking about the whales. Someone radioed in their position, then cut off our communications and stole the food.'

Graham gaped at her. 'You think that was me? God, Sarah! I always knew you didn't like me, but to suggest—'

'Who else can it be?' Sarah leaned all her weight on Mortimer's rump, aware of voices in the corridor outside. 'It's not Geoff, Andrew or me; Joshi's too stupid; and Lisa, Dan and Freddy are dead.'

'How do you know Dan's dead?' flashed Graham. 'Because we found his sample bag? That's dumb! It's *him*, Sarah. It's not me. He's still alive and *he's* the one who dropped us in this mess.'

At that point, Mortimer shot through the porthole and the rope creaked ominously as it took his weight. Sarah started to follow, but Graham was there first, shoving her out of his way in his haste to be next. Fortunately, he was quick, and she was halfway through the porthole when the door opened. It was Zurin, looking for Yablokov.

Twelve

Sarah had just enough time to watch Zurin's reaction to the scene inside the cabin before she swarmed down the sheet rope. There was a flash of satisfaction when he saw Hasim's body, but he went white with shock when he saw Yablokov's. Stunned, he blocked the door for several vital seconds before going to crouch by the first mate's side. It gave Sarah just enough time to clamber into the boat before the guards surged towards the window.

'Go, go!' she yelled.

'What about Dan?' asked Berrister, yanking the starter cord. Nothing happened, so Mortimer pushed him out of the way to do it himself. 'Is he on board as well?'

'Almost certainly,' said Graham. 'But he won't be joining us.'

'What's the plan?' asked Mortimer, still struggling with the engine, while Joshi looked upwards fearfully, waiting for the shots that would end their lives.

Drecki gave a mirthless bark of laughter. 'Plan?'

There was a rapid rattle of gunfire from the porthole, although none of the bullets came close, as the boat was shielded by the curve of *Lena*'s hull. Mortimer gave a muffled bark of satisfaction as the engine roared into life. He twisted the throttle and they were away.

'The fog,' shouted Drecki, pointing. 'Aim for the fog.'

Mortimer did, ducking the bullets that cracked around him, and within moments they had disappeared inside a thick blanket of mist. The sound of gunfire receded.

'Graham,' cried Berrister, as the Scot began to topple backwards. He grabbed him in time to stop him falling overboard, but one side of his hood was dark with blood, and his eyes were open but unseeing. 'They've shot him!'

No one was listening, because they had suddenly emerged from the fogbank, and could see *Lena* again. Two inflatables were being readied to give chase. Mortimer immediately powered their own craft back towards Devil's Point, zigzagging between patches of mist.

'Slow down!' howled Drecki. 'There are

pinnacles just under the surface. If we hit one at this speed, we'll capsize.'

'If we slow down, they'll catch us,' Mortimer yelled back. He swore suddenly, as a rock appeared directly in front of them, forcing him to cut to one side. Another came almost as quickly, and he held his breath as they shot between them with very little room to spare. He eased off the throttle slightly.

'Head east,' called Drecki. 'We'll hide along the shoreline.'

'Too obvious,' countered Sarah. 'Head south – we're going to Deception.'

'Deception?' echoed Drecki. 'We can't reach Deception! The sea's too rough and we don't have enough fuel.'

'There are tourists there,' argued Sarah. 'I heard them on the radio.'

'Heard them when?' asked Mortimer. Something black clung to his fingers – a clump of hair. He didn't recall pulling it out when he had grabbed Yablokov, but supposed he must have done. He flung it away in distaste. 'Because they might be gone by now. We'll be safer waiting for *Worsley*.'

'But that's what these criminals will expect us to do,' snapped Sarah. 'We need to try something different. Head for that fog bank – it'll hide us for a bit longer.'

'She's right,' said Joshi, once they were enveloped in mist again. 'The only way we'll beat them *is* by being unpredictable. We've learned that, if nothing else.'

'Very well, then,' said Mortimer reluctantly.

'Deception it is. I suppose we can always row the last bit if we run out of juice.'

They worked out their course quickly with the compass, although Berrister took no part in it, and only cradled Graham's body in his arms. Then Mortimer eased through the mist, cautiously now as breaking waves revealed the presence of rocks right beneath the surface. Then, abruptly, the fog was gone, giving them a clear view ahead – of a heaving, white-capped sea littered with chunks of ice and several large decaying bergs. He opened the throttle, while Drecki knelt in the bows, and tried to direct him around any submerged pinnacles.

'Here they come!' yelled Sarah, as the first of their pursuers emerged from the mist.

The driver spotted them, and changed direction. Within moments, there was a second boat and then a third. *Lena*'s two had been joined by one from her sister ship.

'They'll call *Galtieri*,' shouted Drecki, turning to look at Berrister with haunted eyes. 'And we know what'll happen then.'

'What?' asked Joshi.

'No – *Galtieri*'s too far away,' said Berrister, struggling to shield Graham's body from the spray, then added under his breath, 'I hope.'

Joshi glanced agitatedly behind him. 'They're catching up. Can't you go any faster?'

'We need to lighten our load,' said Sarah, and looked hard at Graham.

'No,' whispered Berrister, holding the Scot more tightly.

'We have to – he'd understand.'

She was not sure he would, given the brazen selfishness of their last conversation, but something had to be done, because even with Drecki dumping the empty fuel tanks and the emergency supplies, the other boats were still gaining. She prised away Berrister's hands and let Graham roll over the pontoon. The waves played with the body for a moment, before it slipped beneath the surface.

Berrister struggled to pull himself together, unwilling to see the same thing happen to Sarah, Mortimer, Joshi and Drecki. They couldn't outrun the whalers, so they needed a change of strategy. He looked around him. To one side was a huge berg, with a thick band of ice trailing from it in both directions. The band was perhaps half a mile wide, and comprised not only a floating slush of smaller pieces, but some the size of trucks. Negotiating a course through it without damaging the propeller would be next to impossible.

'Head for that,' he shouted, trying to make himself heard over the engine's tortured scream.

'No – we'll be sitting ducks in it,' Mortimer yelled back.

Berrister clambered over Sarah and made a grab for the tiller. Mortimer resisted in alarm.

'It's our only chance!' shouted Berrister. 'Trust me.'

Reluctantly, Mortimer relinquished the controls, and Berrister executed a ninety-degree turn that had them all clinging on for dear life. Behind them, the other boats also altered their courses.

'You've just lost us our lead!' gulped Sarah.

She had doubted his sanity when he had left her to walk thirty kilometres across the ice. Should she be wondering about it again now? His manoeuvre had done them no favours at all – the leading boat had put on a burst of speed and was almost parallel to them, one of its occupants already taking aim with a gun.

Berrister stood, trying to ignore the whine of bullets around his head. He had one chance to save everyone – by hitting a specific slab of ice at full speed in the hope that momentum could carry them clear across it into the clearer water beyond. At the same time, he would have to raise the propeller so it didn't snap off in the attempt. If the ploy failed, they would die for certain – drowned or shot.

With gunfire splitting the air around him, and the terrified shrieks of the others ringing in his ears, he raced towards the ice. The second before they hit, he unclipped the engine from its moorings and swung it out of the water. The propeller howled in protest. They zipped up the ice and then sailed through the air in a graceful arc before slapping down on the other side. Again, their momentum carried them forward, ploughing through the slush until it thinned enough for Berrister to lower the propeller. Cautiously, he chugged forward.

Mortimer's attention was fixed on their pursuers. The first hit the ice several seconds later, a short distance to their left. There was a furious grating sound and it slewed wildly, spilling one of its three occupants overboard. Its engine choked, then died. The driver jabbed the ignition button

– by some miracle his propeller was still in one piece – and turned to follow his prey.

'He's leaving his friend in the water!' Mortimer cried in disbelief. 'Doesn't he know that he'll die unless he fishes him out?'

'He doesn't care,' Sarah responded. 'He's probably been offered a reward for catching us, and what's friendship when compared to cash?'

Moments later, the second two boats met the ice. They had seen what had happened to the first, and were more cautious. Even so, an ear-splitting scream from a propeller ended the chase for one of them. Its driver threw up his hands in disgust, while his companions stood to let off a sustained blast of gunfire. There was a nasty crack as one round hit the wooden transom of Berrister's boat, followed by a hiss as another deflated one of the rubber compartments on the pontoon.

'That'll slow us down,' muttered Mortimer.

More bullets zipped towards them, and Berrister flinched, fighting the urge to duck down. He saw an ice-free channel ahead and aimed towards it. Once there, he was able to move faster.

'Two boats, five men,' reported Mortimer tersely. 'And they're gaining on us again.'

Joshi was crying, worn out by the emotional rollercoaster of so many narrow escapes. In a gesture of helpless frustration, he hauled off his parka and lobbed it at them. It fell uselessly into the channel, but the driver of the first boat swerved instinctively to avoid it, and hit the side of the channel. His engine kicked, sending the boat into a 180-degree turn. Before he could correct it, the second inflatable had ploughed into him. He and his passenger were catapulted into the water.

'One boat, three men,' said Mortimer, astonished that Joshi's coat should have wrought such destruction. 'Our luck's changing.'

But he spoke too soon. The last boat had found a different channel, and was speeding up on their right, while their own way was blocked by a flat, solid floe. They were close enough for Berrister to see the grin of triumph on the driver's face. He looked again, thinking his eyes were playing tricks, then stared aghast when he saw they were not.

Joshi's shriek of fright brought him back to his senses.

'Hold on!' he yelled, twisting the throttle open as far as it would go. The tactic had worked once, so why not again? True, this floe was not conveniently shaped like a ramp, but what other option was there? He narrowed his eyes against the wind and took aim.

For the second time, he managed to raise the propeller before the collision, but it was a much rougher ride. The boat caught the edge of the ice with such force that it careened over it in a wild skid that made the world spin in all directions. Then they were across it, and into more ice-choked water beyond.

The last boat – not from *Lena* but her sister ship *Volga* – should have done the sensible thing and conceded defeat, but the thrill of the chase was hot in her driver. He merely copied what Berrister had done, although at a point where the

252

ice was lower and flatter, which meant his skid was even more violent. His boat raced towards them at a terrifying speed, completely out of control.

They were all bracing themselves for the impact when it hit submerged ice and slewed to the right at the very last moment. The tiller was wrenched from the driver's hand, and there was a metallic screech followed by a bang as its propeller sheered off. The enemy Zodiac spun crazily, before fetching up hard against a berg with towering and very unstable blue pinnacles.

There was a brief silence followed by a crack and a tearing groan. The two gunmen flung their arms over their heads as one of the ice spires toppled forwards, narrowly missing them, but the driver didn't flinch. He gave a diabolical smile and raised his weapon. There was no question of mistaken identity. It was, without doubt, Freddy, their missing cook.

Thirteen

There was a moment of total stillness before anyone spoke. Berrister, Sarah, Mortimer, Joshi and Drecki were in one boat, the motor off and the propeller still raised. They were pressed up against one large, flat floe. Freddy and his two compatriots were on the other side of it, with the iceberg towering above them and their engine torn to pieces. It was Freddy who broke the silence.

'Get out of the boat, real slow,' he called, motioning with his gun. 'Do anything dumb, I'll shoot you.'

Joshi gazed at him in disbelief, while Berrister sat heavily on the pontoon, too drained to feel anything at all. No one made a move to do as Freddy had ordered.

'But I thought you saw his body,' Sarah said, her voice unsteady with shock. 'In the Big Crevasse.'

'He saw Dan.' It was Freddy who spoke, his voice gloating. 'I swapped clothes, then left him on the top of the glacier for Rothera to find. If he was down the Big Crevasse, the wind must've blown him there.'

'But why?' asked Mortimer. He had recovered more quickly from his astonishment than the others and had noticed that the berg behind Freddy was still settling from the thump it had received from Freddy's boat. Could he prolong the discussion until more of it collapsed, giving them a chance to escape in the resulting confusion? He determined to try.

'Because I wanted everyone to think I was dead, of course,' replied Freddy contemptuously. 'And it worked – you all thought I was a goner. Now get out of the—'

'We knew there was a traitor,' said Sarah, also quick to regain her composure, although her shock had given way to rage. 'One who told these bastards about the whales, and sabotaged our communications and stole our food. I thought it was Graham, and he thought it was Dan. But it was you.'

Freddy smirked. 'The reason Graham thought it was Dan was because I'd been hinting for a few days that Dan wasn't a team player. I planned from the start to make you think he told the fleet about the blues, see. It's why I shot him – so he couldn't say otherwise. But the whole thing was a massive cock-up and—'

'*You* shot Dan?' breathed Berrister, shocked.

'You betcha. I shot at him and caused an ice fall. I assumed he was under it, but then I saw him on the glacier. God knows how he made it up there. I shot at him again, and found him later, frozen to death.'

'We heard that,' said Mortimer, nodding and hoping to encourage him to talk more. When Freddy stayed silent, he pressed on. 'Gunfire and a scream. However, a superficial glance at a mangled corpse might have fooled Andrew, but it wouldn't have deceived a pathologist.'

'Never mind that,' snapped Freddy, so that Mortimer saw this hadn't occurred to him, and he was none too pleased to have it pointed out. 'Get out of the boat and—'

'Where did you get the gun from?' interrupted Mortimer. He glanced at the ice. It was definitely leaning more now. If he could just keep the discussion going . . . 'They're banned down here.'

'I always carry one,' replied Freddy. 'You never know when it might come in useful. I just shoved it in with the food we shipped down.'

'We found your good-luck hat,' said Joshi. 'And blood . . .'

'I lost the hat chasing Dan, but I don't know

255

about any blood. A penguin's, probably. There are lots of leopard seals around here now, hunting all the chicks that haven't learned how to avoid them. But enough jawing. Get out of—'

'So, you planned all this from the beginning?' pressed Mortimer, a little desperately. 'You lived with us for three months, knowing we would die at the end of it?'

He sensed the others' bemusement at his eagerness to chat with the man who had murdered their friend, and knew Freddy wouldn't keep answering questions for much longer, especially as his two companions were making their disapproval known with agitated tuts and sighs. He only hoped his efforts would pay off in time.

'Of course not,' said Freddy crossly. 'I tried to get you to go on a hike with me, but you wouldn't come. You've only yourselves to blame.'

'If we'd gone to the Byers Peninsula, we'd have seen *Galtieri*,' Berrister pointed out, while Mortimer marvelled that Freddy's plans should have so many snags; the whole thing was indeed a cock-up. 'It wouldn't have made any difference.'

Freddy shrugged irritably. 'Yeah, well, it doesn't matter now, does it?'

'The missing food and the broken generators,' said Mortimer quickly, as one of Freddy's companions tapped the Australian smartly on the shoulder, telling him to end the discussion. 'Was that you?'

'Yeah, but it wasn't my idea. I was told to do it, just in case I couldn't get you to leave.'

'You little shit,' began Sarah angrily.

Mortimer cut across her, giving her a warning jab in the back at the same time. It would be a pity if she antagonised Freddy into shooting them just when the ice was almost ready to drop . . .

'What possessed you to get involved in the first place?' he asked. 'Money?'

Freddy shrugged. 'What else? I've been working with them for years. There are dozens of us, all round the world – pilots, cooks, researchers, all sorts. We get a retainer, and if we spot whales and the hunt's successful, we get a bonus as well. I'll make a fortune this year. Six blues!'

His crony poked him again, harder this time, and Freddy spun around to glare at him. The man glowered back, but was the first to look away. Purely to show him who was in charge, Freddy continued to talk.

'When I saw them, I radioed it in as soon as I got back to camp. Andrew helped. He told me everything I needed to know – how many adults, how many calves. He even lent me a book on them.'

Berrister felt sick. It had been a magical moment, and one he thought he would treasure. He never imagined it would turn into a nightmare.

'So you decided to sacrifice them and us for money,' said Sarah scathingly. 'And ever since your "death", you've been contacting Rothera, telling them that all's well.'

Freddy nodded. 'But then I started having problems with Noddy Taylor and his bloody krill. We had to get *Lena* to ask you about them.'

Mortimer noticed the pinnacle had slipped

257

another few degrees. He eased towards the engine, ready to yank it into life.

'They'll kill *you*, you know,' said Berrister softly. 'You know too much.'

Freddy laughed harshly. 'Bullshit! I'm vital to their plans, because it's *me* who gets to tell Rothera what happened to us.'

'And what's that exactly?' demanded Sarah, full of disdain.

'Mercury in the water supply,' replied Freddy promptly.

Sarah curled her lip. 'No one's going to believe that.'

'They will. Soon, Rothera's going to start getting some pretty weird messages from me. When they come to investigate, all they'll find is corpses and a rusted canister with mercury leaking out. Some previous expedition left it, see, and it got into our drinking water. And we all know that mercury sends people mad.'

'In that case, you can't shoot us, can you?' pounced Sarah triumphantly. 'Because I assure you, Rothera can tell the difference between mercury poisoning and gunshot wounds.'

Freddy was contemptuous in his turn. 'Anyone I kill will be dumped at sea. Rothera will just assume that you wandered off to the glacier and died up there.'

'It still won't work, dickhead,' said Joshi defiantly. 'Because none of us drank Hasim's poisoned beer. There's no mercury inside us.'

Freddy shrugged. 'Then Mr Orlando will come up with something else. He's brilliant – thinks up solutions to everything. But my friends here think we should be getting back, so get out of your boat, nice and slow.'

'No,' said Sarah, folding her arms. 'You'll have to shoot us where we sit. Of course, if you do, you run the risk of hitting the engine or puncturing the pontoon. How will you get back to your nasty associates then?'

Freddy scowled and brought his weapon to bear on Joshi. The student flinched, and quickly scrambled out to stand on the floe. At the same time, one of Freddy's companions did the same, ready to jump into the captured boat and prevent it from drifting away once it was empty.

Berrister was next to alight, which he did deliberately clumsily, falling to his knees in the process. When he stood again, he held a fist-sized piece of hard ice concealed in each hand. Sarah remained sitting, and so did Drecki, shaking their heads stubbornly when Freddy made threatening gestures with his gun. Mortimer stood slowly, feeling the last vestiges of hope fade. The pinnacle had clearly tipped as far as it was going to go. There would be no rescue for them now.

While all eyes were on Mortimer, Berrister hurled a piece of ice with all his might, aiming to send it smashing into Freddy's gloating face. It sailed clean over the Australian's head, but hit the man on the ice. The man staggered with the force of it, lost his balance and fell heavily against the ice behind him. His friend opened fire, even as Berrister moved to hurl his second missile, and Berrister felt a bullet pluck his jacket.

'Stop!' howled Freddy as his crony aimed at

Mortimer and his finger tightened on the trigger. 'You'll puncture the boat.'

But the man had had enough of Freddy's orders. He pulled the trigger, and the gun rattled off a deadly spray of bullets.

Garik's bloodshot eyes took in the bodies and the open porthole. Zurin sat next to Yablokov and refused to move, while Romanov – the only senior officer still well enough to take command – was struggling to restore order on the bridge, although he was pale and stank of vomit. Pandemonium had erupted over the radio, with Orlando screeching orders and demanding to speak to Hasim.

'He'll blame us if the scientists escape,' said one of the guards, a Colombian named Escobar. His face was white with fear.

Garik regarded him blearily. Hasim's team milled around like lost cattle, confused and waiting for someone to tell them what to do.

'He *should* blame you,' slurred Garik. 'Because you *did* let them escape. Worse yet, you let them kill my first mate.'

'No, we didn't,' argued Escobar. 'Because it was Yablokov who said we could nip off for a fag. It was his own fault – he should've kept us around.'

'Right,' said Garik flatly.

'We'd go to help the others catch them,' Escobar went on. 'But we can't, because you don't have any more boats.'

'It wouldn't matter if I did,' said Garik, making up his mind suddenly. 'Because I wouldn't let you go regardless. We're leaving.'

Escobar blinked. 'Leaving what?'

Garik waved an unsteady hand. 'Here. The Antarctic. All of it. We're going home.'

'But you can't – not without Mr Orlando's permission.'

'Watch me,' said Garik, folding his thick arms challengingly.

Escobar was aghast. 'No! *Galtieri* will hunt us down. You heard what happened to the Poles.'

Garik grinned slyly. 'I'll tell Orlando that we're low on fuel, and that if we don't leave now, we won't make it back home. He won't want millions of dollars' worth of whale meat floating unclaimed on the high seas.'

'Now just a minute,' said Escobar, agitated. 'You're not in charge here—'

'I'm the captain,' roared Garik, making him start back in alarm. 'This is *my* ship, and I'll damn well take it where I like.'

'You're drunk! You should be relieved of command.'

Garik leaned towards him. 'Want to try it? No? I thought not. Zurin, shut this man in the after-deck hold, then do the same with the rest of his cronies.'

Zurin clambered to his feet, heartened by this glimpse of the old Garik. Perhaps Yablokov was right, and Hasim *had* been doctoring the captain's vodka with some mind-dulling drugs. The pair of them had emptied the lot down the sink earlier, in the hope of bringing Garik back to them. Maybe it had worked. Garik had Escobar by the scruff of his neck, and certainly looked more like himself.

'Well?' Garik demanded, when the helmsman made no further move to obey him. 'What are you waiting for?'

'Can't do it,' Zurin said. 'They've got guns.'

'None of which are loaded,' said Garik with another sly grin. 'I saw to it myself. Go – before they realise what's happening.'

'The hold?' asked Zurin, to be sure, and speaking over Escobar's wails of horror. 'With the last of the cargo?'

Garik nodded. 'It's the most secure place on the ship, and we don't want them breaking out and making a nuisance of themselves on the journey home. It'll be cold and uncomfortable, but they'll be safe enough.'

'Don't bet on it,' muttered Zurin savagely.

Even as the gunman turned his weapon on him, Mortimer was yanking the starter cord on the engine. He knew he wouldn't survive now, but he could do one thing before he died – make sure Freddy didn't either. The motor roared into life, and he twisted the throttle, zipping around the floe and aiming directly at the Australian. Bullets flew from both Freddy and his friend, although their aim was wild and most went wide of their targets.

Then the pinnacle began to topple at last, loosened partly by the man who had fallen into it. There was a sharp crack and down it came, burying him beneath it. Wrongly interpreting the sound as an attack from behind, Freddy and his crony whipped around and peppered the ice with gunfire. More of it fell, capsizing Freddy's boat

262

and sending both men flying. The second gunman disappeared into the churning water, and Freddy was sent sprawling across the floe.

'Hold on!' yelled Mortimer, as the sea around them turned into a treacherous maelstrom of waves. Drecki bounced once and was gone. With a cry, Sarah plunged her arm into the frigid water to grab him, but all she could feel was ice.

Water also gushed across the floe. Berrister was swept along with it, but fetched up against a small ridge, which just stopped him from being washed over the edge. Dazed, he lay with one hand dangling into the sea.

Freddy and Joshi were on a higher part of the floe, so only lost their footing. Both noticed something at the same time: Freddy's gun, which lay between them. They lunged, and there followed a fierce tussle.

Mortimer turned the boat and raced towards them, while Sarah scrambled into the bow, ready to leap off and go to Joshi's aid. The moment their boat touched the floe, she jumped onto it and began to run. Seeing her coming, Freddy resorted to desperate tactics: he head-butted Joshi, whose grip on the weapon loosened. With a yell of victory, Freddy ripped the gun away. Sarah stumbled to a standstill as Freddy pointed it at her, clenching her fists, and torn between anger and despair. They had been so close!

Defeated, Joshi slumped to his knees, while Freddy retreated to the far edge of the floe, so he could cover them all at the same time with the gun. For a moment, everything was still. Mortimer was in the boat, its engine idling; Joshi

263

and Sarah were in the middle of the floe; and Freddy and Berrister were at the edge, quite close to each other, but too far for Berrister to lunge at him without being shot first.

Berrister's hand still trailed in the water, and with a shock he felt something brush against it. He drew it up sharply, knowing exactly what had nuzzled at it. He rolled over, away from the edge, his mind working furiously on a final, desperate plan.

'You can't do it, can you, Freddy?' taunted Sarah, regarding him in utter contempt. 'You couldn't kill us the night before *Lena* arrived, even though it would've been better for your employers, and you can't do it now. You're a filthy coward!'

'Yeah?' sneered Freddy furiously. 'Well just watch me—'

'Don't worry, Sarah,' interrupted Berrister. 'He'll be dead in a minute – his bit of the floe is too thin to hold him.'

Sarah shot him a withering glance as Freddy immediately took several steps to his left, to a place where the floe was lower and smoother. Berrister held his breath. Would it work? Had Freddy moved far enough?

'I killed Dan,' the Australian was sneering at Sarah. 'And I can kill you.'

'*Did* you kill Dan?' she asked scathingly. 'Or did he die of exposure? You're pathetic! You were planning to let your friends do it, weren't you? Because you don't have the guts.'

Freddy took aim just as a dark shape appeared in the sea behind him. There was a spurt of

264

movement, and he was suddenly flat on his stomach, feet knocked from under him. The gun skittered from his grasp.

Startled, he turned to see what was happening, and was rewarded by the sight of a large reptilian head looking back at him. The leopard seal lunged again, teeth closing around one tantalisingly close ankle. Then it pulled and Freddy began to slide towards the water. Terror suffused his face as he clawed at the ice, frantically trying to save himself.

'Help me!' he screamed. 'It's got my leg!'

'Get to the boat!' shouted Berrister to the others. 'From under the ice, we all look like penguins.'

He did not need to remind them that leopard seals ate penguins. Sarah and Joshi raced towards the inflatable, almost capsizing it in their desperation to jump in. They stood, transfixed by the sight of Freddy being dragged inch by relentless inch towards the water.

'Sit down,' ordered Berrister, following them more sedately. 'Or it'll be in here with us.'

They sat quickly, then looked back at Freddy. At the last moment, the Australian managed to kick free of the seal and crawl back on the floe, where he lay gasping for breath. Berrister could have warned him that he still wasn't safe. But he didn't.

'You can't leave me here!' Freddy screeched, as Mortimer turned the boat towards the open sea. 'Come b—'

His words ended in a scream, as the seal shot out of the water and grabbed his leg again. With a careless flick of its powerful head, it sent him spinning across the floe and into the sea. He vanished with a splash. Moments later, he broke the surface some distance away, howling in pain and fright. He was jerked underwater again, only to emerge spluttering and coughing a second time.

'God!' said Joshi unsteadily, unable to look away. 'Should we—'

'No,' said Mortimer shortly. 'Now let's go to Deception.'

Berrister was awakened from a restless doze by the sound of the motor sputtering into silence. He sat up, every muscle aching from cold and tiredness. The little boat wallowed, made heavy by the ankle-deep water that slopped in the bottom. The waves were larger than they had been earlier, and the wind was getting up. He hoped they were not in for another storm, as they were unlikely to survive it in a Zodiac that had so many bullet-punctured compartments.

He looked for Drecki before recalling with a pang of grief that the geologist was gone, lost when the ice pinnacle had fallen. Sarah thought he had been shot first, which explained why he had failed to hang on to the safety ropes.

There were just four of them left now: Mortimer trying to restart the engine; Joshi shaking the fuel tank, refusing to believe it was empty; Sarah setting the oars in the rowlocks; and Berrister.

'Where are we?' he asked, sitting up and scanning the horizon. He could see nothing but waves in all directions, some topped with white horses.

'Not sure,' replied Mortimer tersely. 'Unfortunately,

266

we made poor time because we're carrying so much water. We've been heavy on fuel as well.'

'We won't sink, will we?' asked Joshi in a small voice.

'Not if we keep bailing,' replied Mortimer, not entirely truthfully.

Berrister looked at the seawater that sloshed back and forth, and wondered how long Mortimer's boots and their cupped hands would cope if a storm did blow in.

'Not much of a rescue, was it?' he said apologetically.

'It was lacking in one or two details,' acknowledged Mortimer. 'Like a viable escape plan. But better this than what Hasim had in mind. At least he can't use our bodies to further his nasty plans.'

'He won't be doing much of anything any more,' said Berrister. 'Not if you gave him a whole ampoule of ketamine.'

'Good,' said Sarah harshly.

'How far from Deception are we?' Berrister stood cautiously, trying to see over the tops of the waves. There was nothing but sea ahead.

'No idea,' said Sarah. 'But I suggest we save our breath for rowing, because we won't last long out here in a gale. Geoff and Joshi can go first, while you and I bail and watch the compass.'

They did as she suggested, and for a while no one spoke, concentrating instead on forcing tired muscles to do what was needed. Berrister's rest had helped him, but his stomach ached from hunger and he couldn't recall when he had last eaten. The crackers Drecki had shared with him, perhaps, although events were such a blur in his mind that he had no idea when that had been.

'I thought they'd shot you on that floe,' said Sarah softly, breaking into his thoughts. 'When I saw you fall . . .'

Berrister had thought the same, and an inspection of his jacket now showed just how narrow an escape he had had – a bullet had passed clean through his pocket, and the watch Sarah had lent him was nothing but a mass of shards.

'Oops,' he said guiltily, recalling that he'd promised to look after it.

'It doesn't matter.'

'But you said someone important gave it to you.'

He supposed it was a partner, but then realised that he didn't know if she had one. All his conversations with her tended to revolve around work.

'It *was* someone important,' declared Sarah haughtily. 'I bought it for myself.'

He was tempted to laugh, but at that point Joshi began to tell him all that had happened since they had parted company. He had already done it once, but Berrister had still been in shock over Drecki's death, and it was clear that he hadn't been listening.

'So you were right to think that someone from the camp was involved,' Berrister said to Sarah when Joshi had finished.

She nodded, grateful that he didn't mention that her chief suspect had been Graham. The

268

Scot's unappealing selfishness was repellent, but he had been innocent of treachery.

'Freddy!' spat Joshi. 'Who shared my tent, ate our food, laughed at our jokes and pretended to be our friend.'

'Don't take it personally,' said Sarah briskly. 'He worked with the Poles before us – he'd have betrayed them just as easily.'

'Toxic waste brought down and whale meat carried back,' said Mortimer, after a brief silence when they all reflected on what Freddy had been to them. 'That's the business of the Southern Exploring Company.'

'Most countries have a protocol for getting rid of radioactive by-products,' said Berrister. 'They have to account for every gram of the stuff to the international community.'

'Which means it comes from places where nuclear activity *isn't* monitored,' surmised Mortimer. 'Some rogue state. Or some rogue group – terrorists are getting ever more sophisticated. Regardless, we've got to report it as soon as we can, as it means someone dubious might have weapons of mass destruction.'

'Perhaps the Southern Exploring Company *is* a terrorist organisation,' suggested Joshi. 'It makes sense – all those guns and soldier-types.'

'Unfortunately, I think we might soon be in a position to ask them,' said Berrister softly. 'Because they're right behind us.'

Fourteen

Galtieri steamed steadily towards them, while Berrister, Sarah, Mortimer and Joshi watched with a weary sense of helplessness. Would they be taken on board and poisoned after all, so the Southern Exploring Company could cover its tracks? Or would they just be shot to ensure their silence this time?

'No,' said Sarah, gritting her teeth. 'Not now. Row!'

'Why?' asked Mortimer resignedly. 'They'll catch us anyway.'

'We are *not* sitting back and giving up,' shouted Sarah. 'The lives of thousands – maybe millions – might be at risk. We *have* to keep trying.'

Mortimer and Joshi exchanged a glance and took up their oars, but with every stroke, *Galtieri* loomed closer. Mortimer's face was soon red with effort, while Joshi was tiring, so their boat veered to the left as he failed to match his stronger partner. Sarah knelt in the stern and clamoured encouragement, while Berrister bailed furiously in an effort to lighten the load.

Figures clustered around *Galtieri*'s bow, pointing forward. At first, Berrister thought they were gesturing at their quarry, but their attention seemed to be on something further away. He stood unsteadily, expecting to see an expanse of foam-flecked waves again, but there was something else, too: black cliffs with surf surging at their feet.

'Deception!' he shouted. 'We're almost at Deception.'

'So what?' gasped Mortimer bitterly. 'We can't make it there now.'

He was right: *Galtieri* was so close that they could see the rust on her hull. But even as Berrister pulled a shard of Sarah's watch from his pocket – the only thing he had that could be of remote use as a weapon – the warship changed direction, peeling off to the right. At first, he thought he was mistaken, but she was definitely turning.

'They're giving up,' he said, bewildered. 'They're going away.'

Mortimer and Joshi stopped rowing, and they all watched while *Galtieri* completed her turn and headed back the way she had come.

Joshi and Sarah began to laugh, while Mortimer slumped over his oar, grinning in relief. Berrister did not share their relief. He had been through too much over the last few days to have his hopes raised so easily, and there was something about the abrupt abandonment of the chase that did not feel right.

'Come on,' he said, grabbing Mortimer's oar and indicating that Sarah was to take Joshi's.

'In a minute,' objected Mortimer. 'Just give us a second for—'

'No, now,' said Berrister urgently. 'I don't like this.'

'But it's—' began Joshi.

'We need to make for Neptune's Bellows,'

interrupted Berrister. 'It's where we'll find the tourist ships – if they're still there.'

'They will be,' said Sarah. 'They *have* to be.'

'There's one,' yelled Joshi, standing unsteadily for a better view.

They all stood, clinging to each other for balance as the Zodiac tipped and dipped on the waves.

'That's not a tourist ship!' cried Mortimer in dismay, his shoulders sagging and his good humour punctured like a balloon. 'That's another bloody whaler!'

'So that's why *Galtieri* gave up,' whispered Sarah bitterly, as the new ship ploughed towards them. 'To let someone else in her fleet deal with us.'

She slumped in defeat. Berrister put an arm around her shoulders.

'We can row the other way,' he said when she began to cry. It had been her courage and determination that had kept him going, and her resignation now was difficult to bear.

'We were so close,' she sobbed. 'And to fail now, with Deception within swimming distance . . .'

It was a good deal further than Berrister could swim, but he kept his thoughts to himself. He took her oar and rowed alone, unwilling to be taken without at least some show of defiance. The others watched, but made no attempt to help. Behind them, the ship loomed closer, her bow rising and falling with the waves, near enough that he could hear the sea swishing along her sides.

'*Novosibirsk*,' he muttered, painstakingly deciphering the Cyrillic letters. He stopped rowing and stared. 'That *is* a tourist ship! They invited Dan to go with them, to lecture to their passengers. He was seriously considering it as a way to get down here until I offered him a place with us.'

Sarah's head jerked up and a slow smile spread across her face. 'How could we have been so stupid? It doesn't even look like the whalers. Hey! Hey!'

She began waving frantically, although it was clear that they had been seen. *Novosibirsk* gave a short blast on her horn and decreased speed. As Berrister manoeuvred the Zodiac towards her, a hatch opened and two crewmen appeared. Friendly hands reached down to help them aboard.

Novosibirsk was no comfortable cruise liner, but an old Sorokin-class ice-breaker, one of a fleet once used along the Siberian coast. The Russians had newer, more powerful icebreakers now, so the Sorokin-class ships were leased out to tour operators, spending four months a year ferrying rich westerners to the far south.

Red-coated tourists came to watch the newcomers arrive, clustering around them and getting in the way as they jostled to take photographs. Most were in their sixties or seventies – energetic, confident people who had made their fortunes and were now ready to spend them.

Berrister was unnerved by the click and whir of expensive cameras and the babble of questions,

273

and was glad when he and the others were ushered into an office. It was oppressively hot after the chill outside, and smelled of fried food. Two men waited there.

'I'm Leonid Ivanov, the staff captain – that's second in command in layman's terms,' said one in accented but fluent English. He was a tall, angular man with a heavily lined face. He indicated his companion, an overweight Englishman with untidy grey hair and vague eyes. 'And this is Robin Standwick, the expedition leader. That means he oversees the landings and—'

'We urgently need to send a message to Rothera,' interrupted Sarah curtly, unwilling to listen to polite introductions when every passing minute worked to the fleeing criminals' benefit. 'We'll explain afterwards.'

'It really is a case of life and death,' put in Mortimer, aware that needless asperity was unlikely to get them what they wanted.

Pursing his lips, Ivanov led the way to the bridge, the others trailing behind him.

'Is anyone else out there?' he asked. 'If so, we need to pick them up now. There's a storm blowing in.'

'No, we're alone,' said Mortimer. 'Have you heard Rothera trying to contact us?'

'We don't eavesdrop on the bases,' replied Ivanov. 'They wouldn't like it. Is that where you're from? Rothera? You're a long way from home.'

'Got lost, I expect,' said Standwick genially. 'Easily done. Happened to me once or twice.'

Ivanov shot him a withering glance. 'I'm sure it has.'

Tourists greeted them like old friends as they hurried up staircases and along corridors. Most were North Americans, with a smattering of British, South Africans and Germans. Joshi asked how many people were on board.

'About a hundred, I think,' replied Standwick. 'Give or take a couple of dozen.'

Ivanov corrected him crisply. 'Eighty-seven passengers and fifty-nine crew.'

'The other ship,' said Berrister. 'The whaler. Did you see her?'

'Whaler?' echoed Standwick, regarding him askance. 'There isn't any whaling down here – it's illegal.'

'There aren't any other ships in the vicinity,' added Ivanov. 'We're the last of the tourist expeditions this year. The nearest vessel now is *Worsley*, but she's still south of the Antarctic Circle.'

'But you must've seen *Galtieri*,' insisted Joshi. 'She was right behind us.'

'I assure you, no one else is here,' replied Ivanov firmly.

'Hasim told us that *Lena* has unusually powerful radar,' said Mortimer to no one in particular. 'Which means her sister ships probably do, too. They must have picked up *Novosibirsk*, although she didn't see them.'

'I suppose Deception might create a shadow in which they could hide,' mused Berrister. 'It would explain why they abandoned the chase so abruptly.'

'You think a whaler was chasing you?' Ivanov stopped walking to eye them uneasily. 'Perhaps

275

our doctor should check you over before we do anything else. It's—'

'There's nothing wrong with us,' stated Sarah sharply, indicating that he was to keep going. 'Now hurry.'

But the captain, a calm, competent Russian with wavy silver hair, declined to let them loose on the airwaves until he had some inkling of what they intended to say. He invited them to his quarters to tell their tale, but his expression grew more incredulous with every word they spoke. Berrister let the others do the talking, exhaustion overwhelming him now he was safe at last. He sat on the overstuffed sofa in his filthy, sea-soaked clothes and closed his eyes.

When Berrister woke, the first thing he saw was Sarah. She was hovering over him agitatedly, and her fraught expression made him sit up in alarm, anticipating bad news.

'Good, you're awake at last,' she said, although he was tempted to remark that he wouldn't be if she hadn't disturbed him by looming. 'I was beginning to get worried. You've been asleep for hours and I need to talk to you.'

He sat up, blinking to clear his sluggish wits. 'Did you contact Rothera?'

He had a vague memory of being shown to a cabin after their interview with the captain, but he had been too exhausted to register anything other than the bed. He still wore most of his outside clothes, and the meal that had been brought to him sat untouched and congealing on a tray.

Sarah, by contrast, had showered and was dressed in borrowed clothes – blue jeans and an Armani sweatshirt. Her hair was pulled back into a plait, accentuating her finely shaped face, and he was suddenly aware that she was a very attractive woman. He wondered why he'd never noticed before.

'We did, but they didn't believe us.' She stood, and began to pace restlessly. 'Apparently, Freddy had radioed Vince an hour before, and gabbled about whales, toxic waste and mercury in the water.'

'It couldn't have been Freddy – he was dead by then. And Vince will know it wasn't him. He's not stupid.'

'That's what we thought, but then the bloody captain put his oar in – said he'd picked us up from the middle of the sea with a tale of being chased by a ship that *he* hadn't seen, the implication being that we're raving mad. There's a doctor on board, and he had the gall to tell Rothera that we're delusional!'

'Vince will know we're not.'

'Apparently, Freddy's been claiming for days that we've been acting weird, and the story we told . . . well, it does sound too crazy to be true. The Southern Exploring Company is winning, you know. I thought we'd beaten them, but we haven't.'

'I wonder . . .' Berrister faltered, but then pressed on. 'Freddy mentioned that the Southern Exploring Company has agents all over the world . . .'

Sarah's eyes widened in alarm, and she lowered

277

her voice. 'You mean someone here might be in their pay?'

'Or Vince. It would explain why all Freddy's broadcasts were accepted so readily.'

Sarah gazed at him in despair. 'What are we going to do, Andrew? We can't just sit here.'

Berrister shrugged. 'If Rothera won't believe us, one of the other bases will. I assume the captain plans to drop us off on King George soon.'

'Yes, at Arctowski with the Poles, but not until the day after tomorrow. In the interim, we're to be their guests, pissing about with touristy things. We're at Yankee Harbour now, looking at pretty rocks. By the time we reach King George, the Southern Exploring Company will be long gone.'

'Then contact Arctowski – they'll believe us when we explain why they've lost contact with *Jacek*.'

'We did, but they say *Jacek* would never visit Byers without a permit, and insist on continuing the search for her on the other side of Greenwich Island. This is so frustrating! I don't know what to do. Poor Geoff nearly went apoplectic trying to convince Vince. When he saw he was wasting his time, he took himself off to the bar in disgust.'

'Where is he now?'

'Still there – people keep buying him drinks. Joshi's with him.'

Berrister looked around at the cabin. It was basic and functional, although spotlessly clean. Two life jackets lay on the bed opposite, unfastened and ready to wear.

'Did you pull those out?' he asked.

She nodded. 'I keep thinking we might need them. *Galtieri* blew *Jacek* up. What's to stop them from attacking *Novosibirsk* as well?'

'*Jacek* was a tiny ship that had lied about her location. *Novosibirsk* is much bigger, and has a company tracking her progress. Nothing else will happen to us, Sarah.'

'I'm not so sure. I have an awful feeling that they're out there biding their time.'

Berrister took her hands in his. 'They can't, not now we've told our story – if they do, they'll effectively prove us right. And when we get home . . . well, we won't rest until they pay for what they've done.'

They were silent for a while, then she said, 'I'm sorry I doubted you – about walking across the island, I mean. It's just that after your accident . . . well, I thought you'd lost your edge.'

Berrister looked uncomfortable. 'It's not something I like discussing.'

'Sorry, I didn't mean to pry. It must have been terrible.'

Berrister winced. 'It wasn't actually, although I know that's what everyone thinks. The reason I don't talk about it is because it's embarrassing.'

'Embarrassing?'

'I went out alone without a radio and fell down a tiny crevasse. I didn't hurt myself, but its walls were so slippery that I couldn't get out. It was so stupid – like drowning in a cup of tea or bleeding to death from a paper cut. After three days, Dan chanced by. He gave me his hand and that was all I needed to escape.'

'He kept your secret well. Even Geoff couldn't prise it out of him.'

'He was a good man. I'm glad Freddy didn't live to profit from his murder.'

'Is that why you didn't warn Freddy about the leopard seal?'

Berrister didn't reply.

Although it was late, Sarah insisted on using the radio again, and was so belligerent about it that the captain hastily acceded to her 'request'. Vince greeted her coolly, and when she asked for Noddy Taylor, he reported tersely that the biologist had left for home.

Not sure whether to believe him, she tried the Americans at Palmer, but was informed that they never interfered with other bases' personnel. Finally, she managed to raise Arctowski, where the communications officer pretended not to speak English. Berrister used his idiosyncratic Polish, but the station commander came on air and ordered him to stop wasting their time.

'Vince got to them,' said Sarah bitterly. 'He must have told them that we've been at the mercury.'

At midnight, they were joined by Mortimer and Joshi, both of whom stank of alcohol. Joshi wore a silly grin on his face, but Mortimer's mood was dark.

'Noddy Taylor hasn't left Rothera,' he said bitterly. 'Vince is lying.'

Sarah lowered her voice. 'Or in the pay of the Southern Exploring Company.'

'Then what about the communications officers

at Palmer, Arctowski, Artigas, Frei, Ferraz and Bellingshausen?' slurred Joshi. 'Are they all corrupt, too? Freddy did say the whalers had dozens of operatives all around the world.'

'Well, my ex-wife won't be one of them,' said Mortimer. 'And I emailed her all the details of our adventures a couple of hours ago. She'll make sure the story gets out. In a contest between this Orlando and her, I'd back her every time. She'll have him for breakfast.'

Berrister hoped he'd been more sober then than he was now, or it wouldn't be just the bases that didn't believe them. 'We're moving,' he said, feeling the engines start up.

Mortimer glanced at the clock. 'Ivanov said we'd be leaving for Half Moon Island about now.'

'There's an Argentine station on Half Moon,' said Sarah with sudden hope.

'It won't be occupied this late in the season,' said Berrister gloomily.

Sarah went to the window and stared out into the darkness. 'I suppose we should be thankful we're alive – twenty-four hours ago, I'd have been delirious with delight to know that we'd be here. But I can't stop thinking about Dan and Lisa.'

'And Drecki,' said Berrister.

'And Graham,' added Joshi.

'Yes,' conceded Sarah softly. 'And Graham.'

Novosibirsk did not ride well in rough weather. Her rounded hull, which allowed her to break ice, also meant that she had an unpleasant

281

corkscrew motion if there was any kind of swell. In choppy seas, she bucked and twisted like a wild thing. Berrister went back to bed, because it was easier to lie down than try to stay upright, but he hadn't been asleep long when someone climbed in next to him. It was Sarah. She felt warm, and smelled of clean hair and soap. He slipped his arms around her and fell asleep again, comforted by her closeness.

They were awoken early the next morning by an urgent hammering on the door. Before they could move, Mortimer burst in. His eyebrows shot up in astonishment when he saw them together.

'It isn't what you think,' said Sarah quickly. 'I was cold.'

Mortimer waved the feeble explanation away. 'We were wrong about the Argentines on Half Moon – their field station *is* still open, and some are on their way here right now.'

'They are?' asked Sarah, sitting up. 'Why?'

'Free booze, a hot shower and a change of scenery,' replied Mortimer briskly. 'Come on – we need to get to them before someone tells them that we're all off our rockers. Hurry!'

He left at a run. Sarah had dressed at some point during the night – probably for the same reason that she had ensured the life jackets were within easy reach – and she jumped out of bed and raced after him. Berrister threw on some clothes and followed, but decided not to interrupt when he saw Sarah, Mortimer and Joshi in the dining room in earnest conversation with two Argentines. He went to the bridge instead, thinking to pester Vince again.

The door to the bridge was closed. Access was either via inputting a code into a keypad or by buzzing for someone to open the door from inside. Berrister knew the code was 99999, because he had watched Ivanov punch it in the previous day. He was about to do likewise when he heard raised voices within. The captain was arguing with someone. Then there was a loud thump and a cry. Startled, Berrister recoiled, wondering what kind of debates the master permitted on his bridge.

Seconds later, came the sound of breaking glass. The captain's voice, raised in a roar of outrage, was cut short by a sharp crack. Berrister's mouth went dry. He had heard enough gunfire during the last few days to recognise it now. Bewildered and panic-stricken, he ducked quickly into a room marked 'Crew Only'.

He was just in time. Even as his door closed, the one to the bridge was hauled open, and someone hurtled along the corridor and down the stairs. Peering through the crack, Berrister glimpsed a man wearing a life jacket over a coat that was wet from spray. Clearly, he was one of the Argentines who had made the journey from the station. Moments later, he hurried back.

'It's alright, Mr Orlando,' he reported as he pushed open the bridge door. 'No one's about. All the passengers are in the dining room being entertained by the others, while the crew are busy with their duties.'

'I'll shoot you myself if you do something like that again,' snapped someone, presumably Mr

283

Orlando. His accent was clipped and impossible to identify. 'We'd have had a mass panic on our hands if you'd been overheard. Next time, use a silencer.'

'Yes, sir.'

With a growing sense of horror, Berrister realised he had been wrong – the Southern Exploring Company had not given up on the scientists who were trying to expose them. They had been listening to the radio chatter between them and the bases, and knew the incredible story had not been believed. And they intended to keep it that way. He was sure the smashing sound had been the communications equipment being destroyed. There would be no further contact with anyone, because *Novosibirsk* was about to have a dreadful accident.

Fifteen

Muffled voices cut through Berrister's tumbling thoughts. The room in which he hid – a cupboard for spare equipment – was separated from the bridge only by a thin partition. By pressing his ear to the wall, he could hear very well what was being said within. Fortunately, the language was English.

'It won't work,' Ivanov was insisting. A tremor in his voice revealed his fear. 'If the ship they're on mysteriously disappears, everyone will know they were telling the truth.'

'Not after *Novosibirsk*'s final message in which

I – a crewman – scream that they entered the engine room in their mad delirium and caused an explosion. You'll be taking on water fast – too fast for anyone to be rescued.'

'Please, no,' begged Ivanov. 'There must be another way.'

'There isn't,' said Orlando briskly. 'Not now your captain and these officers made it necessary for us to shoot them.'

'I'll say the scientists did it.' Ivanov sounded desperate. 'We can send them ashore with you. There's no need for more violence on the ship.'

'Tempting,' said Orlando, while Berrister agonised, wondering what to do. Run and warn the others? Listen to more? 'But no. You're a witness, you see, and it's those we're trying to eradicate.'

'No one will believe that the scientists blew up the engine room,' shouted Ivanov, beside himself with terror. 'This is a stupid plan.'

'They *will* believe it,' countered Orlando. 'Because the scientists have been drinking mercury-tainted water, and mercury causes brain damage. They're not rational any more, as Rothera and the other bases will testify – they all heard their wild claims.'

Berrister could almost feel Ivanov's bewilderment. 'But if everyone knows they're mad, why are you here? Why not just let them spout tales that no one accepts?'

'Because we're careful,' replied Orlando. 'And because we work for some very dangerous regimes and organisations, which don't tolerate mistakes that put them at risk. They—'

He stopped speaking when someone else entered the bridge.

'The detonators are set, sir,' reported a new voice. 'The first will blow in . . . thirty-seven minutes, and this tub will go down so fast that no one will make it to the lifeboats. Shall I warn the men?'

'The four of us are the only ones who will leave, Enrique. The others will give their lives for the cause.'

'Sir?' asked Enrique. He sounded as startled as Berrister felt.

'Whisking the "Argentines" away suddenly will raise eyebrows, and we want to maintain the illusion that all's well until the detonators blow. We can't risk having survivors.'

'Please,' came Ivanov's voice. 'Don't destroy the ship. I can make sure—'

There was a dull thud, followed by the sound of a body dropping to the floor. Berrister leaned his head against the wall in despair. What could he – one unarmed man – do against criminals so ruthless that even the lives of their accomplices counted for nothing?

Moments later, Orlando began speaking on the radio, putting an edge of fear into his voice. It sounded contrived to Berrister, but he suspected all anyone else would hear were the words.

'Mayday! Mayday!' Orlando screeched. 'This is *Novosibirsk*. We've had a major explosion in our engine room and we're taking on water fast. For God's sake help us!'

There was a confused crackle as two or three

listeners responded at once. One won out over the others.

'This is the US Coast Guard ship *South Star*. What is your exact location?'

'Half Moon Island!' howled Orlando. 'We're listing to port . . . we're rolling over . . .'

'Our ETA is two hours ten minutes,' said the Coast Guard officer. 'Can you hold out until then?'

'Christ,' said Orlando to his men in his normal voice. 'That's close. How come we never picked her up on radar?'

'Must be in a shadow.' Enrique's voice was taut. 'Shit! Our intel said *South Star* was way out west. What's she doing here? And how's it going to look if she tracks us speeding away from a maritime disaster?'

'If we can't see her, she can't see us,' said Orlando decisively. 'We'll just hug the coast until we can make a clean run for it.'

'*Novosibirsk*,' called the Coast Guard. 'I repeat: can you hold out until we arrive?'

'Can we, Enrique?' asked Orlando.

'Not a chance. In an hour, there'll be nothing here but wreckage.'

'We're abandoning ship now,' shrieked Orlando into the handset. 'The scientists . . . they killed the captain. One's got an axe . . . he's attacking the lifeboats . . .'

There was a thud of bullets, and the transmission ended along with the radio.

'Right, let's go,' said Orlando.

'We have thirty-four minutes,' said Enrique. 'And ten seconds.'

The door to the bridge opened and footsteps padded along the corridor outside. Then all was silent. Berrister peered out of the storeroom. The corridor was empty, so he punched the code into the keypad and pushed open the door.

He was greeted by a scene of carnage. The captain, Ivanov and three others were dead, their blood spattered everywhere. Consoles had been smashed, and something hung drunkenly across the window outside – some part of the communications array, which meant that not only were the radios defunct, but Inmarsat, the satellite communication system, was gone as well.

A faint buzz drew his attention to the window. Two Zodiacs were speeding away – Orlando and the lucky three he had decided not to leave on the doomed ship.

Berrister continued to gaze around in stunned horror until the tick of the clock on the wall reminded him that time was passing. He now had exactly thirty minutes to evacuate the ship before it exploded. Blindly, he began to press buttons and flip switches, in the hope that one would sound an alarm, but nothing happened. Then he saw the microphone that allowed messages to be relayed over the ship. Trying to control the panic in his voice, he depressed the 'speak' button, relieved beyond measure when he heard the metallic ping that told him it was working.

'All passengers and crew assemble at their muster stations immediately. Officers report to the bridge. This is not a drill.'

Dropping the microphone, he ran for the stairs. The surviving officers could oversee the evacuation when they arrived – the bodies on the bridge would be explanation enough. Meanwhile he would try to find the detonator and lob it overboard before it did any harm.

He had just reached the bottom of the stairs, and was debating which way to go when a door was wrenched open and a tall, bearded man rushed out. Berrister vaguely recalled being introduced to him the previous night – the chief engineer, Arkady Polushin.

'Did you make that announcement?' he demanded angrily. 'What do you think you're playing at? And where's the captain?'

'Dead,' replied Berrister tersely. 'And the "Argentines" are imposters. They're going to blow up your ship.'

Polushin regarded him askance. 'What are you—'

'Look!' Berrister stabbed his finger towards a window. 'They're leaving.'

'No, they're still in the dining room, talking to the passengers. They—' Polushin stopped abruptly. 'What's *she* doing here? She's a warship.'

'She' was *Galtieri*, nosing out from behind a headland, although it was not long before she slunk out of sight again. Doubtless, Orlando had ordered her back, lest she alert someone on *Novosibirsk* to the fact that all was not well.

But Polushin still hesitated, so Berrister grabbed his arm and hauled him to the bridge, hating the loss of vital moments, but not knowing how else to convince him. Polushin

289

gaped in disbelief at what he saw. Then Sarah and Mortimer arrived.

'God, no!' breathed Mortimer, grasping the situation at once. 'They're here?'

Berrister nodded. 'I said the real Argentines would be gone by now. And *Novosibirsk*'s set to explode in twenty-six minutes – which is two hours before the US Coast Guard arrives. You *have* to get everyone off. I'll try to find the detonator.'

Two more officers appeared, and Berrister felt his stomach churn in despair, anticipating more time wasted in explanations, but Polushin had seen enough. He barked the signal to abandon ship, and ordered his people to ready the lifeboats.

'Come with me,' he ordered Berrister, Sarah and Mortimer, turning and leading the way at a rapid lick down steep stairwells and functional 'Crew Only' hallways.

'D'you know what the detonator looks like?' panted Mortimer, struggling to keep up.

'No,' replied Berrister. 'But it must be quite big if it's going to sink a ship in a few minutes.'

'No – it must be quite small,' argued Polushin. 'The one who asked to look around the engine room – he only had a backpack.'

'And you let him in?' asked Sarah in disbelief.

'He was a fellow engineer,' replied Polushin shortly. 'Of course I did.'

'Hey, Ramon!' yelled Mortimer as they tore past one of the lifeboat stations. 'Orlando has deserted you, so unless you help us, you're dead, too. What does the detonator look like?'

The bogus Argentine's only reply was to dart towards the nearest lifeboat, pushing others out of the way to reach it. He was pale and frightened, but not shocked, suggesting employee loyalty was not one of Orlando's strong points. The moment he was aboard, he began to hand-winch it over the side, ignoring the protesting cries of the crew. Two of his friends leapt over the rail to join him, but one misjudged the distance and fell shrieking into the water below. His terror transferred to the passengers, who surged forward in alarm. The crew fought to impose order.

'What's happening?' demanded Joshi, appearing from the milling crowd.

'Get in a lifeboat,' ordered Berrister. 'The Coast Guard's coming – you *have* to tell them that the Southern Exploring Company did this. Do you understand? You can't fail.'

Joshi nodded, so Berrister ran to catch up with the others.

'Twenty minutes,' gasped Sarah. 'By my reckoning.'

'We'll search for fifteen,' said Mortimer. 'If we don't find it, we'll leave together. Agreed?'

They reached the engine room, where Berrister took one look at the complex jumble of pipes, cables, boxes and spare parts, and knew their task was hopeless. He had no idea where to start.

Polushin briefed the four crewmen who hurried towards him, finishing with, 'It could be anywhere, but near the fuel lines or tanks is a good guess – a small explosion that will lead to a bigger one.'

291

'I hope it's not nuclear,' muttered Mortimer. 'Orlando works for regimes and organisations that have them, doesn't he? Perhaps he bought a couple with him, for occasions such as this.'

It wasn't a comforting thought. 'Seventeen minutes,' said Sarah tersely. 'We'd better hurry.'

But it was impossible. There were so many places that a small device could be hidden, and the engine room was so huge, that it quickly became obvious that they were wasting their time. They soldiered on anyway, unwilling to give up until they had done all they humanly could.

'There's only one thing we can do now,' said Polushin, when Mortimer shouted that there were only four minutes left. 'Contain the explosion.'

'How?' asked Sarah shakily.

'Seal the engine room doors and hatches. The blast will destroy it, but it will give us a little more time to evacuate everyone.'

His crew raced to obey a furious flood of orders, while Berrister, Mortimer and Sarah continued to search.

'Fifteen minutes is up,' yelled Mortimer. 'Everybody out.'

'But there hasn't been enough time to get everyone off,' cried Berrister desperately. 'And this is our fault. If we hadn't come aboard—'

'Getting blown up won't make it right,' declared Sarah. 'So out – *now*!'

The abandon ship signal was deafening, and the passengers were a shoving, terrified mass. Their disorderly panic frightened the crew, some of whom had elected to leave them to it and save themselves instead. They had launched two of the six lifeboats, and although a few enterprising passengers had managed to jump into them, both had gone out mostly empty. Ramon had taken a third, while a fourth had been lowered with about twenty passengers in it, which left two boats for roughly eighty people. It would be a tight squeeze.

'How much longer?' asked Mortimer, as they joined the frantic melee.

'Not sure,' said Polushin. 'Maybe a minute.'

The words were no sooner out of his mouth than there was a shuddering explosion, followed almost immediately by a far bigger one. Flames shot from the hull, rising in a great ball of fire, and the whole ship listed to one side. Passengers screamed as they struggled to keep their balance. The fifth lifeboat – which was only half full – swung crazily on its cables before they snapped, plunging it down into the sea. Dense black smoke started to pour from the ship's shattered side, rising in choking clouds to swirl around them.

'We won't all fit in the last boat,' whispered Sarah, appalled. 'There're too many of us.'

'We can get the remaining passengers off,' said Polushin, looking around and doing some hasty calculations. 'That will leave some crew, including us. So we'd better hope we don't sink before the Americans arrive.'

A groan from below suggested that was unlikely.

'We'll use the Zodiacs,' determined Berrister. 'How many do you have?'

'Four, but two have been packed away. The others are on the afterdeck, along with yours.' Polushin turned to the young, white-faced third officer. 'Get the passengers on the last lifeboat and go with them. Hurry!'

'Will everybody else fit in three inflatables?' asked Mortimer doubtfully.

'Just,' replied Polushin. 'There are also four crew on the bridge – we'll need to leave room for them as well.'

He ran quickly to where the three boats were lashed, Berrister, Sarah and Mortimer pounding behind him along the now seriously listing deck. Getting the inflatables into the sea wasn't going to be easy – the explosion had knocked out the electrical winches, so they would have to be lifted over the railings by hand. Moreover, it had started to snow heavily, making it difficult to see and turning every surface slick.

'Those bastards didn't mess around,' muttered Polushin. 'If we hadn't managed to seal the engine room, we'd have been feeding the fishes by now. Thank God you warned us.'

'How much longer can we stay afloat?' asked Berrister, brushing flakes out of his eyes.

'Not long enough for *South Star*. You'll need these.'

He shoved life jackets at them. They all donned them except Mortimer, who claimed it would get in his way. His face was grim, and it occurred to Berrister that he had made a decision – that if they failed to get the boats off in time, he would rather drown quickly than die of hypothermia in the freezing water.

It took the combined strength of everyone to get the first inflatable over the side. It landed stern first and there was an agonizing moment

294

when they thought it was going to flip. By some miracle it didn't, and a crewman quickly clambered down a rope ladder towards it. He leapt in and held it steady while his workmates followed.

'That's enough,' shouted Berrister, aware that it was becoming dangerously overloaded. 'Cast off.'

Three more crew managed to cram themselves on board before someone started the engine and drove it away.

Minutes ticked past as they fought to cut the lashings on the second boat. The snow was coming down harder, and Berrister could not stop shivering – there had been no time to grab a coat and the wind was bitter. The knife he was using slipped from his frozen fingers, and he struggled to pick it up again.

'Hurry,' yelled Sarah, as smoke drifted across the deck. 'If we don't get away before she sinks, she'll suck us down with her.'

Terrified, one of the crew grabbed a fire axe and began hacking at the straps before anyone could stop him. The blade bit through ropes and rubber hull alike. There was a sharp hiss.

'Stop!' yelled Berrister, but the man was too frightened to listen, and shoved him away with a strength born of terror. They wasted more valuable seconds wrestling the axe away from him.

'Now get her in the water – quickly!' howled Mortimer when the last strap was gone. 'We're going down fast.'

The sharp angle on the deck helped them this time. The boat slithered down it, fetched up against the rail, and pitched overboard of its own accord. It landed beautifully, and Polushin used a long hook to draw it under the ladders.

'Sarah, go,' ordered Berrister, bundling her towards it. 'And Geoff, put the damn life jacket on!'

But there was a vicious scrum as the remaining crew fought to be first off, and Sarah was knocked to the deck by a flailing elbow. Then the third officer arrived – he had launched the last lifeboat, but said there had been no room for him on it. In his wake were several more crew, and once again, there were too many people for the remaining craft.

'Tell the bridge officers to come down now,' shouted Polushin. 'They can't do any more up there.'

Even as he spoke, there was a roar and more flames exploded from the hull. *Novosibirsk* listed even more violently, and there was a scream as one of the crew fell from the ladder.

'Third Zodiac!' shouted Mortimer.

Berrister chopped frantically at the straps, cursing whoever had been so thorough. Snow spat into his eyes, and his hands were beyond sensation. Finally, it was free, and they manoeuvred it down the deck, over the rail and into the water – which was decidedly closer than it had been. The little boat was far too small to hold the remaining fifteen or so people safely, and he hoped their weight wouldn't capsize it. He looked over the side – a number of heads bobbed in the water, some calling for help, but most not.

'Geoff!' he snapped. 'Put your life jacket on.'

'No point,' said Mortimer softly. 'Look.'

296

Galtieri had appeared during the chaos. She had launched her boats, and four of them were speeding towards the floundering *Novosibirsk*. Berrister didn't need binoculars to tell him that they would be bringing men with guns.

Sixteen

There was another boom, and *Novosibirsk* rolled farther onto her starboard side. The passengers on the lifeboats were screaming at the officers to take them to a safe distance. The officers refused, and continued to pluck survivors from the sea, although everyone knew they were too close to the stricken ship, and thus in danger of being dragged under when she went down. Already there were terrible creaks and groans emanating from *Novosibirsk* as she underwent stresses her structure was never designed to take.

The whalers were closer now. The dying ship gave another tearing shudder, and her deck tilted yet more crazily. A greasy black pall of smoke belched towards the shore, and patches of oil burned on the water. Absently, Berrister wondered how much would wash up on the beaches, to foul birds and seals. He felt a sudden spurt of rage towards the men who had brought it about – and who would commit more horrors in the future unless someone survived to tell the truth.

The remaining officers and crew were skidding

down the slick deck to clamber aboard the last inflatable. It was already overloaded, but there were still another seven people to go. Polushin was keeping a dogged grip on the hook that held it to the ship's side, but those aboard were trying to knock it away, knowing the little craft would be swamped if everyone got on it.

When *Novosibirsk* lurched again, Mortimer lost his footing. He managed to grab a hatch and hung there, only the tips of his fingers preventing him from slithering into the sea. He was still not wearing his life jacket. As fast as he could, Berrister grabbed one of the severed straps. Wrapping one end around a stanchion, he threw the other towards the dangling glaciologist. Mortimer snatched at it, but the desperate movement displaced his tenuous hold. With a howl, he tumbled down the deck and hit the water with a splash.

'No!' cried Berrister in horror, when Mortimer did not reappear.

He tossed the life jacket to where his friend had fallen, willing him to rise to the surface and take hold of it, but nothing happened. Then there was another ear-splitting groan from the ship, and she listed further still. Berrister lost his own balance, and was only prevented from following Mortimer into the water by seizing the strap himself.

At the same time, he heard the rattle of gunfire as *Galtieri*'s people reached the first of the life-boats. Agonised screams drifted across the waves, audible even over *Novosibirsk*'s death throes. It was the boat that Ramon and his cronies had hijacked.

Berrister looked at Sarah, who was clutching a railing nearby. He stretched out his free arm and wrapped it around her, to hold her close. She let go of the railing and hugged him hard. Their combined weight was too much for him, and he felt his hand slide down the strap.

He was about to let go, so they would fall together into the churning waves, when there was a deep, powerful blast from a ship's horn. At first, he thought it was someone on the bridge, performing some strange maritime ritual as *Novosibirsk* gave up the ghost, but it sounded further away. He looked across the water. There, steaming towards them, was a smart red and white vessel with the Stars and Stripes flapping on her bow.

'*South Star*!' he gasped, struggling to keep his grip as she sounded her horn again. *Galtieri*'s men were already racing away in the opposite direction, and he could hear Joshi cheering insanely from one of the lifeboats.

Even as they felt their hopes rise, Berrister's frozen fingers slipped down the last of the strap. Sarah flailed frantically as they slithered seaward, and managed to clutch a rail with one hand and the sleeve of Berrister's sweater with the other. *Novosibirsk* tipped further.

'Let me go,' he shouted. 'I'll swim to the closest boat.'

'No,' hissed Sarah through gritted teeth as she struggled to keep hold of him. 'You won't make it.'

But the sweater began to tear from her hand, and even though she fought with every ounce of

299

her strength, she felt it snap from her fingers. Berrister slid feet first into the icy sea and disappeared. She waited for him to bob up again – the life jacket would not let him drown.

'He needs to inflate it manually,' called Polushin. 'So do you. There's a toggle on the bottom.'

But she had not known that, so why would Berrister? She watched the last Zodiac chug away from *Novosibirsk* as fast as its little engine would take it. It was dangerously low in the water, and she wondered if it would capsize before *South Star* reached it. She glanced at Polushin – they were the only two left now. Sobbing, she swung her empty hand up to get a better hold on the rail, and closed her eyes in grief.

Fortunately for Sarah and Polushin, *South Star* had a helicopter, which soon winched them to safety. At the same time, the overloaded inflatables were relieved of their shivering, terrified occupants, and the lifeboats were escorted to a safe distance. By the time *Novosibirsk* finally slipped beneath the waves, Sarah was wrapped in a warm blanket on the helicopter, surrounded by efficient but kind Coast Guard personnel. She watched a fountain of water gush up from where the ship had been, but soon even that was gone, leaving behind a greasy slick and a mass of floating debris.

The canteen on *South Star* had been converted into a makeshift hospital, where survivors were being stripped of wet clothes, and treated for shock and hypothermia. She went to look for Joshi.

'Are we safe now?' he asked hoarsely, turning a white, exhausted face towards her. 'Or will the Southern Exploring Company send an even bigger ship after us?'

'We're safe,' she replied, slumping down next to him. 'Even they can't take on the Coast Guard – it would be like declaring war on the United States.'

'What if these people don't believe us either?' he pressed miserably. 'No one has so far, so why should anyone start now?'

'Don't worry,' said Sarah. 'They will – I promise.'

She was surprised to find anger beginning to replace the despair that had crippled her since Berrister and Mortimer had gone. She looked around her, taking in the sobs of an elderly couple huddled on a makeshift bed, a man in a wet toupee sitting stoically upright with his arm in a sling, and Polushin, whose head was swathed in a bandage.

It was Rothera's fault, she thought bitterly. Or rather Vince's, and she would see he spent the rest of his miserable life regretting it. If he had done his job, the alarm would have been raised days ago, *Novosibirsk* would have been ordered out of the Antarctic, and no one else would have died.

'Where are you going?' asked Joshi, as she stood suddenly, all grim resolution.

'To demand an audience with the captain – get him to order Vince's arrest before the little shit does any more harm.'

She pushed through the milling mass of people,

looking for an officer who would conduct her to the bridge. Then she spotted a familiar face, but not one she had expected to see. It was the krill-obsessed Noddy Taylor. She gaped at him in astonishment.

'You! But what . . .'

'Thank Vince,' he explained. 'He knew something was wrong when Freddy started making all your broadcasts – long before poor Graham tried to send a message via the krill data. Unfortunately, it took a while to secure the right kind of help.'

'But everyone thinks we're mad from mercury poisoning . . .'

Noddy regarded her with raised eyebrows. 'We're scientists, Sarah – we happen to know that mercury doesn't work like that. However, we had to pretend that we did think that was what was going on, to give the Coast Guard time to get here.'

'And the other bases? Palmer, Arctowski and the rest?'

'Helped with the ruse, yes. The Southern Exploring Company eavesdropped on our radio conversations, but not our emails. We all worked very hard to lull them into a false sense of security – all the bases together.'

'But you came too late,' she said, feeling her legs unsteady beneath her. 'People are dead.'

'Yes,' he acknowledged. 'There were several fatalities on one of the lifeboats, although they were men linked to the Southern Exploring Company and were apparently shot by their own people. And an as yet undetermined number of passengers and crew of *Novosibirsk* died in the water.'

'You should've ordered *Novosibirsk* to leave the area completely.'

'We did. Unfortunately, the second officer was in the pay of the Southern Exploring Company, so the message never got delivered. She was one of the four shot on the bridge at Orlando's order. So much for the rewards of loyal service.'

'But Andrew and Geoff,' said Sarah miserably. 'They . . .'

'Over there,' said Noddy, pointing. 'Making sure the captain has all the information he needs to put out a general alert. They were rescued shortly after you.'

Sarah whipped around and saw Berrister and Mortimer sitting at a table with two men in uniform, one of whom was listening intently, while the other typed their statements on a laptop. A third officer was standing nearby, carefully peeling apart the printed emails that Yablokov had given Mortimer, sodden with seawater but still perfectly legible. She felt her jaw drop. Abandoning Noddy, she raced towards them.

'I thought you were dead!' she sobbed, grabbing Berrister and holding him tightly.

'Did you?' he asked in surprise. 'Why? I told you I'd swim to the nearest boat. It wasn't too bad, once I'd got the life jacket inflated, and I was fished out of the water very quickly, thanks to Geoff.'

'It was the overloaded one,' explained Mortimer. 'And its occupants were loath to let anyone else on, lest it capsized. So I threatened to throw a

303

couple of them overboard to make space for him, and miraculously a spare corner appeared.'

Sarah felt almost sick with relief. 'You might have told me,' she mumbled, embarrassed by her display of emotion. 'I was worried.'

'We assumed you knew,' said Berrister with an apologetic shrug. 'And we needed to get the story out as soon as possible. When you didn't come to help, we just thought you needed a bit of time to yourself.'

Sarah sniffed. It was the last thing she wanted.

'I've just told Joshi that it's all over.' She gazed up into Berrister's face. 'Please tell me it's true.'

'It is,' he assured her. 'The story's all over the internet, and the Southern Exploring Company's days are numbered. According to *South Star*'s radar, they're already running north.'

'You mean they're escaping?'

'They're being tracked, and the navies of a dozen countries are ready to intercept them, no matter which way they turn.'

Sarah heaved a slow sigh of relief. 'We won, then,' she whispered. 'We won.'

Epilogue

England, four weeks later

'I just had a call from Noddy,' said Berrister, standing at the door to Sarah's office.

She was sitting on the floor, surrounded by the specimen jars and notepads that represented the meagre remnants of the data she had managed to salvage. It wasn't much for three months of hard work, but it was better than nothing.

'And?' she asked, shaking a bottle and holding it up to the light.

Berrister sat on the desk, pushing his hands in his pockets. '*Volga* tried to offload her cargo in Japan, to sell on the black market there. So, that's it: all six ships have now been caught.'

He went to stare out of the window. Spring was in the air, although the remains of a late snowfall still lay on the ground in slushy, frozen heaps. A group of high-spirited students were lobbing snowballs at each other in the dim light of an early dusk.

'Was *Volga*'s whale meat contaminated, too?' asked Sarah, coming to stand next to him. 'Like it was in the holds of the other five?'

'Noddy said it virtually glowed in the dark.'

'And the scum who killed the whales and poisoned the sea? How are they?'

'Not good. Even Orlando is sick, and he knew

305

exactly what was in the cargo, so kept his distance. Apparently they scrimped on the sealing process this year, to cut costs. He can't believe they didn't tell him, and is avenging himself by turning informer.'

'Informer against whom, exactly? Who runs the Southern Exploring Company?'

'According to Noddy, a group of criminals who supply rogue regimes and terrorist organisations with dirty weapons – not just nuclear technology, but chemical and biological as well. Weapons of mass destruction.'

'Bastards! But Orlando's grassing them up?'

Berrister nodded. 'To a joint task force including Interpol, MI6, the CIA, and a number of other parties interested in combatting that kind of threat.'

'That's good, I suppose, but so much damage has already been done – it won't be easy to retrieve the leaking barrels, while the whales are dead. And all in the name of profit. I'm glad the crews are getting what they deserve.'

'Most of the sailors did it to support their families – the cod industry's collapsing in the Arctic, so they were easy prey. Others were mercenaries, who knew to avoid the holds, but even they're showing a degree of contamination. Incidentally, *Lena*'s crew insist that Yablokov was going to help you escape.'

Sarah looked disgusted. 'Only when he found out that the Southern Exploring Company had poisoned him.'

'They say he decided before that.'

Sarah tried to feel empathy for the people who

had almost killed her, but found she could not do it. 'They murdered our friends, Andrew. That's unforgivable. Lisa, Dan, Graham and that nice Drecki who died trying to rescue us . . . none of them deserved that.'

They were silent for a while, both thinking about the people who had failed to come home. Outside, the students shrieked with laughter as their snowball fight escalated.

'We owe Vince a good deal,' said Berrister eventually. 'Without him, we'd be dead for certain – and so would a lot of people who would have eaten contaminated whale meat.'

'It would have served them right,' said Sarah harshly. 'It's their taste for the stuff that keeps these criminals in business. Part of me wishes they *had* stuffed it down their unscrupulous throats.'

A snowball hit the window, and the guilty student gazed up in alarm. Berrister smiled at him, although Sarah would have given him a piece of her mind, had she been alone. She went to her desk and pulled out a bottle. It was almost six o'clock, and time to stop work for the day.

'The whole world knows about the Southern Exploring Company and what it's done,' she said. 'Conservation groups are lobbying governments everywhere about the dead blues, and the Antarctic is being proclaimed as a place that *must* be protected. Perhaps something good has come out of it all.'

'It won't last,' predicted Berrister. 'Some other scandal will come along and people will forget about the far south. And when they do, other unscrupulous sods will be down there to see how they can exploit it for personal gain.'

'Then we have to make sure they *don't* forget it,' said Sarah, handing him a glass. 'Joshi's got himself a job with Greenpeace, Geoff writes a weekly blog with a growing number of followers, and you and me – well, we're university lecturers, responsible for shaping young minds.'

At that moment, her phone rang. While she answered it, he gazed out at the fading day, thinking about Dan Wells and how much he had learned from him. They had been unable to retrieve his body, but Berrister thought he wouldn't have minded. Wells would have been quite happy with a glacier as his final resting place.

Then something in the tone of Sarah's voice made him look at her sharply. She sat down suddenly, clutching the phone so hard that her knuckles were white. Eventually, she disconnected the call and looked at Berrister with shocked eyes.

'That was Noddy. Apparently Orlando wasn't as sick as he led everyone to believe, because he got out of bed, killed his guards and calmly walked out of the hospital. And according to his interrogators, he holds *us* responsible for his capture. They think he might pay us a visit.'

'I doubt he'll make it,' said Berrister. 'Too many people will be looking for him – not just half the world's police forces, but the Southern Exploring Company, which he betrayed.'

'But that's just it, Andrew – he *didn't* betray them. It transpires that nothing he shared held

308

up, and now so many of his underlings are dead or dying . . . well, there's no one left to tell the truth.'

Berrister stared at her. 'So we were wrong. It isn't over.'

'Worse,' said Sarah. 'I have a bad feeling that it's only just beginning.'